The Bad Quarto

Also by Jill Paton Walsh

THE IMOGEN QUY MYSTERIES

The Wyndham Case

A Piece of Justice

Debts of Dishonour

WITH DOROTHY L. SAYERS

A Presumption of Death

Thrones, Dominations

NOVELS

Lapsing

The Serpentine Cave

A Desert in Bohemia

JILL PATON WALSH

The Bad Quarto

An Imogen Quy Mystery

St. Martin's Minotaur
New York

www.minotaurbooks.com

Library of Congress Cataloging-in-Publication Data

Paton Walsh, Jill, 1937–
    The bad quarto : an Imogen Quy mystery / Jill Paton Walsh.—1st U.S. ed.
    p. cm.
  ISBN-13: 978-0-312-35409-1
  ISBN-10: 0-312-35409-6
    1. Shakespeare, William, 1564–1616. Hamlet—Fiction. 2. University of Cambridge—Fiction. 3. Quy, Imogen (Fictitious character)—Fiction. 4. Women detectives—England—Cambridge—Fiction. 5. Nurses—Fiction. 6. Scholars—Crimes against—Fiction. 7. College theater—Fiction. 8. Cambridge (England)—Fiction. I. Title.

PR6066.A84 B33 2007
823'.914—dc22

                                                        2006100618

First published in Great Britain by Hodder & Stoughton,
a division of Hodder Headline

First U.S. Edition: April 2007

10 9 8 7 6 5 4 3 2 1

To my son Edmund, hoping he may enjoy it.

All the quotations from *Hamlet* in this novel are taken from the 1603 First Quarto in the Clarendon Press edition of 1965. This is known as the Bad Quarto.

ACKNOWLEDGEMENTS

I would like to thank John Kerrigan, Jean and Colin Normand, Declan Flanagan, and Walter Aylen for directing my reading in their various fields of expertise, and Ian Kerr for information about court procedure. Of course any errors and misapprehensions remain exclusively my responsibility. I would also like to apologise to the astonishing 'Whipplesnaith' for fictionally introducing my fictional college into his terrifying masterpiece, *The Night Climbers of Cambridge*. If he is still alive I hope he will forgive me. As always, I owe a debt of gratitude to my husband John Rowe Townsend for unfailing help and support.

JPW

The Bad Quarto

I

Thus twice before, and jump at this dead hower
With Marshall stalke he passed through our watch . . .

It was much later than usual when Imogen Quy, the college nurse of St Agatha's College, Cambridge, locked up her office in the college and went to fetch her bike for the ride home. There was a lot of writing up notes to catch up on, it was examination time and the final-year students were all stressed and excitable. She had seen many of them in the last week. Later she was mortified to be unable to say at exactly what time she had left. She didn't mind cycling home after dark: her cycle lights were in order, and there was a provisional and unemphatic quality about the darkness on summer nights.

She took her bike from the college bicycle shed, and wheeled it out onto Castle Hill and her way home. She passed the end of Patten Alley as she went. The usually deserted little alley was packed with people, for some reason. Glancing down it she saw a crowd, backs turned to her, and heard a commotion of some kind – a muted commotion. Then someone turned and saw her – she must have been passing the pool of light cast by a lamppost at the corner and called out to her. 'Miss Quy! Come quick!' The note of anguish in the cry was unmistakable.

Imogen propped her bike against the wall and ran forward. She had to elbow her way through the press of people. And there, lying face upward on the stones of the little street, was a fellow of the college. John Talentire, glamorous, outspoken, provocative John Talentire, the best research fellow for years. Imogen knelt down on the stones beside him, taking his wrist to feel his pulse. It was very faint. His eyelids fluttered and closed.

'Has someone called 999?' Imogen asked.

'Yes, ages ago!' wailed a young woman close by. But Imogen knew very well that minutes seem like centuries in such a scene as this.

She pushed something off his chest to put her ear to his ribs and listen for his heart. She couldn't hear it. She smelled beer on his breath. The sporadic lights in the alley were not bright, and the onlookers cast nearly solid shadow over the scene. Then someone shone a torch at her. She saw that a pool of blood was gathering around Talentire's skull; he had fallen very hard, not, surely, just fallen over, or else he had been viciously struck on the head. At that moment the faint pulse in the wrist she was holding faltered and stopped.

A wailing siren a little way off indicated the arrival of ambulance or police. Too late, Imogen thought. He had died this minute, while she knelt beside him. How odd and distressing that a man that she didn't like, and who didn't like her, should die with her holding his hand. She sat back on her knees. She looked curiously at what she had pushed off his chest to listen for his heartbeat: it was a coil of rope. It was still attached to his belt by a shackle. Then she looked up.

Overhead on one side of the alley the lovely Jacobean buildings of the college rose in an elaborate tower, marking the corner of the court. The topmost casement of this tower was wide open, maybe fifty feet above them. And on the other side of the alley the pediment of the New Library jutted out against the stars, coming to within ten feet or so of the window.

'Of course,' Imogen murmured. 'Harding's Folly.'

2

Is it a custom here?

It was not unusual for Imogen to find herself applied to for non-medical consultations by members of her college. Lady Caroline Buckmote, the Master's wife, asked often for Imogen's counsel on college matters, the two of them having developed a friendship based on instinctive sympathy, and a shared concern for the welfare of Sir William Buckmote, a great man who had from time to time found the stresses of his position deeply trying. On a fine March morning, Lady Buckmote recruited Imogen for advice about what to do about the tower room in Fountain Court. This room, one of the best in the college, had been empty, unused and locked since the terrible accident two terms ago, in which John Talentire had lost his life. But accidents and deaths, however tragic, are only moments in the life of colleges, which encompass years in hundreds and brilliant fellows in dozens of dozens.

Imogen followed Caroline Buckmote, up the ancient spiral stone staircase that led to the disastrous room, and waited while she unlocked first the 'oak' – the heavy outer door with which ancient college rooms were provided to preserve privacy when required – and then the handsome panelled door into the room itself.

It was an extraordinarily pleasant room. It was nearly

square, with a window in each wall, and a window-seat below each window. It would, when occupied, have been lined with books, but now was lined with vacant bookcases. It was a bed-sitting room, with a bed against one wall, and a little lobby containing bath and basin and lavatory concealed behind a panelled door. It was perfectly comfortable in spite of the oddities of the space. The ceiling was high, and supported from corner to corner by a massive diagonal beam, carved with running vines and fruits in low relief. At each end of the beam, supporting it, was a vertical prop, in effect an upright beam, standing a little clear of the wall as though the builders had not quite trusted the ceiling beam with the considerable span, and the weight of the stone roof overhead. Light poured into the room from all directions. The two women instinctively walked round looking through each window in turn. One opened onto Fountain Court, the famous and beautiful main court of St Agatha's. Seen from this height – four storeys above the pavements – it looked like the diagrammatic engravings of college buildings beloved of the eighteenth century – charming compromises between pictures and plans – which one bought at huge expense on King's Parade.

They moved on to the second window. This looked sideways along the roof ridge of one side of the court, across a slope of Barnack stone tiles running down to a parapet decorated with saints and gargoyles; a sensible, solid, water-shedding roof hiding behind the architect's fancies about what ought to show from the ground. The third window looked into the Fellows' Garden, and was dominated by the huge mulberry tree planted by the college's first botanist, who was, of course, not a scholar, but a gardener; and so they came round to the fourth window. This last window was the cause of all the grief.

It was startlingly near the New Library, which had been squeezed onto an old burying plot the college had acquired in the nineteenth century. As they looked out now the New Library reared up alongside them and the angle of the pediment pointed directly at the tower, reaching its closest point about three feet below the window where they stood, and perhaps eight feet distant; it was hard to estimate. Far below them at ground level ran a narrow street, a little medieval lane, Patten Alley, which had once led to the burying ground, and was a public street, although St Agatha's now stood on both sides of it. From the street, as Imogen had often had the chance to observe, the gap between the corner of one building and the window of the other looked very small indeed – close enough to jump, and that was the trouble. The gap was known as Harding's Folly after the first student to have jumped it. His survival, alas, had set an example to all who came after him, so that the college had been faced with a savagely dangerous tradition, a tempting dare to all its hot-heads, which in the eighty-odd years since the New Library was built had claimed four promising young lives.

Thirty years back St Agatha's had refused admission to a perfectly well-qualified young aristocrat whose father and grandfather had both attended the college, and both jumped Harding's Folly. He had promised not to try it, and he had not been believed. Rightly; he had been admitted to King's, made friends at St Agatha's, tried the jump and broken his neck.

'You see?' said Lady Buckmote.

'It has to be said,' said Imogen thoughtfully, 'that it looks much worse from up here than it does from down below. One might have to be a touch tipsy, don't you think?'

They were joined at this point by Malcolm Gracie, St Agatha's new bursar. 'Ah, a conference, I see,' he said.

'Our natural reaction to all this, ladies, was to propose putting bars on the window; but it seems one needs listed building consent, and the Society for the Protection of Ancient Buildings is appalled at the idea, and English Heritage is muttering about not giving grants in future to institutions which cannot be trusted with the curatorship of what they have got. All very tiresome, as I'm sure you can see.'

Imogen thought about it. 'Do we need consent if the bars are not visible from outside?' she asked.

'I'm not sure,' said the bursar. 'How would that be done?'

'Well, after all,' said Lady Buckmote, 'there isn't anyone out there on top of the New Library who can look right in; suppose we fixed the bars on the inside of the thickness of the wall, just here.'

'Making the window-seat inaccessible,' said Gracie.

'Leaving three window-seats in use, after all,' said Lady Buckmote.

'It would nevertheless look a bit odd,' said the bursar, 'and leave a space that the housekeeper couldn't reach to dust.'

'Then what about putting a sealed double-glazing unit right across the window aperture, leaving the present casement just as it is?' offered Imogen. 'That wouldn't show from outside, would it?'

'It would look a lot nicer than bars, too,' said Lady Buckmote. 'Whose room is it going to be?'

'Don't know,' said the bursar gloomily. 'We knew, of course, that we couldn't put an undergraduate or graduate student in here, in view of their potential as suicide candidates, but we did think it would be safe to put a fellow in here, however young and brilliant. But as you know we were sadly mistaken. I wondered if we have anyone old and doddery enough to be absolutely certain not to go jumping out of windows, but the trouble with our extensive selection of brilliant old dodderers is that they are perfectly capable of going off to the south of France for a week leaving their room unlocked. And then anyone could get in. I suppose you wouldn't consider it, Imogen?'

'Golly, what a temptation!' Imogen said. 'In some ways this is the best room in Cambridge. But I don't think so; it's such a long way up for people to climb to come and see me, and naturally they are often feeling a bit dicey when they want to come. It's just not accessible enough to be practical, I'm afraid.'

'I'm afraid you're right,' said Lady Buckmote. 'What a shame.'

'Ah, well, we'll think of something. But I think we should attempt to get permission to close off that window impenetrably somehow, whatever we are going to do with the room.'

'Oh, yes, Malcolm. Better safe than sorry. Pity we didn't think of it earlier.'

'I have been lying awake at night with that thought, Caroline,' said the bursar ruefully.

And with that they left him to lock up securely behind them.

Back in the Master's Lodge having a quiet coffee and chat together, Imogen and Lady Buckmote were joined by the Master himself. Ultra-sensitive to Sir William Buckmote's state of mind, for she had known him a long time, and nursed him informally through several crises, Imogen perceived at once that sunshine and cheer were not the prevailing mood-music.

'Trouble, my dear?' asked Lady Buckmote.

'Not exactly,' the great man replied. 'But I see trouble coming. We have to appoint a new fellow in English. We will have feuding and squabbles over it all term, I'm afraid.'

'Why, William?'

'Well, it's no good asking me!' he exclaimed. 'Nature of the subject, I suppose. It's corrupting, I think. But then I'm only a poor bloody scientist. What could I know about it?'

'If English is corrupting, William,' said Lady Buckmote, 'then the college has been debauching young people by the dozens for many years. Do you want some coffee?'

'No time, thanks. Yes, I rather think the college has been perpetrating damage. Not just English, either, though it's English on my mind at the moment. Any course called Something Studies, for example.'

'Rather an extreme view, dear?'

'Well, it is, I suppose, extreme. It wouldn't make me any friends on the college governing body if I uttered it in public. But I'm not exactly joking, either. I seriously think that subjects in which there is no such thing as a wrong answer are debilitating when one is young. I must be off.'

His two companions watched him go, ambling across the vast space of the living room, under its elaborate ceilings, past its portrait-laden walls.

'Do you think my better half is becoming rather odd, Imogen?' asked Lady Buckmote.

'Not really. Not as heads of house go.'

'They go potty in large numbers, you mean?'

'It's a stressful job. And it hits people when they are entering the home straight, so to speak. How long has William to go before he retires?'

'Three more years, officially. I hope he isn't going to upset the English faculty. There's tension enough between arts and sciences here.'

'I know, though I don't understand exactly why.'

'Well, roughly, the arts people think that science is about

facts; and facts involve only mechanical rote learning. And the scientists think that subjects as subjective as English, almost devoid of discernible fact, are too wishy-washy to train the mind, and just self-indulgence.'

'Therefore bad for the young who are too self-indulgent already?'

'Exactly.'

'I must go,' said Imogen. 'I have a surgery in a minute. I mustn't be late.'

There is a curious aspect of life in Cambridge, which can seem exhilarating, and can induce a mood of autumnal sadness. Those who stay put in Cambridge all their lives get older with the passing years; but the crowds around them are the young, endlessly replenished. There are two large universities in the place, and every year another throng of golden lads and girls arrive, and begin to walk and shop, and cycle and row, and sprawl talking on the grass of the open spaces in summer weather, and get drunk in the pubs. Imogen's clients were mostly undergraduates, with a range of slight problems, or sports injuries – those were sometimes serious – or feeble excuses to request sympathy and attention from a kindly person, for sometimes all that ailed them was that they were missing their mothers. They would of course have been horrified and mortally insulted had Imogen offered that diagnosis. Increasingly they seemed to Imogen too young to be there, far too young to be taking their lives in their own hands, studying and thinking for themselves, taking lovers, making choices that would follow them for years. But she realised that she herself had been fully adult and mature at eighteen, in her own opinion. The greenness of her clients didn't really measure change in them, but, awful thought, in her.

That morning brought a random set of problems into Imogen's room. The only serious one was James Shelford, a chemistry student, who was feeling wheezy. He hadn't had asthma before, and Imogen reached the conclusion that he had been inhaling something in the laboratory that had done him a bit of no good. When she asked him what the fumes would have been he reeled off a molecular structure which left her none the wiser. Even if she had known, she wouldn't have had an antidote in her simple medicine cupboard. But when she said, 'Off with you to Addenbrooke's. I'll write you a note for the casualty officer,' young James demurred.

'I can't tell them what it was,' he said. 'It's new research – it's got to be secret.'

'But you've just told me,' said Imogen.

'Well, I knew you wouldn't understand it.'

'You shouldn't take risks with your health, James. Go and get seen to in A & E.'

He shook his head. 'My supervisor wouldn't like it. We're supposed to keep it strictly confidential till we're ready to publish.'

'Who is your supervisor?' asked Imogen, lifting the phone.

Dr Appleby, of course, could see what was what. He didn't need a health-and-safety inspection of the lab; he didn't need a sick undergraduate with a grievance; he needed to know at once if anything going on under his supervision was potentially dangerous; he didn't need a horror-story in the tabloid press putting off next year's applicants to read chemistry: in short he could see beyond the end of his nose, and when Imogen handed the phone to James he gave strict instructions to go to Addenbrooke's at once, and come to see him afterwards. By now James's breathing was audibly rough, so Imogen called the lodge to have the college porter order a taxi.

'I can't afford a taxi,' said James, resistant to the last.

'It'll be on the college account, James,' said Imogen. 'Look, various other people have some responsibility to make sure you don't come to any harm; but you have a duty to be sensible too.'

Behind James came an assortment of relatively minor complaints. Imogen dispensed paracetamol, and advice, wrote a couple more notes, showed a girl how to use a pregnancy testing kit, and suggested measures of self-defence, and was just closing up shop when Samantha Barton appeared. Samantha couldn't sleep for worry. At first Imogen felt rather severe about this problem: all that was worrying Samantha was her approaching exam, part one of the English tripos, and Imogen thought that others might have rather more serious worries to think about. But she let Samantha run on, as she always did; it was the chief means by which she got into a position to help people. And Samantha's complaint was not unreasonable. She didn't know whether the examiners would be structuralists, post-structuralists, deconstructionists, new historicists, etc. etc. There was even a possibility that the examiners would be looking for close reading, fine judgement, and enjoyment of the set text. Samantha, Imogen gathered, had worked hard, and would be able to provide whatever form of commentary would get her good marks. But not knowing what sort of thing would count as clever and correct was making the exam seem terrifying. What if she gave historicist answers to an anti-historicist examiner? It wasn't fair, it wasn't fair!

No, it wasn't. And undergraduate memories are short; Samantha didn't know that only a few years back the English Department had been riven with feuds which made the Montagues and Capulets seem like good chums. Imogen could remember a few terrible terms in which brilliant students had had nervous breakdowns over this sort of problem; in which college tutors hated, resented, scorned the views of distinguished lecturers, and the whole thing had come to a simmering head over the honorary degree proposed for Jacques Derrida and then vetoed by Regent House.

Could all this be starting up again? It sounded uncannily like the Master's lament about appointing a new English fellow. Imogen offered as much common-sense soothing as she was able. Was it the nature of English to generate hatred and infighting?

'The only thing you can do, really,' she suggested to Samantha, 'is make up your own mind between these schools of thought. If you know what you think yourself, you could describe the different views, and come down between them.'

'Who cares what I think?' wailed Samantha. 'I just want to know what to say and I'll say it.'

'But you're in Cambridge to learn to think for yourself,' said Imogen crisply. 'You could get sleeping pills from a doctor; or you could try a hot drink and a couple of aspirins last thing at night.'

She waited for Samantha to depart, and the girl did get as far as the door before turning back. 'There is something else, Miss Quy, only I don't really know – I mean I'm not sure if I ought to tell you. Is it all right to consult you about somebody else?'

'That rather depends, Samantha. I'm not going to encourage you to tell me something you were told in confidence, for example, unless you think it's a matter of life and death.'

'I haven't been told anything. I haven't been sworn to secrecy, but there's someone I'm a bit worried about.'

'A fellow student?'

'Yes. She's my new room-mate, Susan Inchman.'

'Well, she's in my parish as much as you are. What about her?'

'You won't tell?'

'I won't rush up to her and tell her you have been talking about her, if that's what you mean. But until you tell me what this is about, I can't say what I might do about it.'

Samantha hesitated a moment more, and then said, 'She's got a most awful temper!'

After the build-up Imogen almost laughed. But she managed a straight face. 'Throwing books, you mean?'

'No, she doesn't throw books. She has respect for books. She moans if someone has made notes in a library book, or mended a tear with Sellotape, or anything.'

'A right-minded young woman. Go on.'

'She sort of raves. She gets incredibly angry about stuff, and works herself up about it, and can't talk about anything else for hours.'

'She's obsessive?'

'People are starting to avoid her. They don't want to hear all that crap.'

'But you can't avoid her because you are sharing a room?'

'I do my best,' said Samantha, grimacing. 'But I did just begin to wonder if there was something wrong with her. Getting things out of proportion.'

'Give me an example.'

'Well, last year some time she was kept waiting half an hour for her supervision, and then her supervisor had to hurry off, and didn't replace the missing time.'

'Well, anyone might be cross about that.'

'Yes, but she's still on about it! saying all sorts of things, like as how he only did it to her because she wasn't from a posh school and her family didn't score, and he knew he could treat her badly and trash her work without conse-quences, and other people didn't have to put up with that sort of thing, and on and on and on. And she seems *really* angry, Miss Quy, I mean not, like, cross, but savage about it. So I did just wonder . . .'

'How long has this been going on? I mean, is it endemic?'

'I don't know how long. She was moved from sharing with someone else who couldn't stand her. And I offered to give it a go. We've only been room-mates this term.'

'Are you regretting it? I could ask the bursar to move one of you again.'

'Well, no. I mean, she's all right most of the time. And she's interesting. A bit different, if you know what I mean.'

'OK. Look, Samantha, you are right to mention this to me. And if you get a chance, try to persuade her to come and see me, and I'll perhaps be able to help.'

'Thanks, Miss Quy.'

'Oh, and Samantha, if any of this rage is ever directed at you, or at somebody actually present at the time, let me know at once, will you?'

'You bet! It would be scary. But she hasn't so far.'

'Just in case.'

'Yep, sure,' said Samantha, departing at last.

She left Imogen wondering if the point of the consultation had actually been about Samantha's own worries at all, or if the whole thing had been designed to complain about Susan Inchman. On reflection she thought not; Samantha's own woes had seemed genuine enough. But she should look up the file on Susan Inchman some time when she had a moment. Moments seemed harder to find than usual, just now. Imogen's mind was partly on other things.

Frances, Imogen's long-term lodger, had once described Imogen, in her overhearing, as 'sharp as needles and soft as butter' which had given her a much needed boost of confidence at the time. But now her confidence was at an all-time high, and her concentration at an all-time low; in short Imogen had acquired a lover. The lover was not as she might have hoped, a handsome, well-meaning, middle-aged available man, the sort of fellow Frances would have prescribed for her, but a frail, elderly scholar, a fellow of St Agatha's, living in retirement just down the road, whom Imogen had taken to visiting while he recuperated from pneumonia, and who made her laugh. More to the point he made her think. The question whether he still needed daily visits from the friendly neighbourhood nurse was delicately on hold at the moment, while he played for time, to hold her attention, to keep her near at hand. And Imogen was touched. She had not before experienced this kind of love – a sort of disinterested bloom on the surface of friendship. Able to show itself because at Dennis's age it was past all practical consequences. To the best of Imogen's knowledge, Fran was completely unaware of Professor Dobbs. She aimed to keep it that way.

The possibility that English studies were bad for the young was a subject for discussion with Dennis. Which need not wait longer than tomorrow; they were trying an experiment, a walk slightly longer than anything Dennis had accomplished since his illness. They were going, weather permitting, to have lunch at the Ditton Plough. Imogen would drive them to the end of Riverside, past the new flats and houses, on which she expected Dennis to have strong opinions, and then they would walk along the river bank on Stourbridge Common. This walk was newly made easy by the provision of a walkway under the railway bridge, which had previously barred the way along the bank and enforced a detour. The two friends were eager to try it.

They set out mid-morning on Imogen's nearly free day – her 'surgery' was at five o'clock on Wednesdays – in bright clear weather, with just a bite in the air. Imogen was carrying a bag with a spare sweater for Dennis, and a bottle of water and a chocolate biscuit in case they didn't reach the Ditton Plough soon enough for comfort. As Imogen had expected, Dennis was volcanic on the subject of the new developments along the river, and it was a relief to park the car, and to cross on foot through the cattle-gate onto Stourbridge Common. This common had been the site of one of the most ancient fairs in England, and Dennis regaled her with historical facts about it. There were still cows peacefully grazing on the lush water-side grass. But something had changed greatly since Dennis had last walked here, and that was the arrival of canal boats.

All along the bank a line of boats was moored, boats of every description. There were some plastic palaces, 'Plastic ducks, more like,' growled Dennis, of that large family of boats that looks as though undecided between peaceful river cruising and setting out to sea. But most of the boats were narrow boats, some few full length, and even one or two in working trim – that is with the hold still under canvas instead of cabined over. The boats were in various states of repair, from spanking paintwork, lovely traditional lines, painted roses and castles, carefully coiled rope-work, and gleaming brass tillers and tiller-pins, all the way to the most horrendous state of dereliction, with dirty windows, stained and rent canvas covers, rotting hulls, rubbish of various kinds piled on the roofs or on the bank alongside. Floating slums, in effect.

There was interest too in the names people gave to boats: *Unthinkable, Costabomb, Flowing English, Swan of Avon, Nor-*

folk Lass, Gonzoogler, Ratty and Mole, Out of Phase, Athene Noctua . . .

The two friends walked and looked. Clearly there were people living on some of these vessels. There were yellow plastic bags of coal piled on the roof, and masts with wind-power fans mounted on them to recharge batteries, and television aerials, and, on some of them, prolific flowering tubs and baskets. Nobody, surely, needed sixteen bags of coal on the roof of a boat used for holidays.

'Whatever are they like to live in?' wondered Dennis aloud.

Immediately a man popped his head up through the sliding trap at the stern of the nearest boat, and said, 'Want to take a look, mate?'

They did indeed want to take a look. The boat on offer to view was *Wild Thyme*, a splendid, full-length beauty in dark navy, with none of the usual decoration. Inside they found themselves in the galley, a narrow, beautifully fitted kitchen done out in mahogany. It boasted a fridge, a small cooker, a little sink, a few cupboards; the owner was beaming at their surprise. He showed them a living area, with settees and a TV set, and a tubby little multi-fuel stove, a folding dining table, a bookshelf, pretty brass lamps on the sloping upper cabin sides, and then a shower and toilet, and three cabins, one with a double bed, and two with bunks. Then they came out at the front of the boat, into a well with seats on either side, where it would plainly be lovely to sit as the boat proceeded gently along the river.

'Whatever does all this cost?' asked Dennis tactlessly.

'If you bought this new from a boatyard, eighty K, I should think,' said the owner, not a whit offended. 'But my son and I fitted this up from a shell. He has a job in Cambridge, and he can't afford a house.'

'Well, I congratulate you on your work,' said Imogen. 'Who are we talking to?'

'Graham. Everyone calls me Gray.'

'It's a bit different from the only time I went narrow-boating,' said Dennis, 'in the Midlands somewhere. That was just sleeping under the canvas, and using some stuff called Racusan in a bucket for calls of nature. Fun in its way. Young man's game.'

'Well, it's all the heart could desire, now,' said Gray. 'With holidays, you just pull up the mooring stakes and set off. Plus if his job moves to Oxford, his house goes with him.'

'Oxford?' said Dennis. 'Bit risky, wouldn't it be? Across the Wash?'

'No, mate, you're out of date,' said Gray. 'It used to be that you couldn't get here through the Fenland drainage channels; there was a tight bend at Whittlesey that used to stop you getting anything through the Levels longer than about thirty-five feet. The canal freaks got going, and dug it out. You can take a full-length boat round it now. Easy. There's more and more boats coming.'

'What's the company like?' asked Imogen. 'What sort of street is the river bank?'

'Mixed,' said Gray. 'Retired toffs, and working profs, and lots of drop-outs. Druggies. Losers. Hard-up youngsters that can't afford a house, and think it's a caravan. Don't know a thing about a river; danger to themselves and others. Some of them can't undo a knot, leave alone tie one. I actually heard an eejit yelling for his sister to come and help him undo the mooring rope once. All sorts. Tend to stick together, though. Help each other out.'

Imogen thanked Gray, watched anxiously as Dennis stumbled down the sloping plank to the bank, and they went on their way. There were quite a few boats further down-stream of the Green Dragon Bridge, and Imogen inspected them with heightened interest. This was an aspect of Cambridge life that she had not encountered before, living as she did south of the city, where the river was a meandering stream, out of reach of anything larger than a punt.

The walk was too much for Dennis. By the time they reached the Ditton Plough it seemed best to down a pair of pints while waiting for a taxi to rescue them, and to leave both eating together and talk for another occasion.

3

I'd rather heare a towne bull bellow
Then such a fellow speake my lines

'There are,' remarked Frances Bullion to Imogen, 'only two parts for women in *Hamlet.*'

Imogen looked up from the *Telegraph* crossword, and said, 'Three.'

'How do you make that out? Gertrude and Ophelia. Makes two.'

'You've forgotten the Player Queen,' observed Imogen serenely. 'Who was Cinderella of Rouen? 4–2–3?'

'Joan of Arc. Now *that* would be a good choice of play.'

'How many women's parts in that?'

'Well, only one to speak of, but what a part!'

'Were you hoping to play Ophelia, Fran dear?' Imogen contemplated Fran: a nice-looking girl on a robust frame, able perhaps to play Rosamund, or Beatrice, but rather too tough-looking to manage going mad and floating away singing.

'Not a hope,' said Fran, 'but we have this delicious young fresher, perfectly beautiful and very talented. Name of Amy Parturian. Just the person to do a feeble, fading sort of girl easily knocked off her rocker by a footling prince.'

'You seem to me,' said Imogen, 'to be rather hostile to *Hamlet.*'

'You bet I am!' cried Frances. Then she quietened down, and sat on herself the other side of the kitchen table. 'Well, I am hostile to anything being forced on us by that prat Mottle.'

'Shakespeare has nothing to do with it?'

'Not,' Frances admitted with her usual lop-sided smile, 'as such.'

'Good,' said Imogen. 'I have been used to regard Shakespeare as an unassailable star. But I was recently assured that he is not. Not even particularly good. Just admired by a conspiracy of the right-winged because of his cryptofascist views.'

'Cripes!' said Frances. 'Who have you been listening to?'

'Percy Venton-Gimps.'

'Oh, him,' said Frances.

'I would be sorry to think you were of his way of thinking,' said Imogen.

'No, no, of course not. This isn't even about Shakespeare. But it is serious. Golly, look at the time. I must fly.'

Frances seized her jacket, and disappeared through the back door towards the bicycle sheds. Seconds later she put her head back round the door to say, 'Imogen, I forgot to ask: can we have the committee meeting here tonight?'

'Yes,' said Imogen. 'What's a word for Greek terror in five letters?'

'Panic. Thanks.'

'Be warned,' Imogen called after her, 'there are no biscuits left in the tin, and no crisps that are still crisp.'

She couldn't be sure if Frances had heard this last, and so later on she got her bike out and pedalled off to the Co-op to stock up. Biscuits were not an official part of her deal with her lodger, but she had a kind heart. The house rules at Imogen's place had changed a good deal over the years. Once she had taken three or four lodgers, never from her own college, and had learned to padlock the larder when a biscuit was about. But now her only lodgers were Fran, with her partner Josh Collihood, living in Imogen's rambling upstairs flat until they could afford a place of their own. Since they were both young academics, Josh doing research at the Science Park, and Fran doing a PhD, this didn't seem imminent. It was a good arrangement. Imogen didn't waste time dreading the empty house, and she had relaxed the larder rules. She liked both her lodgers.

'But if it isn't about Shakespeare,' she wondered to herself, 'what is it about? And who is the prat Mottle? I'm out of touch.'

For getting back in touch, there would be nothing like eavesdropping on the committee meeting, about to take place in her living room, with the aid of folding chairs from the summerhouse. Imogen expected it to be amusing.

It wasn't amusing; it was too serious for that. The young men and women who assembled for the occasion were clearly gloomy and apprehensive in the highest degree.

They were called to order by Simon Malpas, the chairman of the society – the Kyd Players. They were quite a large committee: seven of them present, of whom two were at St Agatha's and known at least slightly to Imogen. The others were strangers to her. There were also quite a few members not on the committee, but anxiously present. They were as flamboyantly dressed as she would expect of members of a long-established university dramatic society, but seemed tonight much less confident.

'Is Debbie here?' asked Simon Malpas.

'Not yet,' he was answered.

'Damn!' said the chairman. 'We can't start without her.'

'You can forget Debbie,' said a young woman sitting at the back of the room. 'She won't show up. I think she has resigned.'

'That won't help her,' said Nigel Snow. 'She's in it up to the neck like the rest of us.'

'She's in denial,' offered Fran.

'Can someone else take the minutes?' asked Simon. 'We've got to have this minuted, for heaven's sake.'

There was a silence round the room. 'Can't anybody just write it down?' implored the chairman. 'It doesn't have to be the official secretary. Just someone who can write!'

Still silence. Then: 'Actually, Simon, minute-taking is a bit tricky,' said a young man sitting near the door, 'even if everybody isn't all talking at once. I tried it once and I made an awful botch of it.'

'I'll take the minutes for you,' offered Imogen. Her eternal disposition to be helpful had landed her in trouble-taking once again.

'Oh, would you really?' cried Simon. 'How kind of you, how awfully kind.'

'I don't know who everyone is, though,' said Imogen. 'You'll have to run round the room giving me names. Fran, get me the ruled notebook from my desk, would you?'

'We've got a proper minute book,' Simon said.

'I'd rather work in rough and copy it into the book later, if you don't mind,' said Imogen.

'Anything you say. We are so grateful to you. Wait till I get hold of Debbie.'

'Tell me who everyone is,' said Imogen, trying to move the discussion along.

'Simon is chairman, and our director,' said Fran. 'The

cowardly Debbie is secretary; and I'm the new treasurer. Robert, the old treasurer, went down last term.'

'I'm Nigel Snow, publicity,' said a young man on Imogen's right.

'I'm Hugo Brown, fund-raising,' said another.

'I'm Antonia, casting manager,' said a small and pretty girl on Imogen's right. The lighting manager and the costume manager then introduced themselves.

'The others here are just members, not committee members,' said Simon. 'They can listen but not speak or vote.'

'All set, then,' said Imogen. She had made a quick diagram of the names arranged according to where people were sitting. Her pen was poised.

'OK then,' said Simon. 'Chairman's report. I'm afraid it's very bad news, everyone. As you know we have – we had – rehearsal rooms just off Parker's Piece. As I'm sure you recall, there was a bad fire there last term, and Mr Fleet, our part-time caretaker, was injured. He got a lung full of smoke and fumes. He is still off work, although I'm glad to say he is a bit better. You probably also know that the next-door premises – that printing shop – were also damaged. You know that the fire officer thought the cause of the fire was a bank of stage lights left switched on overnight, rather too near a curtain on stage. That means it is our fault; negligence on our part. What you probably don't know is that we weren't insured.'

'Yes, we were,' said Hugo Brown. 'I saw it in the accounts.'

'It was entered in the accounts,' said Fran, 'but the dear departed treasurer forgot actually to write and post the cheque.'

'So we don't get a lovely lump sum to rebuild the rehearsal rooms,' said Antonia. 'Shame. We'll manage.'

'You haven't realised,' said Simon Malpas wearily. 'Mr

Fleet has a claim against us. So does the print shop. We haven't any money to meet the claims.'

'Well, it's Robert's fault, isn't it? They must go after him,' said Hugo.

'I'm afraid not. The whole committee is responsible. "Jointly and severally" is the phrase. They can go after *us*.'

'Didn't we have director's liability insurance?' asked Hugo.

'Yes; we let it lapse along with the buildings insurance.'

'Oh, God,' said Hugo.

'Well, can't pay, won't pay,' said Antonia. 'They can't get what we haven't got. We can just close down the Kyd Players.'

'After a hundred and two years?' wailed Fran.

'I've been talking to a lawyer,' said Simon. 'Not a real lawyer, we couldn't afford that. A friendly academic lawyer. He thinks the print shop won't sue us because they themselves will be insured, and they will be told there's no point going after us precisely *because* we can't pay. "Men of Straw" was his name for us. He thinks the same will apply to Fred Fleet. But – wait for it – there is something called employer's liability insurance which we were by law supposed to have. He thinks it might even be a criminal offence to employ someone and not have it. And Fred Fleet is a member of a trade union which might want to go for us and make an example of us.'

'Can't we get off the hook by going bankrupt?' asked Hugo.

'I thought of that,' said Simon. 'We could. We would be dropping poor Fred in the shit. But also once we have been bankrupt we won't appeal to many employers. And we will be disqualified by many professional organisations. We won't easily become lawyers, or accountants, for example.'

'How much money can we rake up between us?' asked Antonia.

'Well,' said Simon, 'I'm from a rather hard-up family. My

parents remortgaged their house to help me through Cambridge. I can't imagine even telling my father what we have done. How about anyone else?'

'I've got a bit in the building society,' said Antonia. 'It wouldn't do Fred's lost wages for more than a month.'

'Will the university in any shape or form help us?' asked Nigel.

'Some time back a Kyd Players committee made a great palaver about being independent of the university,' said Simon. 'They were trying to escape dead-hand control of what plays they could produce, but the result is I think nobody could now assert that the university was responsible for us, I'm afraid. And, look, friends, I am dreadfully sorry. I know you all joined just for the fun of acting, and nobody knew what responsibilities they were incurring. I'm sorry. But there is just one other possibility. Someone has offered to bale us out. Martin Mottle. But if we accept his offer we have to accept his conditions.'

'Mottle . . .' said Hugo. 'That name rings a bell.'

'You'll have heard of his father,' said Simon wearily. 'A huge, multi-multi-millionaire. Invented something that makes fruit ripen without rotting in container ships.'

'So Mottle junior is loaded?'

'Beyond the dreams of avarice. He funds his college climbing club single-handed while they scramble expensively round the top of the Himalayas and the Andes.'

'Why does he want to rescue us?' asked Hugo. 'Is he a mad do-gooder? Loves his fellow men? I mean if he was keen on acting, he would be a member of this or the ADC or something.'

'I cannot fathom his motive,' said Simon. 'I have trouble enough with his conditions.'

'Well, spill the beans, Simon. What are these conditions? Do we have to put on a show for the Sherpas, or what?'

'Some of you already know about this,' said Simon. 'For the benefit of the others, it's this. We have to put on *Hamlet*, and let him both direct it, and play the lead role. I can be assistant director. And there must be total secrecy about all aspects of the production or he will pull out.'

'And if we agree?'

'He'll pay a hundred thousand into our bank account the day after the first night of the play.'

'Whew!' said Hugo.

'And that,' said Simon, 'will compensate Mr Fleet, and probably repair the building as well.'

'Let's go for it, then!' said Hugo. '*Hamlet*'s all right. By a reputable author. What's the problem?'

'Difficult role. Completely untried and incompetent actor. He'll make a dog's dinner of it and we shall all look bloody fools. All our rival dramatic societies will be laughing their heads off; bang goes any chance we might have had of getting talent-spotted and going on to greater things.'

'Well, we backstagers won't be disgraced,' said Antonia. 'We can stage it properly. But I do see it's rather hard on Simon. I mean directors do get the blame for dying ducks.'

'Just the same,' said Nigel eagerly. 'None of that is a bit as dreadful as what we were looking at just now. Think of it, friends: no charred building, no crippled caretaker on our conscience, no bankruptcy, probably need never tell parents about it at all. I mean what's a bit of artistic disgrace compared to that?'

Simon quietly put his head in his hands.

'We've got to accept this offer,' said Nigel. 'And put up with it. It won't last for ever, and it might not even be that bad. I mean, how do we know Mottle can't act?'

'You haven't met him,' said Antonia.

'Tell you what, though,' said Fran. 'I think we will all have to promise to stand by Simon through thick and thin. We can't just decide for Mottle's plan and then desert the ship. Simon deserves our loyal support if he is going to carry the can for the whole committee like this. No more Debbies. OK?'

'Are we sure he'll keep his word?' asked Antonia.

'We would have to draw up a contract,' said Simon gloomily. 'That could be done.'

'Put this to the vote,' said Fran. 'It's too important to just discuss it, and pass on.'

'Before we vote,' said Simon, 'I'd like to just point out that we could turn down this offer. We could say our artistic integrity demands that we do. That we'd rather just face the music.'

'Well, your artistic integrity would then leave Fred Fleet on the dole, with no compensation for his suffering and his loss of wages,' said Antonia. 'Funny thing to call integrity, isn't it?'

'Not everybody has got the kind I'm talking about,' said Simon. 'I do realise that. The theatre is just a game for some people . . .'

'Hold on, Simon, don't get het up,' said Nigel. 'We need to keep this cool and civil, otherwise heaven help us.'

'We don't disagree, anyway, do we?' said Hugo. 'We all feel terrible about Fred; we all hate the Mottle plan. We haven't got a clash of values here, just a really hard choice.'

'Well said,' said Fran. 'Look, before we vote, I am going to formally move that we decide that a vote for the Mottle plan commits the person who casts it to participate in the production, to remain on the committee until the end of the year, and to give Simon all the support he needs. Anyone who doesn't accept that need not cast a vote. I propose; who will second it?'

'I will,' said Nigel.

'Anyone opposed to that? Nem con, I see,' said Fran. 'OK, the main proposition. Do we accept Mr Mottle, subject to contract?'

'I propose we do,' said Antonia.

'Anyone second that?'

'I will,' said Hugo.

'Right. In favour?' asked Fran. Hands went up all round. 'Against?'

Only the hapless Simon voted against.

'Carried,' Fran said. 'Sorry, Simon.'

The meeting broke up almost at once. Imogen saw with amazement that the plate of biscuits was untouched. They had actually been too miserable to eat.

It wasn't long at all before Imogen heard more about the troubles of the Kyd Society. Fran seemed to regard Imogen's minute-taking as putting her in the loop, and talked freely about it all. Imogen had, as promised, copied the minutes carefully into the official book, which had minutes at the front, and accounts at the back, and had observed the carefree chaos in which the book had been left by her predecessors. It is completely illogical, she told herself sternly, to hold that someone who cannot spell and who uses green or violet ink and writes crookedly all over the page is exactly the sort of person who *would* forget to insure a building. But Imogen had not herself enjoyed the privileges of a fine education; she had thrown over reading medicine for love, and followed someone to the States, where he had abandoned her. It is almost superhuman when one has lost a chance oneself not to feel severe about people who have gained it and who seem unworthy of it. Imogen was, however, very sympathetic towards the harassed Simon, the more so when Fran told her more about him.

'He's bloody brilliant,' Fran declared, sitting on the floor beside Imogen's gas fire one evening. She was playing with a beautiful toy she had just bought, allegedly for her nephew, a Noah's Ark, complete with pairs of animals and birds, all ready to be set out along the carpet, two by two. 'And it's probably the end of his glorious career before he's got started,' she said, putting a pair of ducks in line behind the giraffes. 'You have to admit it's hard.'

'Why is it as bad as that?' asked Imogen.

'He's in his second year,' said Fran. 'Next year is finals year; like everyone else he'll have to apply himself to work, or risk his degree. So now is his last chance to put on a big show. But quite often, Imogen, there are talent scouts for the professional theatre at the big production of a Cambridge dramatic society. Simon really did stand a chance of following Richard Burton and Tom Stoppard and others onto the London stage.'

'Couldn't he still?'

'Well, what chance is there of impressing anyone with his production skills with a goof like Mottle in the lead role?'

'I don't know anything about Mr Mottle. Is he really a goof?'

'I sat in on one reading,' said Fran. 'He's awful beyond belief.'

'Can't remember his lines?'

'Oh, he can remember them all right. He just can't speak them properly. He's, like, "Oh-that-this-too-too-sol-id-flesh-would-melt . . ."' Fran began to speak in a monotone drone, giving every word the same flat-footed weight. '"Thaw and-resolve-it-self-in-to-a-dew." Not even Shakespeare, Imogen, can withstand it. It's unbearable. The only consolation is that

Simon has found a very short version. The Bad Quarto. It's a crap version, a prompt copy, or remembered rather badly by one of the actors, or pirated by a scribbler in the audience. But its shining merit in Simon's eyes is that it is only two thousand-odd lines. As little as possible of the dreadful Mottle.'

'It's early days, surely. Won't young Mottle get better as Simon coaches him?'

'I don't think he *can* get better. And think what a part it is, Imogen: something the greatest actors aspire to. People go and see Branagh do it and come away muttering that they preferred Gielgud. Our friend Mottle would make a hash out of playing a Teletubbie!'

'You are harsh, Fran dear.'

'And what I don't get is his motivation. He looks and sounds miserable all the way through rehearsals, and yet the whole thing is his idea and his alone.'

'Well, wanting to play Hamlet is a not unknown crazy ambition.'

'No,' said Fran thoughtfully, 'that's not it. I mean, you are quite right about the crazy ambition, but I was not quite right to describe him as miserable. Tense, and buttoned up. Angry perhaps? Well, perhaps just mad. Aha, worse luck for us.'

'Better luck for you, Fran. Nobody is going bankrupt, and Mr Fleet is getting compensation. Remember?'

'It's an odd thing about human nature, isn't it?' said Fran musingly. 'One's attention is always switched on to what trouble one actually has; one forgets in a minute the worse that might have been. Animals quarrelling in the ark, forgetting the flood outside.'

'Talking of human nature, lodger dear,' said Imogen, hauling herself out of her deep armchair, 'it's time for bed.'

*   *   *

Of course it was not any part of Imogen's duties to engage in the scholarly disputes that raged from time to time through the seemingly calm courts, halls and gardens of the college. But to wash her hands of them was to accept that she did not and would not grasp one of the factors influencing the life of those around her, and impinging on her work, as it had done in talking to Samantha. Had Imogen's advice to her been correct? Perhaps, Imogen thought, as she cycled home across Lammas Land, she was too idealistic by far. Perhaps what Samantha ought really to do was to try to find out about the examiners and write as required. The ghost of Dorothy Sayers, the deep idealism about university life in *Gaudy Night* might have misled her. She had heard *Gaudy Night* being very scathingly attacked. And it might be, rightly. It might be that such an Arcadian view of scholarly detachment and concern for truth was a chimera living on past its time chiefly in the minds of people like herself who had not had a university education. And yet . . . Imogen knew the scholars and students she worked with very well. When it came to the students, firsts were the spur that the dull spirit did move; but the senior members of colleges were not what they were. In her father's time the dons had had a comfortable, one might say cushy life; they were well fed, well cared for by their colleges, and safely ensconced for life, however odd and dysfunctional they became. And posts were reasonably well-paid, and very reasonably respected. Naturally in those conditions there were reasons for seeking to live as a don that had nothing to do with a love of learning. Imogen supposed that most of her father's colleagues had started out with a scholarly bent; if the urge to think and study left them, they had usually stayed put anyway, rather like the nineteenth-century vicars who stayed in the Church ministering to parishes when they no longer believed in God.

Not now. Now anybody bright enough to go through the

motions of university teaching could get a better-paid job somewhere else, and many people found the comfort-blanket of college life stifling. Especially in the sciences, the college fellows were teaching youngsters who earned three times their salaries the moment they went down. Money talks, louder than it used to do, and the profession of scholar was no longer an automatic passport to a bit of respect. Those who stayed were detained neither by lust for money nor desire for glory; only the love of learning accounted for it, and however false *Gaudy Night* had seemed to the sour Leavises, it had quietly become true again now. Or so Imogen thought. Of course, Cambridge was in England. People no more talked openly about a love of learning than they did about loving anything else. All deep motives were unavowed, and in need of deduction.

Imogen resolved to talk over feuding in the English faculty with Professor Dobbs the following afternoon, when they were planning a picnic together.

4

O, these Players cannot keepe counsell – thei'le tell all!

'One would have thought,' said Fran to Imogen next morning, 'that the Bad Quarto was short enough. Bad enough too, come to that. But the prat Mottle won't have it. He won't have the dumb-show – we're cutting it out and going straight to the play-within-the-play. Oh, and we're not supposed to tell anyone that, either.'

'He does have very decided ideas, doesn't he?' offered Imogen. 'But then, for a hundred thousand pounds I suppose he would have.'

'The whole show will be over in about an hour,' said Fran. 'People will want their money back.'

'But it wasn't young Mottle who chose the Bad Quarto, was it? I thought you said it was Simon.'

'In self-defence, yes,' said Fran. 'You know, Imogen, I just don't like the feel of all this. Makes me very uneasy.'

'Understandable. But you're honour bound. Is the dumb-show essential, in your eyes?'

'Nope. To be honest I can't see what it's doing there at all. And the original producer – Hamlet himself – doesn't seem to like it much either. He mutters to Ophelia all through it.'

'Miching mallecho?'

'Whatever that means – yes.'

'We could look up what it means.'

'Mmm. I have. The great OED says: "*Occurs only in the Shakespeare passage quoted and echoes of it*. Of uncertain form, origin and meaning." '

'So it just means: here comes trouble?'

'Yup. And why? He, Hamlet, I mean, has just arranged all this, and he ought to be expecting it. Directors are not usually astonished at what is happening on the stage – unless they are poor Simon, of course.'

'But you don't think the play is maimed if the dumb-show is cut?'

'Not personally, no,' said Fran. 'But what do I know? I'm not a Shakespeare scholar, just a poor bloody historian. Must fly . . .'

Imogen, who was not a Shakespeare scholar either, took *Hamlet* to bed with her that night. She didn't have a copy of the Bad Quarto, but made do with the beautiful Folio edition of the Tragedies that she had bought second-hand in the Haunted Bookshop a little while back. What she had remembered from a school production was 'The play's the thing, in which I'll catch the conscience of the King.' Hamlet organises the troupe of visiting players to enact the story of his father's murder related to him by his father's ghost. If the ghost has told true this should upset King Claudius enough for his discomfiture to show, and Hamlet has Horatio briefed to watch Claudius carefully.

Imogen read late into the night. She had remembered correctly, in a broad-brush sort of way. But she had contrived not to notice how odd it is that the dumb-show and the play-within-the-play repeat each other. She had not remembered how genuinely doubtful Hamlet seems about the ghost: it might be a fiend from hell, set on trapping him into murdering someone. And yet wouldn't it, in that age, have been almost expected of him to murder a man who had usurped the crown, without benefit of ghosts? Wasn't the crown rightfully his? Isn't Claudius nervous of him for that very reason? So why does it matter so much whether the ghost is 'an honest ghost' or not? This would certainly give her plenty to discuss with Dennis Dobbs.

The following afternoon Imogen was sitting comfortably on a bench in the lovely gardens of Anglesey Abbey, beside the very man. They were achieving a more restful expedition this time. They had not after all brought a picnic with them, but instead had eaten an early cream tea in the refreshment room. Now they were quietly watching the wind in the trees. Lord Fairhaven, who had laid out the grounds of the abbey, had liked trees more than flowers; his gardens were austere and grand. The scene was shared by classical figures on plinths in statuesque poses, and by wandering visitors.

For a while the two friends were companionably silent. Dennis Dobbs was one of those fortunate men who keep their good looks into old age. He was lean and white-haired, with a narrow face, which had crinkled into thought-lines, giving him an air of distinction. He had very pale blue eyes, and a steady gaze. The illness he had just survived had put a sort of cosmic calm on him. It had also demolished any reserve between himself and Imogen. She had washed his clothes and his bed-sheets and every inch of his person for weeks together last year, when the hospital had dumped him home, and there had been nobody to nurse him through convalescence. Imogen had extended her college duties to include him, because he was a college fellow, although long retired. Also she had always liked him. She knew him now as closely as in youth one knows a lover, and it was very plain to her that he now loved her.

'Dennis,' said Imogen in a while, 'would you think a production of *Hamlet* much the worse if it went forward without including the dumb-show before the play-within-the-play?'

'Hmm,' he said. 'I have seen it produced like that. But personally I think the dumb-show is necessary.'

'Why? I had a quick look myself, and I couldn't see what the point was. Of having both, I mean. Don't they rather repeat each other?'

'Yes. I think it was to increase the tension, by letting the audience know what was coming, so that they could all watch the King as keenly as Horatio is doing to see his reaction.'

'But Claudius is there for both. If the idea is to upset him with the ghost's story, why does he sit through the dumb-show quite calmly and then go berserk during the play?'

'It ought to be staged with Claudius's attention clearly elsewhere during the dumb-show. But the stage directions have maybe got lost or garbled. You need to read Dover Wilson, *What Happened in Hamlet*. I'll lend it to you when we get home. Why the sudden interest?'

'Oh, just something I heard,' said Imogen evasively, aware that all this was supposed to be a deep secret. 'In confidence,' she added.

'Aha! A nice girl like you could never imagine how much bile and venom is expended on matters of Shakespeare scholarship,' said Dennis gleefully. 'Structuralists and anti-structuralists, historicists, feminists, allegation and counter-allegation, traditionalists calling people Marxists, Marxists calling everyone imperialists, reputations broken and trampled, hatred riding into battle, assassination by footnote

. . . it gets almost homicidal. Dover Wilson belonged to a calmer and more reasonable age. You can read him without nightmares.'

'Don't we have a fellow in college who is into all that?' said Imogen. 'Mr Venton-Gimps?'

'Oh, him,' said Dennis. 'Don't rate him overmuch, myself. Now that young fool of ours who broke his neck a couple of terms ago was an altogether different kettle of fish. Gave one of the best Arden lectures I have ever heard. He knew how to put the cat among the pigeons. Completely put paid to a saying of my own dear tutor, long long ago to the effect that one should bear in mind that new remarks about Shakespeare are *wrong*.'

Imogen laughed. 'I take it we are talking of John Talentire?'

'Yes. What do you have against him, dear Imogen?'

'Have I said a word against him? I only spoke his name.'

'Tones of voice speak volumes,' said Dennis Dobbs. 'Of course I would expect any friend of the college to look askance at idiotic horseplay that turns suicidal. Is it that?'

'Well, I can't approve of trying Harding's Folly. Such a waste of a young life.'

'But that's not all, I perceive,' said Dennis.

Imogen sighed. There was a downside as well as an upside to being very well known to Dennis; he was, among other, better things, a gleeful old gossip. And Imogen's feelings were uncomfortably transparent to him.

'Well, I'm not proud of this, Dennis. But some college fellows, especially since I was made a fellow myself, pass the time of day with me when I happen across them, and talk to me like an equal. And others don't. It tends to affect how much I like someone. Prejudice, of course. Pride, maybe.'

'But completely natural. And Talentire was one who didn't stoop to bid you good day? Pity that. A blot on his scutcheon.'

'Dennis, while you are educating me would you like to tell me whatever a scutcheon is or was?'

'Look it up,' said Dennis crisply. 'So how do you feel about the prospect of having another Talentire in the college? The late John's dad is about to retire, and I hear there's a move to give him the Postgate Fellowship.'

'Yes, I heard a rumour about that,' said Imogen. 'I've never met Sir Duncan Talentire. I have no opinion about giving him a fellowship, or even about giving him good morning. I suppose he would be an ornament to the college. Isn't that what a Postgate Fellow is supposed to be?'

'Naturally. A distinguished man just retired, to spend three years as a college fellow, with no formal duties, but three lectures to give.'

'He might, don't you think, Dennis, having lost his only son through a St Agatha's window, shudder at the very thought of spending time there?'

'Well, we wouldn't give him the tower room, I suppose,' said Dennis, grinning malevolently.

'His revulsion might not be confined to one particular room,' Imogen said.

'He seemed very attached to the place while his son was alive,' said Dennis. 'John was always bringing him to dinners as a guest. I'm afraid you might have to put up with being snubbed by Talentire senior just as you were by Talentire junior. Poor you.'

'I'll survive,' said Imogen drily.

Imogen's journey between her home in Newnham and the college could take a large number of nicely varied routes. The day after her conversation with Dennis Dobbs, having promised to buy him some new socks, she was pushing her bicycle down a little alley between King's Parade and the market square, where Marks and Spencer stands, a way that took her past the Haunted Bookshop. She often paused to admire the window display of this little second-hand book dealer; quite often she could stare at old editions of children's books, deeply familiar from her own childhood reading, and gasp at the price these copies could now fetch. The run of books in her attic might be part of her pension, if the bookseller had gauged things right. Once or twice Imogen had bought something there, replacing a well-loved and missing title with a copy not in first-quality condition, affordable and good to have.

That morning her eye was caught by a very expensive volume: *The Night Climbers of Cambridge* by one 'Whipplesnaith'. It hardly needed the quotation marks to show that a name like that was a pseudonym. The jacket showed a madman ascending the gate-tower of St John's College, holding on to a narrow plinth, and with one foot on a carved Tudor rose, and the other dangling, apparently in search of a foothold. In the light of the conversation about the Talentires that she had been having with Dennis, Imogen went in and asked to look at the volume. It was full of blurry photographs, all taken at night, of young men engaged in heart-stoppingly daring and foolish ascents of various monuments of Cambridge architecture. Worse, to Imogen's fascination and dismay there were detailed descriptions of these climbs, listing handholds and footholds, and amounting to an insane person's guide on how to risk your life on college walls and roofscapes. There were chapters on particular colleges: St John's, Pembroke, Trinity, King's and Clare. When Imogen saw there was a chapter on St Agatha's, she took the copy to the till and bought it, winning at the astronomical price: thirty five pounds was a small fortune on her salary.

*   *   *

It was always a pleasure to be invited to the Master's Lodge, unless, as sometimes happened, the invitation was a professional one concerning the Master's medication, or state of mind. For all his serene demeanour, his widely admired skills at overseeing college affairs, and his towering scholarship, the Master was not robust. He took things far too much to heart, and had in the past been prescribed tranquillisers which he had had terrible difficulty getting himself off. Imogen had once had his medication in her own cabinet to be doled out to him carefully at moments of real need. He was independent of them, and her, now, but she had become a close and trusted friend of both him and his wife, and often found herself drinking sherry with them in the Lodge before hall dinners, or sharing some expedition with Lady Buckmote.

She had meant to mention the feuds in the English Department, and the confusion of students like Samantha, next time she had a chance to talk quietly with the Buckmotes, but the conversation turned instead to another lament: the problem of the Postgate Fellowship. The college had money from a bequest to run this rather desirable position, which fell due every three years. The current Postgate Fellow, an eminent historian, was retiring at the end of the academic year, having performed admirably, living in college, running a historians' debating society, being charming at High Table, writing canny letters to *The Times* giving his address as St Agatha's, and above all using the time the appointment gave him to write a splendid history of the Middle East, which was plastered with acknowledgements to the college, and was being reviewed everywhere. No more than this could be expected of any recipient of the fellowship.

That made him a hard act to follow. Further, Imogen learned there was a sort of informal agreement that the fellowship should be occupied alternately by an arts and a science fellow. A distinguished scientist was now required.

'That should at least be easier than dealing with the English faculty,' said Lady Buckmote, pushing her shoes off her feet, and settling comfortably on one of the vast sofas in the drawing room.

'I thought it was all done and dusted,' said the Master. 'I thought it would be Talentire. But there are difficulties. Someone is objecting – well, that's rather strong – someone is uneasy.'

'Oh?' said Lady Buckmote. 'I thought Talentire was the ultimate expert witness. Haven't I been reading his name in law reports these twenty years at least?'

'Don't ask me, beloved,' said Sir William. 'The law reports are not my cup of tea. They take too long in the morning.'

'I think I'm right, though,' said Caroline Buckmote. 'He's usually for the prosecution, isn't he? Didn't he give evidence in that rather distressing case last year?'

'Yes. I remember that,' said Imogen. 'A woman who had apparently killed three of her children.'

'That's the one. There was a piece about Duncan Talentire in the papers when the case was all over. Made him out the bee's knees on forensics.'

'Are we allowed to ask who is uneasy?' said Imogen.

'Appleby,' said the Master.

'Oho, our most senior fellow in the sciences,' said Lady B. 'The plot thickens. Why is he uneasy?'

'Can't quite get him to say. Perhaps he just doesn't like Talentire. Unusually, this time the college has had plenty of chances to get a look at someone before appointing him.'

'But it must be something more than his table manners, or

an irritating laugh, if it's Appleby objecting,' said Lady B. 'He hasn't a frivolous or unfair bone in his body.'

'Oh, agreed. Splendid chap. But so careful not to be unfair that all he will do is shake his head and tell me he'll let me know later what he thinks.'

'Better consult the bursar, too,' said Imogen.

'Why, Imo?'

'To make sure Talentire, if appointed, is given a ground-floor room.'

'That's not in the best possible taste,' said the Master, grinning at Imogen. 'Quite surprised at you.'

'Don't be a prig, William,' said Lady B.

Imogen left them exchanging amiable insults, and took her leave.

As she passed through the porters' lodge, the junior porter, known to one and all as 'James', called out to her.

'Have you a minute, Miss Quy?'

'What is it, James?'

'We have an intruder in the Fellows' Garden. Blotto or under the influence or something. I would have thrown him over the wall, so to speak, but Mr Hughes said to ask you to have a look at him first in case we are wrong and he needs help. You'll have to hold your nose,' he added. He came round from behind the counter in the lodge, and walked with her towards the Fellows' Garden. This was a choice enclosed area of the grounds, with a huge mulberry tree – the eighteenth-century fellows had fancied raising silk-worms – valuable plants, and even more valuable peace and quiet. The college grounds were open to the public every day from dawn to dusk; the inner part of the Fellows' Garden was open only twice a year. 'I wouldn't like to criticise Mr Hughes,' said James as they went.

'Indeed not,' said Imogen gravely. Mr Hughes was the head

porter, a man of immense dignity and sapience, whom even the Master would be loath to criticise.

The intruder was lying on one of the Gothic benches provided for fellows to sit upon in contemplation. He was in filthy clothes, his hair was matted, and he seemed unconscious rather than asleep. Imogen stooped to examine him closely. Sickly complexion, pallid, blotched and moist with sweat. Lips blueish, lightly frothing. Not an old dosser: he couldn't have been above his mid-twenties, perhaps younger. He emitted a reek of cannabis enough to knock you over, though what actually made her recoil was the sight of body lice crawling on his neck.

'Pleasant sight, Miss Quy,' remarked James. 'Another part of the rich tapestry of life in beautiful Cambridge. Can I manhandle him, do you reckon? Tip him in a wheelbarrow and trundle him off?'

'Just a minute, James,' said Imogen. She took the dangling wrist of the intruder in her fingers, to find his pulse. But that woke him up. He lurched into a sitting position, saying, 'Whaaa? Get off me, you sodding pervert!'

'Right,' said James. 'That's it. Out with you now!' He tugged the youngster to his feet.

Fully awake now, though with speech still slurred, the youth let rip a stream of invective. He hadn't done no one no harm, only having a rest in the sodding college, just sat down on a sodding bench for a moment, let go of him, and much more. Imogen followed as the stumbling wreck of a man was frogmarched out of the Fellows' Garden, across the court, and out into the street. Various undergraduates moving through the court witnessed the little scene. One young man called out to James, offering help. A group of girls fell silent as they passed. Imogen saw, for the split second in which she looked at these, an expression of deep distaste crossing faces like a cloud shadow skidding over the immaculate lawn.

'Do we have a lot of bother with intruders?' Imogen asked James, when the man had been ejected.

'Scum like that?' asked James. 'Now and again. You'd be surprised, Miss Quy. They have excuses, mind you. Got lost trying to cut through the college to the station, for example.'

'But the station is right at the other end of town!'

'Just so. Or thought we were the Department of Social Security, or thought we were a drop-outs' hostel. Lots like that. Usually got something to say for themselves, other than the truth, which is they were looking for an unlocked room where they could nick something to buy drugs. Mr Hughes had someone last term trying to sleep on a bench in the grounds, saying he was waiting for his sister. Couldn't remember her name, though. I ask you! As for the number of times the gardeners find syringes and needles in the flower-beds . . . I've lost count.'

'Some of those, James, I regret to tell you, may be ours – the doings of one of ours, I mean.'

'I know, Miss Quy. Whatever is the world coming to?' he said.

'This is supposed to explain it all,' said Imogen, waving Dennis's copy of *What Happens in Hamlet* at Fran and Josh, found making supper in her kitchen when she got in late and exhausted that evening. She had been invited to share the pasta and pesto meal they were making, having arrived just as Fran was putting the linguini into the pan of boiling water. Josh grated extra Gran Padano, and Imogen contributed an apple cake bought at the Women's Institute stall on the market that morning, to serve as pudding. They often mucked in in this way, on the understanding that it was always by invitation, and nobody took offence if it didn't suit. This was one way in which Imogen's settled tenants were ideal for her. She had the advantages of living alone and independent, but she never needed to be lonely: she had easy access to company.

Conversation soon returned to *Hamlet*, and the prat Mottle. Imogen retailed Dennis Dobbs's views on the dumb-show, and Fran said that made perfect sense, but — she shrugged eloquently — 'What can we do? I think I'll not mention it to Simon, it would only upset him. He's sort of gone dogged and calm, and is making what he can of the thing. The Bad Quarto misses out most of the best bits, but it's damage limitation. I'd have called it the garbled quarto myself. Simon doesn't need any more aggravation.'

Josh said, 'You wouldn't think people could get this worked up about Shakespeare after all these centuries.'

'Philistine!' cried Fran, putting the dish of fragrant pasta in the centre of the breakfast room table. 'I might be just about to announce that I'm writing a biography of the Bard.'

'Don't do that, Fran dear,' said Imogen. 'I gather the whole field of Shakespearean scholarship is a seething snake-pit of biting vipers. Murderous, even. Keep clear.'

'Murderous?' said Josh. 'Wasn't that St Agatha's fellow who broke his neck last year a Shakespeare scholar?'

'He wasn't murdered, though. Silly ass fell out of a window,' said Fran.

The talk veered away to settle on Josh's research.

5

Why, what should be the feare?
I do not set my life at a pinnes fee.

The Night Climbers of Cambridge was not a suitable bedtime book. Imogen started by looking through the illustrations, each and every one of which showed a young man in a hideously dangerous position, clinging to the walls or pinnacles of a well-known building in imminent danger of death. A laid-back bravado informed the captions: 'The Tottering Tower: at the moment of taking the photograph the top cross, which the climber is holding, was swaying,' Imogen read. She shuddered. She was one of the many people with not much head for heights. The book was as terrifying for a mature woman with experience of human injuries as a horror comic might have been for a small boy. Just as the small boy would have done, Imogen continued reading. The book revealed a strange freemasonry of the night among the undergraduates of yore. They surveyed every vertical surface in Cambridge in search of ways of risking life and limb. Pursued by the proctors, the college porters and the police, they fled across rooftops and down drainpipes, and melted into the night. They acquired strange obsessions like a wish to 'introduce goutu onto the roof of the Gibbs building' and pursued the idea with flights of madness. Imogen continued reading, unable to release herself and go to sleep.

'The easiest way, which may perhaps be considered an evasion, is to climb the face of Caius and drop across the Senate House Passage, a distance of about seven feet . . .'

How, then, would one climb the face of Caius? The instructions were detailed and precise, but Imogen skittered over them.

> . . . a hand traverse along a ledge to the left, past the pipe, until the left foot can reach the curved flange, projecting for an inch from the wall above the archway . . . standing on the steel bar of the windowsill and with one hand on the crossbar, you can just reach a small ledge above your head . . . laying the left forearm flat on the lower ledge to the left, and holding the upper ledge with the right hand, pull with the right hand and push up with the left . . . at this stage of the climb one is acutely conscious of how much depends on the soundness of the stone of the two ledges. Fortunately all the stonework except the gargoyles on this building is in excellent condition . . .

Feeling slightly nauseous, Imogen got up, put on her dressing gown, and went down to the kitchen to make herself some warm milk. She tried a less dizzying section of the book, a chapter called 'For Beginners Only'. This contained a discussion of the desirability or otherwise of using a rope, following a careful distinction between mountaineering and night climbing. Imogen learned that using a rope was a controversial matter: 'it is the writer's opinion that no climb should be attempted on a rope that the climber would be incapable of achieving unroped.' However, the writer went on to specify the quality of the rope, and the minimum length for maximum utility.

Sipping her milk, deciding that the chapter on St Agatha's

would be best left unread until bright morning, Imogen reflected on the strange subculture revealed between the covers of Mr Whipplesnaith's magnum opus. Published in 1937. Did the wild boyish crew who indulged in this suicidal folly already know, already guess, that their lives would be thrown away wholesale in another world war? Did they think, as who would not have thought, that if there was another war the slaughter of the First World War would be repeated and exceeded, that they would die innumerable like the leaves falling from the trees in autumn? Did they choose to throw away their future on their own terms, rather than waiting for military service to do it for them?

No, surely she was moonshining. Whatever time of night was it? Three a.m. Too late for common sense. These chapters were not written with death in mind: they were written by and for the immortals. The devil-may-care, the golden lads, for whom risk is a heady brew and harm is something that happens to other people. Their successors rode motorcycles at a hundred miles an hour, and took up hang-gliding, white-water rafting, or anything else they could think of that threatened life and limb. It was as unfashionable to be self-preserving as it was to be a swot.

Surely she was tired enough now to put the book aside and go to sleep? The book had a lot yet to tell her, but it would wait. She put out the light, and went to her bed.

'Will you do something for me?' Dennis asked when Imogen called in on him after breakfast.

'If I can.' She was regularly doing his shopping, or his laundry.

'Will you take me to the theatre? I don't feel as if I ought to go by myself anywhere.'

'A pleasure, Dennis. What do you want to see?'

'This production of *Hamlet* the Kyd Society are putting on.'

'I understand it will be a shambles.'

'It will be the Bad Quarto; I've never seen that. Is there any difficulty about it? About you taking me, I mean? I'll buy the tickets.'

Dr Appleby called in on Imogen during her office hours, and settled himself comfortably in a chair in front of her desk. 'Young James,' he began.

'He seems quite all right now.'

'I'm sure he is. Look, I'm sorry he made a mystery about what he had been inhaling; there's no reason why he should have done.'

'You hadn't sworn a whole lab full of students to secrecy?'

'No, I hadn't. They had sworn themselves to it. They thought they were on to something wonderful, and I didn't. They were inflamed with talk of patents and fortunes to be made. And full of conspiracy theories. The young fool might have harmed his health for nothing.'

'I'm sorry. More fun for everyone if there really had been a great discovery.'

'Those are few and far between. And best met with caution and further tests. Real proofs are hard – harder than most of my young men and women realise.'

'Of course they are. In medicine especially so.'

'Yes,' he said thoughtfully. 'Many pharmacologicals are fatally flawed because the basic verification is defective.'

'Really?' Imogen prompted.

'Well, there is a bothersome ethical problem with a proper trial involving a control group, and blind testing. If something looks effective – say it seems to be slowing the growth of tumours – then everyone wants to abandon the trial and give the thing to the control group as well. It seems wicked to withhold it just because of a scientific quibble.'

'So the trial is suspended incomplete?'

'And then nobody knows exactly where we are. A lot of medical procedure is like that too. Never properly verified. But people love certainty – so dramatic, so newsworthy. The qualified truth, full of ifs and buts and as far as we know so far, is so relatively boring.'

Imogen laughed. 'So while we are rubbishing medical science, do you feel like telling me what you have against Talentire senior for the Postgate?' she asked.

'Mmm,' said Dr Appleby. 'What a sharp lass you are, Miss Quy. Well, he has been telling courtrooms, and more than once, that cot death doesn't run in families.'

'So where there have been several . . .'

'The mother is a murderer. He has been giving incredible odds against the thing striking by pure accident twice or more in the same place.'

'Once is misfortune, twice is highly suspicious, three times is murder?'

'Well, that exact phrase was what some other expert is supposed to have said. But something like that, yes. Then the grieving mother goes to jail.'

'But are you saying that in fact cot death does run in families?'

'I haven't the faintest idea,' said Dr Appleby. 'But neither has he. The research on the question as far as I can discover has not been done.'

'That juries believe him?'

'Juries are impressed by expert witnesses. I can't prove him wrong, mind you, and I don't suppose he is in bad faith. After all, he is on oath. But I don't quite like it, Miss Quy, and I'd rather we didn't give him an honorific, you see. Reputation of the college, and all that.'

'But Professor Talentire stands very well in terms of reputation, surely?' said Imogen.

'Vulnerable. Genetic research is galloping rapidly along and producing knowledge in the place of guesswork all over the place. Someone is sure to be working on cot death, or SIDS as we are supposed to call it. Sudden Infant Death Syndrome.'

'But it would be much easier to find that there really was a gene for it, or predisposing to it, than to find that there wasn't,' said Imogen. 'Negatives are hard to prove.'

'You mean he could be vindicated, but is unlikely to be exposed, during the term of a Postgate fellowship?'

'Well, wouldn't the entire human genome need to be completely understood before one could be sure he was wrong?' asked Imogen.

'And that won't happen quickly? But even if he is found to be right, you see, that wouldn't satisfy me.'

'Because he isn't right now, and there are women in jail because of him?'

'Well, not just because of him. It takes teams of people to put a woman in jail. But it takes more than proving something to be true to justify having held it to be true ahead of the proof of it. I think, Miss Quy, that entertaining certainty more than the available knowledge justifies is, in scientific terms, the sin against the Holy Ghost.'

'So no Postgate for Talentire?'

'Not unless the Master overrules me. Perhaps this conversation had better not go beyond this room, do you think?'

'Of course not. I'm used to the secrets of the confessional!

But you'll need an alternative nomination for the Postgate, I should think. You'll carry the matter easily if you have a better name to suggest.'

'I'll think about that,' he said, taking his leave.

Imogen was not expected to work on Sundays. But the next Sunday was one of those spring mornings like a crisp new apple, when the air blows across the Fen from the north, cool and cleanly bright, a morning on which it is a crime to be indoors. Imogen invented an errand for herself. She had forgotten to look up the file on Susan Inchman. A cycle into college would take her right across the city through the glories of the Backs, past one amazing building after another, and could easily take her through the market square, which on Sunday mornings contained a farmers' market with home-made cakes and jams and organic vegetables. It was quite early when she set out, as the best things on the stalls were snapped up by the first-comers. The Lammas Land was bright spring green. The pallid sun was picking out the dew on the blades of grass, so that everything was glinting like scattered diamonds. Her cycle tyres skidded slightly on a patch of wet path as she cornered by Newnham Pool, and she changed down a gear, and rode more sedately.

The market was always fun. The stall-keepers were stamping their feet and blowing their fingers to keep warm, and the square was full of the loud brazen rejoicing of the bells of Great St Mary's. Imogen bought a rhubarb pie, a bunch of earthy carrots still with their tops on, and was considering ostrich-meat sausages from a local farm when the bells completed their mathematical dance and tolled a count of ten and fell silent. You could hear yourself speak again. And in the silence someone was indeed speaking, declaiming rather, and drawing everyone's attention.

Standing on the steps of the city hall was a desperate, ragged tramp, his hair grown in a dirty tangle to his shoulders, his beard matted and long, the tracksuit he was wearing heavily stained and quite insufficient for the cold. His hat lay on the pavement below him.

'Blow wind, and crack thy cheeks!' he cried, raising his eyes to the serenely china-blue sky. '*Rage! Blow!*

> You cataracts and hurricanoes, spout
> Till you have drenched our steeples, drowned the cocks!
> You sulphurous and thought-executing fires
> Singe my white head!

The speaker had an enormous voice, commanding attention without benefit of microphone. And he had a subtle and perfect intonation, complete with the appropriate tremor of self-pity that went with what he spoke.

The people were migrating along the aisles of the stalls, past the flowers, the cakes and fruit and veg, past the shining gewgaws on the craft stalls, to stand in the open space in front of the city hall and listen. Some of the stall-holders were not best pleased.

'Leave it out, Granddad!' yelled one of them as Imogen passed him, going with all the others to listen. 'Give us a break!'

Someone tossed a few coins into the hat.

'Change the record, can'tcha?' cried the angry stall-keeper. 'Don't suit the weather. We don't want it to blow, do we?'

Some more coins fell in the hat. The speaker stopped. He said to the stall-keeper, 'What would you like instead? Any where in Shakespeare?'

'*Hamlet!*' someone called. 'Give us some *Hamlet!*'

The tramp suddenly leaned backwards, and put up his hands as though to fend off a blow.

'Angels and ministers of grace defend us!' he said, softly, but perfectly audibly.

> Be thou a spirit of health or goblin damned,
> Bring with thee airs from heaven or blasts from hell,
> Be thy intents wicked or charitable,
> Thou com'st in such a questionable shape
> That I will speak with thee. I'll call thee Hamlet,
> King, Father, Royal Dane, O answer me!

Imogen was not the only one to look round to see what threatened him. By now a considerable crowd surrounded him, and his hat gave an answering chink to every new coin thrown in.

'Don'tcha know anything cheerful?' said the stall-holder despairingly. 'Get'm in the mood to buy my nice damsons, and I'll pay you myself.'

The tramp put his chin in his hands, and began again, with a puzzled frown:

> Oh, what a rogue and peasant slave am I!
> Is it not monstrous that this player here,
> But in a fiction, in a dream of passion,
> Could force his soul so to his own conceit
> That from his working all his visage wanned
> Tears in his eyes, Distraction in's aspect
> A broken voice, and his whole function suiting
> With forms of his conceit? And all for nothing!

'Well, not quite for nothing,' said an amused bystander. 'You've got a quid or two in that hat now.'

'And that's enough for today, thank you very much,' the stall-holder was saying. 'Move along, Granddad, or we'll call the police.'

But the crowd didn't like that. Someone had bought a fruitcake, and put it in the hat. A young woman brought him a coffee from the coffee stall.

'You must have been an actor,' she said to him.

'I was of that company, yes,' he said to her. 'And when they fall, they fall like Lucifer, never to hope again.'

With that he stooped, scooped his takings out of his hat, put coins in one pocket, cake in another, and bowed to his audience.

'Beggar that I am, I am poor even in thanks,' he said, shuffling away, his paper cup of coffee clutched in his hand.

'My God, he's good,' said someone at Imogen's shoulder. 'I'd kill to direct him!' It was Simon Malpas.

'Someone must know who he is,' said Imogen. 'He's obviously done this before.'

'Only in Cambridge,' the young woman who bought the coffee was saying, 'could one busk with Shakespeare.' She sounded smug at the thought.

Perhaps also in Oxford? wondered Imogen, putting her shopping in her bicycle basket, and riding away.

Susan Inchman's file, when Imogen got it out of the college filing system, was full of interest. For one thing, she had never presented herself to see Imogen. Even the most robust students had usually appeared in Imogen's office by the time they had been in college for a term or two – for a flu jab, or travel inoculations, or in hope of a remedy for hangovers, or some small thing or other. Not Susan. Well, that was all to the good, surely, but it explained why Imogen couldn't put a face to her.

She was interesting, just the same. She was older than most undergraduates, having taken her Os and As later than usual, at an evening college. Reading on, Imogen saw why: she had spent a lot of her childhood in care-homes, before eventually being adopted by a kindly schoolteacher when she was sixteen. Presumably by then there was a lot of time to make up. Imogen recalled reading, appalled, that it was very unusual for any child in care to get any school exam qualifications at all. But Susan Inchman had obviously managed very well from a late start. Just the same, she had not won a place in competition with others on a level playing field: she was one of St Agatha's three-a-year special admissions, a scheme referred to in private by the dons as the lame-duck scheme, which existed to give a chance to somebody who looked as though they might have underachieved so far as a result of bad luck in their family or their schooling.

Imogen reflected on all this. St Agatha's admission tutors must have been rather good at spotting such people, because most of the lame ducks turned out to be pretty good swans, and had done well in the college. Imogen could recall a young Asian boy who had spent most of his early childhood in an iron lung, a victim of polio, and who walked on crutches, but got a first in maths. Then there was a girl who had been dragged around the world by her mother, a famous rock-star, supposedly being home-taught. The lessons had been attended to, if at all, by a hairdresser travelling in the entourage. That almost completely ignorant girl had achieved a lower second, and gone on to train as a teacher. Imogen remembered, smiling to herself, how the flashily named Orchid had been sharing all her lecture notes and reading lists with the hairdresser, who one year later got an external degree from a northern university, those two having dragged each other into the life of the mind.

But Susan Inchman . . . If Samantha was right about her temper tantrums she was having difficulty with her golden opportunity. Imogen wondered how to get an interview with her, tactfully, to see if help was needed. Perhaps the easiest first step would be to see what her supervisor made of her. Imogen made a mental note to talk to Dr Venton-Gimps soon.

So when later, glancing out of her window, she saw the unmistakable figure of Venton-Gimps wandering across the court towards the senior common room, she made her way there in quest of a morning coffee and a chance to chat.

Dr Venton-Gimps was in a wide low armchair, concealed from view behind the *Sunday Sport*. One of the many privileges of the St Agatha's senior common room was the array of daily papers spread out on a Georgian side-table just inside the common room door. This enabled dons to read stuff they would not have dreamed of being caught buying.

'Have you a moment, V-G?' Imogen asked. 'It's shop, I'm afraid.' He had once asked her to call him Percy, but everyone in practice called him V-G.

'I was just about to get a coffee,' he said, lowering the paper and smiling at her.

'Don't let me stop you,' said Imogen, sitting down in a facing chair, and putting her own coffee on the table between.

She thought for a moment that he was considering replacing the hint with an outright request to her to fetch the coffee for him, a move she was used to fending off. Then he heaved himself out of his chair and went to fetch it himself. Mildly amused, she watched him go. He was as usual very oddly dressed. He was a little older than Imogen, perhaps approaching forty. But he affected to be an old fogey of the finest vintage. He was never to be seen without a dark suit and a colourful waistcoat, worn with open-necked shirts and cravats instead of ties. This morning his cravat was deep purple with little ducks embroidered on it, and his waistcoat was mustard-yellow moleskin. The really odd thing was that his manner of dressing and his manner of scholarship were so at odds. No literary theory, however extraordinary, failed to have his enthusiastic endorsement when it was mint-new and outrageous. He had been among the most vociferous campaigners for the honorary degree proposed for Jacques Derrida, and the most excoriating critic of the opposition. Imogen knew that Dennis Dobbs despised V-G, but knew also that he commanded the slavish admiration of some of the cleverest students, and was one of the few whose lectures were attended – packed out, indeed – by students not studying his subject. He had made English trendy.

V-G told Imogen that Susan Inchman was rather promising really. A bit sulky. He had to coax contributions from her, and she was apt to lace her perfectly cogent opinions with remarks like 'Who cares what I think?' and 'This is going to be wrong, but I think . . .'

'A sort of Eeyore of a girl, and such a frump, Imogen. I suppose your pastoral care of the wenches couldn't be extended to help with their dress-sense, could it?'

'Certainly not,' said Imogen.

'Pity,' he said. 'Now you yourself, if I may say so, are always a pleasure to the eye.'

'An interesting compliment, coming from you,' said Imogen sweetly. There's a kind of misogyny that is completely invisible to the perpetrators. They can't see the condescension in their choice of compliment. 'You yourself are always dressed to please,' she tried.

The feint went wide. 'Oh, do you really think so, Miss Quy?' he said, beaming at her. 'How very kind.'

As discreetly as she could, Imogen enquired about any problems with punctuality at supervisions.

'Can't remember any,' said V-G. 'She and her group are usually waiting for me when I arrive, I'm afraid. I get deeply into something in the library and lose track of the time. Have I made her fearfully cross? I do make some of the students cross, I realise. Sheer absence of mind. No malice in it.'

Part of the act, thought Imogen grimly, but she didn't say so.

'She's rather good, actually,' V-G continued. 'Somewhat to my surprise. Very bright indeed. And in a way her lack of the proper education has helped her. She just writes what she really thinks; she's an original. Nobody has taught her to have the accepted reactions. She's an iconoclast. Likes theories that wipe the smirk off posh faces.'

Cross Susan could teach Samantha something, thought Imogen.

'She's not first-class material,' he said, musing. 'An upper second, I should think.'

'And she's perfectly calm in supervisions?'

'Oh, perfectly. Unless you count it as un-calm to be argumentative. Why are you asking? Is she ill? Is she going to have a breakdown, and waste our investment in her?'

'Oh, nothing of the kind,' said Imogen. She took her leave hastily, before he asked any more questions.

6

The Princes walke is here in the galery . . .

S omehow having taken the minutes for them had per-
suaded the Kyd Society committee members, not least
Fran, that Imogen was one of them. A quest for a venue for the
production was now rather urgent, and Imogen's advice was
being sought. Delicately it was intimated to her that there
would be no chance of paying for the nurse whose attendance
at a public performance would be required. Since perhaps
Imogen would like to cover the performance for them – how
exceptionally kind she was – would she also like to trot round
with committee members to inspect various possible places to
mount the play?

Imogen considered. 'What would be wrong with the dining
hall at St Agatha's?' she asked them.

'A dining hall?' said Simon doubtfully. He was at Churchill,
Imogen remembered, a new college in new buildings.

'Not *any* dining hall,' she explained. 'Ours is about con-
temporary with Shakespeare after all.'

The little group sitting round Imogen's table looked at her
blankly. 'The thing is,' she said, 'I heard of a démarche some
little time back when the undergraduates in a famously
wealthy college were demanding that the college build a
theatre for their dramatic society. And the bursar was horrified

Jill Paton Walsh

at the expense. He pointed out to them how suitable the college hall was for staging productions, and they reached a compromise: no new theatre, if the hall was made available for three nights once a year. I went to *Romeo and Juliet* there, and it worked rather well.'

'Would St Agatha's let us? After all, we're not a college society.'

'You could always ask,' said Imogen. 'But you'd better have a look first. If you'd like to meet me there after my office hours some time, I could let you in.'

'Is tomorrow any good?' asked Nigel Snow. 'It's getting urgent to print some flyers. Word has got out, and I'm being inundated with enquiries.'

'*What* word has got out?' cried Simon.

'Cool it, Simon,' said Nigel. 'Our sworn secret is safe. The only word that has got out is that we are staging the Bad Quarto, and lots of people want to see it. I've even got someone wanting to bring a party from the National.'

'Oh, God,' groaned Simon.

'It seems,' Nigel went on, oblivious, 'that the Bad Quarto is hardly ever put on. The general public expect the Folio, but the Shakespeare buffs are fascinated by the other versions. We'll sell out, for certain sure.'

'I was rather hoping we might play in an obscure corner to a nearly empty house,' said Simon gloomily, 'and limit the damage.'

'Well, Simon, there wasn't really any hope of that,' said Nigel. 'The whole of Cambridge is buzzing with talk about Mottle playing Hamlet. Everyone thinks it will be a fabulous pratfall, and they would be fools to miss it. They'll come flocking like the groundlings of old, with bags of rotten tomatoes at the ready.'

'Were tomatoes around in time for Shakespeare's ground-lings?' asked Antonia.

Fran took the relevant volume of Imogen's *Oxford English Dictionary* from the shelf behind her chair. 'First recorded in 1604,' she reported.

'Well, there you are then,' said Antonia. 'The Bad Quarto is 1603.'

'I think tomatoes got here in 1597,' said Hugo learnedly. 'But people grew them as decoration at first. They didn't realise they could be eaten. Honestly, I don't think they could have been around in sufficient numbers for rotten ones to have been widely enough available.'

'Oh, bother the botany!' said Nigel. 'Rotten eggs, then – let it be rotten eggs.'

'It hadn't better be either if I'm to recommend you to St Agatha's bursar as reliable enough to borrow the hall,' said Imogen. 'I can make tomorrow at four.'

St Agatha's Hall was one of the finest things in Cambridge, but college halls are less accessible to the public than college chapels, and St Agatha's was not on the famous Backs, but slightly off the beaten track. To a large extent it enjoyed two things not often found together in Cambridge: beauty and peace. Evidently nobody on the Kyd Society committee had ever seen it. Malcolm Gracie brought the keys, for the hall was kept locked when not in use, and joined the little party around Imogen. They walked in to an enormous and lofty space, with long narrow tables stretching down it, and a dais with a table crosswise at the far end, where the dons sat. The black oak of the ancient tabletops contrasted with the white glint of silver candlesticks. The walls were panelled halfway up, and painted plaster above, with portraits of college worthies hanging high.

Above the painted highbrows in period dress the room rose to a magnificent hammer-beam roof, with a lantern in the middle, where the smoke-hole would have been under yet more ancient arrangements.

'The tables are all trestles, of course,' said Malcolm Gracie. 'We can move them and provide folding chairs in rows.'

'There's absolutely no backstage, though,' said Simon. He was looking at the dais on which High Table was laid out. Solid panelled walls surrounded it, and a very grand bay window on one side lit it with dim splotches of Gothic colour from the stained glass.

'There's a door for the kitchen staff, isn't there?' asked Antonia, staring at the panelling, in which there was indeed a nearly invisible door.

'Could we curtain off that bay window?' asked Hugo doubtfully.

'No, no, friends, you haven't seen the beauty of it,' said Gracie eagerly. 'For a theatrical performance you turn the room round. The dais isn't the stage. Come and look.'

They trooped along between the tables, and, mounting the dais, looked back at the other end of the room. Facing them was the screens passage, a division of a narrow strip of the hall with a spectacular Jacobean carved oak screen, pierced left and right by two elegantly arched doors. Above the screen was the minstrels' gallery, likewise entered by two doors. Having entered through the screen doors, they hadn't appreciated this layout till now.

'There's your stage!' said Gracie expansively. 'After all, Jacobean plays were written to be performed in halls just like this. In livery company halls, in great houses, even in colleges, no doubt.'

'And it has just what the Globe had, except for a raised

platform stage,' said Simon. 'Two doors under a gallery; two doors in the gallery, space in front . . .'

'Some people even think that the design of the public theatres was based on the arrangement of great halls in the first place,' said Gracie happily. Imogen had known how much he loved the fabric of the college, but had not heard him before talking like a historian of the theatre. She warmed to him.

'Try it,' he suggested to the youngsters.

Hugo ran down the room, disappeared through the left-hand screen door, and clambered rather noisily up to the gallery, reappearing stage right. Below him Simon and Nigel had advanced to stand between tables and screen.

'Thou art a scholar, speak to it, Horatio!' cried Nigel. 'Looks it not like the King?'

'So then Hamlet climbs up to the gallery while the others try to stop him, and appears upper stage left . . .' Simon was thinking aloud. 'Very nice. Splendid.'

'Quite authentic, I assure you,' said Gracie.

'What about the audience?' asked Nigel. 'What about emergency exits?'

'We can provide seats all across the floor-space, with an aisle in the middle, and more seats on the dais. You can charge a little extra for those: they are further back, but safer from a tall chap sitting right in front. There are actually two doors in the panelling on the dais, which lead through to the modern kitchen, so those would be emergency exits. It has always worked well for college productions, though we haven't had one recently. St Agatha's own drama society is a bit moribund at the moment, but you know how undergraduates are – things come and go.'

'I think this would be really good,' said Simon. 'We would need some rehearsal time here, because it isn't a bit like what we are used to working in.'

'We'll arrange that,' said Gracie. 'But look here, Malpas, I'm not deaf and blind, you know. I have been hearing rumours about your proposed production. If you're going to make a complete ass of yourself I'd as soon you didn't associate it in any way with St Agatha's.'

'We'll put a disclaimer for you in the programme,' said Nigel. 'Clearly worded.'

'Thank you,' said Gracie.

'I'm not going to make any more of an ass of myself than I can possibly help,' said Simon glumly.

Gracie looked at him, considering. 'I'm sure you're not,' he said gently. 'The college will be glad to help out over this. One more thing: I take it Imogen will be in attendance to deal with fainting fits and heart attacks and the like?'

'We've asked her to be the statuary nurse, but I'm not sure she answered,' said Nigel.

Imogen tried not to laugh. A wild vision crossed her mind of herself ministering to fallen marble figures in shady gardens, or helping amputees like the Venus de Milo.

'I'll do that for you willingly, Nigel,' she said.

'For that I'll cook you a slap-up supper tonight,' said Fran.

But Imogen was not destined to enjoy her reward. Before she locked up her office there was a real emergency. This presented itself as the arrival of Susan Inchman, crashing through Imogen's office door in a flat panic. She had found Samantha lying on the floor of the room they shared, and she couldn't wake her. Imogen seized her emergency box and her mobile and ran down the stairs and across the court at Susan's heels.

Samantha was lying face down on the carpet in front of the gas fire, one hand under her head, the other at her side. She was breathing heavily. Imogen knelt down and rolled her over, and saw at once the slight frothing of spittle on her breath.

'She's taken something, Susan,' she said. 'Look for a bottle or a pill bottle. Quickly.'

She lifted Samantha's limp wrist in her fingers, and took the pulse. It was slow but steady. Imogen sat back on her heels and sighed. Was this foul play? Hardly. Drink? The girl's breath didn't smell of drink. A serious suicide attempt?

Susan was back from the bathroom holding an empty bottle of aspirin. 'When did Samantha expect you to come back?' Imogen asked.

'For dinner. We were going to a film together after hall.'

So it was a phony suicide. A dangerous game. You take an overdose, but you calculate that you will be found and rescued. Your calculation had better be right. Samantha suddenly convulsed and vomited, voluminously, over the hearth rug. The white specks of chewed undissolved aspirin were visible to Imogen in the mess. She had to decide at once what to do. Call an ambulance? Probably not necessary: forcing the girl to drink an emetic would do the trick, but it was beyond Imogen's official responsibility. She thought quickly. Samantha had been worried about Susan, and being worried about anybody else was untypical of suicides. Untypical of false suicides too, come to that. But she had also been worried about exams.

'When was Samantha taking her Part One exam?'

'Starts next Monday. Oh, God, Miss Quy, she will be all right, won't she?'

'Yes. Just as well you came back when you were expected.' Samantha was groaning and vomiting again. Imogen decided. She was reluctant to be implicated in this; this was an attempt to get out of having to face an exam, and admitting the girl to casualty would undoubtedly help that. The examiners would 'allow' the exam; that is let the students continue with their studies as though they had passed it, while if they sat the exam and failed it they could not. That was all very well, but if Imogen was wrong, or wrong about the amount of aspirin that Samantha had taken, or wrong in assuming that she had taken nothing else, then that might be life-threatening. Sighing, Imogen dialled up the porters' lodge on her mobile and set in motion the calling of an ambulance.

While they waited for it, she turned her attention to Susan, who was deeply distressed. 'What did she want to go and do that for?' the girl kept asking. 'Couldn't have been as bad as that! To go and do a wicked thing like that!'

'I don't think she really meant it, Susan. She didn't expect to die; she expected exactly this to happen: you to come back, to fetch me, to start a drama, to escape the exam . . . You can work it out.'

'But she might have got it wrong! Stupid cow! These kids rabbiting on about exams, and how they're in love and not in love, and what gear to ask Mummy to buy them for the ball – they don't know they're born, if you ask me. A bit of real grief would do them a power of good. I've had horrible things happen, and I never tried to top myself.'

Imogen studied Susan. She was flushed and fidgeting, showing every sign of being really upset. Wildly angry? No; just upset; and she had reason. This self-pitying gesture had scared her, and to say the least had exploited her as part of the drama.

'It's a horrible thing to do,' the girl was saying. 'It leaves people all around you in the shit.'

'Yes,' Imogen said. She was preoccupied taking Samantha's pulse again.

'When the ambulance comes will I have to go with her?' Susan asked.

'No. I'll do that,' said Imogen. 'And I'll see if someone can come and clear up the carpet. You just go to hall, and perhaps don't talk about this yet.'

'Oh, I don't mind clearing up the sick, Miss Quy,' said Susan, surprisingly. 'I've done worse than that.'

The ambulance men could be heard pounding up the stairs. Imogen thought that perhaps having something to do would steady the girl. 'Well, it would be a help if you could tackle the worst. The housekeeping staff will all have gone home till tomorrow.'

The girl nodded, and stood back into the window bay to make way for the stretcher and the paramedics.

So Imogen was not home in time for her reward dinner. She let Fran know on the phone. She spent the evening in Addenbrooke's while the casualty staff administered a stomach pump to Samantha.

'Not strictly necessary, in all probability,' said the casualty officer cheerfully to Imogen, 'but nasty enough to discourage a repeat performance. Someone ought to keep an eye on her for the next few hours. Can we discharge her in your care, or must we find a bed for her? We're a bit tight for beds,' he added.

'No, I'll look after her,' Imogen said.

'Sure you can manage?' the casualty officer asked.

A passing nurse looked round. 'Oh, that's Imogen,' she said. 'She'll cope.'

'Thanks,' said Imogen.

'Bloody Cambridge,' the young doctor said. 'Everybody always knows everybody.'

It was after eleven by the time a bedraggled and tearful

Samantha, wrapped in a blanket and still shivering, was returned to her college room.

Susan had made a good job of it: the rug was hanging out of the window to dry and the whole place smelled of Dettol. Imogen through a haze of tiredness noted the unexpected competence of it. But the room was cold, and Susan had found somewhere else to sleep.

'Look, Samantha, you'd better have the bed in the sick room beside my office for tonight,' Imogen said. They retreated there. The sick room was equipped with a bell that rang Imogen's pager. She settled Samantha under several blankets, and showed her the bedside bell.

'I'll be all right, Miss Quy, honest I will. I don't want to be any more trouble.'

'Let's hope you can get some sleep,' said Imogen.

However, where was she to sleep herself? The armchair in her office was an uninviting prospect. She couldn't go home; although the pager would ping as far away as Newnham it would take her too long to respond, and it would entail rousing the night porter to let her back into college. She considered her options. She couldn't do what Susan had probably done, and billet herself on the floor of a student room. She could try a sofa in the senior common room, but that was a long trek across the college to the sick room. Then she remembered the tower room. It was two floors above and one wing along from the sick room. A five-minute run at the most. And she could be sure it was empty. She went across to the lodge to get the key before the night porter locked the outer gates, and retired to his somnolent mode.

On her way back she looked in on Samantha, and found her fast asleep.

'You got away with it this time, Sarah Bernhardt,' murmured Imogen, and left her.

She took two blankets and her emergency nightdress from her cupboard, and up the stairs, along the moonlit gallery, and up the spiral staircase to the tower room she went, key in hand. The room was heavily scented with dust and beeswax, and had that closed-in feel of unvisited and locked-up places. Imogen threw her blankets on the bed, turned the radiator knob to get some warmth, and opened the window. Instinctively she opened the one that faced the moon. Then she lay down to get what sleep she could.

Sleep did not come easily. She was too tired, and the place was unfamiliar, and triggered some atavistic sense, often induced by a bed one has not slept in before, that it would be unwise to sleep deeply. Also there was the chance that the pager would go off if Samantha needed her. And she had nothing to read. Like many avid readers Imogen always read at least a paragraph or two last thing at night. She lay on her back, looking into the shadowy heights of the room. Where could she find something to read? The college library was across the lane outside, and would be locked. She had some medical reference books in her office, which would not entertain, distract, or console. There would be journals and newspapers in the common room, but that too was a distance off; really, she thought, it was ridiculous to be so addicted to anything, even literature, that one could not sleep without it. Pull yourself together, she admonished herself, and get on with it. But pulling oneself together is not soporific.

In spite of all this, she was, by and by, deeply asleep.

7

Afore my God, I might not this beleeve,
Without the sensible and true avouch of my owne eyes

I mogen was abruptly awake, pulse racing. Something had disturbed her . . . She glanced at her pager, but the warning light was not flashing. The room was full of moonlight, and rather cool; was it chill that had woken her? But she was quite warm under the blankets. And there was a deep silence, except for a softly hooting owl hunting somewhere in the college gardens. No, there wasn't – was there a slight scrabbling sound somewhere? Gone as soon as listened for. She looked with momentary anxiety at the open casement, until she remembered how high it was. Five storeys up; and as the thought comforted her the faint scrabble sound came again, and something dark broke the bright rectangle of the window-frame against the moon. Imogen sat up abruptly in bed, her skin prickling with alarm.

As she tried to decipher the shape in the window it changed. What she had at first seen was a pair of gloved hands grasping the sill; now a head was slowly raised into the window-frame, then lifting itself on its arms the torso appeared in outline against the light. Then a knee was brought up onto the sill, and for a short second a man stood crouched before leaping into the room. During the long minutes while the intruder had hung in the casement, over the lethal drop onto the stones of the alleyway below, Imogen's terror had been as much for him as for herself. Now he was in the room, her fear was for herself. The spectre was stumbling about, apparently looking for the light-switch.

He found it before she had time to roll off the bed and conceal herself; the room was flooded with light, and he saw her. He startled in every limb, and jumped backwards to spread-eagle himself against the wall, saying, 'Christ!'

Imogen was sitting upright with the blankets clutched instinctively up to her chin. She saw across the room a young man with a mop of red hair, wearing a black sweater, dark tracksuit bottoms, black gloves, and the kind of black plimsolls that Imogen hadn't seen for years. It is hard to be very frightened of somebody who is visibly alarmed himself.

'Christ, you frightened me!' he exclaimed.

'*I* frightened *you*?'

'I'm sorry. I wasn't expecting anyone. I was told,' he said, sounding aggrieved, 'that this room was out of use.'

'Mr Whipplesnaith, I presume?' said Imogen.

'I'm one up on him. He and his chums concluded this tower was impossible. Drainpipe too near the wall, and square in section.'

'It certainly should be impossible. Whatever possessed you?'

'Needs must. I have a particular reason for wanting to see inside this room, and no charm, blandishment or bribe could achieve it. The college porters here are sea-green.'

'I'm glad to hear it. So they should be.'

'Even proffered cases of Moët et Chandon wouldn't sway them. I've sneaked past them and tried the door over and over but it's always been locked. So when I was passing just now, on my way home a bit late from dinner, and I looked up ruefully, and I saw that the window was open, I just slipped home to change out of my dinner jacket, and came along to have a bash at it.'

'And what is the reason that leads you to take such ghastly risks?'

'Well, that's the problem. Can't say, won't say. And people are horribly untrusting. They won't accept that I might be in earnest even if I can't explain.'

'I accept unhesitatingly that you are in earnest,' said Imogen. She was beginning to recover her composure.

'That's decent of you,' he said, offering a tentative smile.

'So now you have effected an entry, what then?'

'All done. I've been looking round while we have been talking.'

'That's all? As easy as that?'

'Yes. I'll be off now and let you get some sleep.' He walked over to the window-seat.

'*How* are you going?'

'I thought of going down the way I came up,' he said. 'Do I have any alternative?'

'I absolutely forbid you to climb out of that window,' said Imogen, horrified. Her voice came out squeaky with fright.

'Do you have the keys to the citadel?' he asked. 'Can you let me out another way? Just for your peace of mind, you understand. I personally have no objection to climbing down.'

'We'll get the night porter to let you out.'

'Oh, no. If I have to admit to having got in I'll be in trouble. It's never been done before, and the news will get out.'

'You'll be famous all over Cambridge I should think,' said Imogen, getting out of bed.

'Well, I don't want that. I'd rather climb down.'

Imogen had positioned herself between him and the open window. 'Over my dead body,' she said.

'Well, my dead body would be more likely than yours,' he said, offering his boyish smile again. 'But neither is very likely. This sort of thing is safer than it looks. I don't want to manhandle you out of the way, so we seem to have stalemate,' he added.

Imogen thought for a moment. 'I will escort you downstairs, and allow you to climb out of a ground-floor window,' she offered.

'Locked. They will all be locked. I've tried them all,' he said. He was right; they almost certainly would be.

'If I let you out of the building into the gardens, can you cope with the garden wall?'

'Oh, that's a doddle,' he said. 'There's a weak spot. You have crowds of people doing that every night.'

'You must tell me where. We need the place to be secure.'

'Couldn't tell. Scout's honour.'

'Look, whoever you are. How will you feel if you don't tell me and then an intruder rapes a young woman?'

'Mmm. I wouldn't feel good about that. Look for the branch of a plane tree very near the top of the wall. And some spikes missing. And please don't tell anyone I told you.'

'As I don't know who you are, that wouldn't be very likely.'

'I'm Martin Mottle,' he said, holding out his hand. 'Whose sleep have I had the pleasure of disturbing?'

She was so surprised that it took several moments before she gave him her name. 'You are already famous all over Cambridge,' she told him, as they began the descent to safer levels. 'You don't need to seek glory ascending drainpipes.'

'It would be exceptionally helpful if you wouldn't spread it around that I have been Wipplesnaithing,' he said, as she opened a garden door for him, and he slipped out. A gust of night air, and a faint grey light came in through the door. Somewhere across the garden a bird sang, softly, as if not to wake the whole chorus. 'All's well,' he said. 'The bird of dawning singeth all night long.' He started across the garden, and she shut the door on him, in a state of some amazement.

There were a lot of adjectives she might think of applying to her night visitor. He was stocky, but well-knit and agile. He was charming, but guarded. Well, after all, one might well be guarded on being witnessed breaking and entering. There was a formidable feeling about him. He was quietly purposeful. Judging by that parting shot about the bird of dawning he was well able to articulate a line of Shakespeare if he was in the mood. A word it would never have occurred to Imogen to apply to him was the word *prat*.

Imogen slept off her interrupted night by not waking till nine – horrendously late for her – and she found Samantha dressed, waiting for her in the sick room, ashamed and apologetic. Imogen accepted the apology. 'But it's Susan you should really apologise to,' she told the girl. 'She cleared up after you. And she bore the brunt of it. Have you thought what would have happened if Susan hadn't come back to your room when expected?'

'I'd have died, and serve me right, you mean?'

'If you hadn't been found promptly you might have died. How would Susan have felt about that, do you think? Picture it, Samantha: Susan meets a friend and goes off for a drink instead of keeping to her arrangement with you, and as a result you are found dead. How do you imagine Susan would feel about that? Lifelong?'

'I didn't think,' said Samantha miserably.

'Did you think having the examination allowed would be a way out of finding the right opinion for the examiners?'

'What's "allowed"?' Samantha asked innocently. She wasn't a very good actress.

Imogen stared her down. 'I'm going to refer you to the student counselling service, Samantha,' she said. 'And are you going to tell your parents, or shall I?'

'Tell my parents? Oh, surely they don't have to know, Miss Quy. Please. And I don't need counselling either.'

'You tried to kill yourself. Of course you need help.'

'Well, I didn't exactly . . . I didn't mean . . .'

'You didn't mean it to work? But what if it had? Someone would have been telling your parents about it then.'

This was enough. She changed tack. 'All right, Samantha. I'll take you on trust. You were just dramatising, you are not really a suicide risk. But you must come and see me in each of the next three weeks before your exam, and let me see for myself how you are coping. Any wobbles and you get referred for counselling. OK?'

Samantha accepted this bargain eagerly, visibly cheered up, and went off for breakfast.

The capacity of the young to bounce back with a healthy appetite never ceased to impress Imogen. She was feeling rather ragged herself, after her late evening and her broken night. She resolved to get home as soon as she could, and take an afternoon nap.

But Imogen got home to an emergency meeting of the Kyd Society. A dispute was raging. Nigel wanted to run *Hamlet* for three nights, and cash in on the huge interest the production was attracting. Simon wanted a one-night stand.

'Mottle didn't ask us to put on a run of the damn thing,'

Simon was saying. 'Just one night will meet his terms. That's all we undertook, and that's all we are doing.'

'But Simon, *think*. Most of the expenses are fixed; costume hire and props and so on. Lighting hire covers a minimum three-day period. The marginal extra costs of two more nights come down just to the booking fee for the college hall; but the gate will raise nearly a thousand each night. One hundred and fifty seats at six fifty a punt. Whatever we have to pay out to Mr Flood, whatever the repairs cost, we'd be set up for next year, we'd be in full funds for the first time in living memory.'

Listening from the door, Imogen reckoned living memory for an undergraduate society at a maximum of five years: they stayed for only three years, and they could have heard in their first year from people then in their third year, so, unless there were graduate students on the committee in which case . . . heavens, she needed some sleep!

'Mottle will only play Hamlet for one night. I'm sure he said that. He wasn't interested after the first night.'

Hugo said, 'That's a massive chance for you, Simon. You play Hamlet on nights two and three. And Nigel can gently suggest to folk from London and afar that the first night might be a little shaky, and—'

'Talking about shaky,' said Fran, 'we all have to be around for the dress rehearsal on the afternoon of the first night. And we have to stay around; Mottle proposes to sequester us with hampers from Fortnum and Masons.'

'You mean we can't leave the room, like naughty children in detention?' cried Hugo.

'Like juries in mid-trial, I think he means. He promises to feed us well.'

'He's just bloody well a bit much. Why do we have to take orders from a prat like him?'

'You know why, Hugo,' said Simon sadly.

Once more Imogen tried to fit the prat Mottle as seen in Kyd Society eyes with her friend the night climber. She couldn't do it. She left the meeting to get on with it, and went upstairs for a soak in a bath, and a nap.

'You're joking!' said Malcolm Gracie.

'I'm not,' said Imogen. She had just told him about the intruder entering the window of the tower room in the middle of the night.

'Not possible,' said Malcolm firmly. 'You must have been hallucinating. Dreaming, I mean, my dear Imogen.'

'A long and circumstantial hallucination,' said Imogen. 'No, Malcolm, I'm serious.'

'My God, how terrifying, Imogen – how awful for you.'

'I was scared, till he started to talk to me,' Imogen admitted. 'However, in the course of discussing with the villain his possible means of exit, he told me that there is an easy hop over the garden wall, being used by our undergraduates in droves every night. I wondered if we oughtn't to get that fixed.'

'Did he say where?'

'Look for a tree branch overhanging the wall and some missing spikes.'

'That should be findable. And the sun is shining now. Have you a minute?'

'Certainly.'

The two set out to walk the circuit of the college wall. It was part of the old castle wall, since the college garden had simply filled in the castle bailey, including the motte, a large pudding-shaped mound now sweetly landscaped, and giving from its top a view of the city. The wall was high – at least twenty feet from the outside, though rather less from the path which led round it within. It had a narrow walkway round the top behind battlements, and steep steps down at intervals. Sentries had patrolled it once, and borne the brunt of arrow-showers, giving their lives for the fierce certainties of the civil war. Now it was just a mellow and pleasing background to the splendid herbaceous borders which were the pride of the college gardeners. There was indeed a tree, an ancient and magnificent plane tree, growing on the slope down to Chesterton Lane, which had a stout branch extending over the wall. The moment you spotted the branch you spotted that a section of the rotating iron spikes with which the top of the wall was fitted had gone missing. If you could climb the tree you could hop over the wall.

Malcolm and Imogen climbed to the top of the wall and looked over. The tree was forked and gnarled, and even had a sturdy iron bolt or two banged into its trunk to give firm footholds. 'I'll send someone round at once to remove those,' said Malcolm.

'Can you? Is it our tree?'

'No, but I'll lay any money the bolts are our doing. If by "our doing" you mean perpetrated by some member of the college. Who else would want them?'

'A love-sick suitor of one of our fair maids?' asked Imogen.

'You're dreaming, Imogen. Nowadays there's no obstacle at all to the love-sick. They don't have to climb in, they just walk in and it's none of our business where they sleep or how long they stay. But perhaps this entry was arranged in the good old days when we had rules and curfews and prowling proctors, and we defended the young against their errors.'

'How nostalgic you sound.'

'Well, I'm an Oxford man myself. And it did have romance about it, all those years ago. If you got a young woman back to

Lady Margaret Hall after midnight, you had to help her climb in. And she was often in a very posh frock. She would shed it to make the scramble, and you would give her a leg up, and then toss the dress over the wall to her. I remember the rustle of expensive silk sliding to the ground, and the moonlight on a nearly naked young woman in extraordinarily scanty underwear. We weren't used to such sights in our repressed and respectable youth. Kissing a girl goodnight with most of her clothes over your arm, and an ear cocked for the tramp of the proctor's feet . . . those were the days. Can't believe they have more fun these days. Where were we?'

'Dealing with intruders.'

'Of course. And the very fact that the love-sick don't need to climb in means that anyone who does climb in might have much worse things in mind than trysts. We must get the bolts out of the trunk, the branch cut short of our wall, the missing section of spikes replaced. I'll get moving.'

As they returned through the gardens, he said, 'Now how in the name of all the saints did someone climb into the tower room? We must look at that, too.'

They left the garden by the side gate into the alleyway between the old college boundary and the purlieus of the New Library. There was a facing gate that led to the library, so in daylight when the gates were open one just walked straight across. Imogen and Malcolm walked a few feet along the alleyway and looked up at the outside wall of the tower. It looked dizzying. They were standing right underneath Harding's Folly, looking up at the very window through which the feat was performed.

'How in hell does someone climb up there from here?' asked Malcolm.

'I don't know,' said Imogen. 'I've got a book about it. I'll look it up.'

As they walked back to their respective offices she told him about the book. He was fascinated. 'I've heard of it, but never seen a copy,' he said.

'I'll lend it to you,' said Imogen. 'It makes my head spin.'

'You know, while I was up at Oxford a section of the college wall fell down,' he told her. 'An ancient wall; it just fell off its foundations and was breached right to the ground. And a notice appeared in the gap, saying: "Will gentlemen please not avail themselves of this opportunity." So we didn't. We continued to climb in up a drainpipe and via a window ledge right alongside the open gap.'

'You'll enjoy the book, Malcolm,' said Imogen.

'One thing,' he said as they parted. 'There's clearly no point in trying to block Harding's Folly by barring the window, if there's a way up to it from a public roadway, and a published set of instructions for climbing to it from outside. No point at all. Problem solved.'

Imogen looked up St Agatha's in *The Night Climbers* as soon as she could. It described Harding's Folly 'falling across the gap' as childishly easy. It described the climb up the outside wall to the window as very difficult. Only for the most expert. Climbing down it described as so much more dangerous than the jump to the corner of the library that it had never been attempted in the knowledge of the writer. She put the book on the hall table to remind her to take it to Malcolm Gracie.

It was late in the afternoon when she climbed on her bicycle to go and have tea with Dennis Dobbs. She let herself in to his house, and went through to the kitchen to put a kettle on. Dennis was snoozing in a deep armchair by the fire, with a book held slackly in his sleeping hands. The gas fire hissed gently to itself, punctuating the sound with occasional pops.

Imogen sat down in the facing chair, and waited for Dennis to wake. He looked so frail and old when he was sleeping.

Imogen's friend Lucy had told her sharply that there was no future in Dennis, and clearly there wasn't; not in any way that would have made sense to Lucy. Only an ongoing conversation. And most of that was just gossip. In a minute he would wake up, and be transformed. His face would light up to see her, and he would begin to flirt and charm her with his clever talk. Talk was all there ever would be to Dennis now; but that seemed to Imogen like a good reason to talk as much as they could. The kettle began to whistle feebly in the kitchen, and she went through to make the tea.

When she came back with the tray he had woken up, and looked about twenty years younger.

'What's the news, my dear?' he enquired.

Imogen launched into an account of her night in the tower room. Dennis was fascinated. 'I never knew!' he said. 'I never knew!'

'Never knew what, Dennis?'

'That there was a possible climb up that tower. Too late now, I'm afraid.'

'Too late? When could it have been in time?'

'Ah, well, when I was a green youth I was quite good at all that. I've been up one of the pinnacles of King's, to put a banner on it. Quite exciting.'

'What did the banner say?'

' "No attack on Nasser." It was in vain. And it offended the purists.'

'How come?'

'It politicised the game. They thought only umbrellas and potties and the like should be left as proofs of achievement.'

'I thought there had already been a banner up there saying

"Save Ethiopia"',' said Imogen. She had learned this from her book.

'Ancient as I am,' said Dennis, ' "Save Ethiopia" was before my time. Look, Imogen, I'm afraid we can't go to *Hamlet* together. It's all sold out. I can't get a seat.'

'We'll see about that,' said Imogen.

8

I will have sounder proofes.
The play's the thing
Wherein I'le catch the conscience of the King

There's really nothing as scary, as tense, as excited, as backstage of the amateur production of a play. It was the afternoon of the dress rehearsal. The college hall was sequestered, and food was being served in the common rooms. A marquee had been hired to serve as a green room. Malcolm Gracie was jittering about the place worrying about the placement of the stage lighting; nothing could be fixed to the walls, and hanging lights from the roof beams entailed finding long ladders. Or at least he thought it did; the trick was accomplished somehow without them when his back was turned.

Imogen entered the marquee and found it humming with excitement. Costumes were hanging on rails, a table was spread with stage make-up, and the cast were drifting about, partly in costume, muttering their lines, or being coached by friends holding prompt-books. The nervous energy was enough to drive the light-bulbs. Imogen was looking for Nigel, and an extra ticket. He was perfectly obliging about it. 'Not everybody turns up, even when they've paid,' he said. 'And if they all do turn up we'll squeeze an extra seat in the front row.

You don't look very wide, Miss Quy; we'll get someone in beside you.'

'I need to sit at the back, ideally, to keep an eye on the audience. Beside the emergency exits.'

'Fine. We'll reserve a couple of seats for you there.'

With that matter settled, Imogen left them to their dress rehearsal, and went off on some errands of her own. These included collecting her dress from the dry-cleaners, and collecting Dennis from his house to drive him into college. She settled him into the senior common room, where Venton-Gimps greeted him as an old friend, and promised to bring him over to the hall in good time.

Imogen left him and re-entered the maelstrom of the green room. The panic was still rife, but it had a different timbre. She bumped into Simon and asked him how the rehearsal had gone.

'You know what,' he said, sounding amazed, 'it went well; really well. Keep your fingers crossed, Miss Quy.'

Fran rushed up to her. 'Imogen, can you help? Ophelia has ripped her dress, and we're short of anyone who can sew.'

'Where's the dress?'

'She's in it. Over here.'

Imogen saw the famously beautiful Amy. She was slender and short, and very dark-haired. Long glossy locks fell to her shoulders, but her eyes were light. She was standing in her torn creamy silk, holding her part and running over it in a whisper.

> Oh my deare father, such a change in nature,
> So great an alteration in a Prince,
> So pitifull to him, fearefull to mee
> A maiden's eye ne're looked on . . .

Imogen knelt at Ophelia's feet, and set herself to running a line of stitches to repair the rent in the dress. Ophelia meekly turning round when ordered, and holding her hands above her head, out of the way, said, 'Wait till you see the ghost, Miss Quy!'

'Where is he?'

'I think he's asleep behind one of the costume racks. He got a bit tipsy, and Simon told him to sober up.'

'I hope he's the only one tipsy.'

'Oh, I'm sure he is. We've just got to get through tonight, and then Simon is in full charge again, and we can play it properly.'

Just then Simon walked across, and laid a hand gently on Amy's cheek. 'All right, love?' he said. 'No nerves?'

'Lots of nerves,' she said, smiling at him. 'And it's quite all right. Don't worry, Simon.'

Imogen got to her feet and tiptoed away.

She was immediately waylaid to help with make-up. There was a long trestle, covered with stage paints, beards and moustaches, cheap glass jewellery, all the clobber of the job. Three girls were working expertly at making up the cast, starting with the minor ones, like Marcellus, odd soldiers, odd courtiers, an ambassador, the gravediggers and Fortinbras with his men.

'Don't smudge it!' said Antonia as she finished a face. Imogen could save expert time by applying foundation and gluing on facial hair. Everything had a rather warm hue, as though the actors were all heated; Antonia said that was because the stage lighting had a cold blue tinge. 'They'll all look like corpses unless we warm them up.'

But soon there wasn't any more work for Imogen, and the thought of joining Dennis in the senior common room for a drink before the performance seemed very attractive.

As she was leaving there was an argument going on just outside the marquee. There were two young men there, carrying a large wicker trunk. The girl at the door was trying to deny them entry. 'This is only for the cast,' she was saying. 'You can take your seats in the hall in about twenty minutes, or less.'

'We're friends of Martin's,' the taller of the two strangers said. 'Let us in.'

'I'm not letting anybody in,' she said stoutly, 'and certainly not anybody carrying luggage. There's hardly room to breathe in there as it is.'

'Friends of Martin. Martin Mottle. He's expecting us.'

Curious, Imogen stood watching. And it seemed Mottle really was expecting them. He appeared in the gate of the tent, clad all in black, with a white ruff, and said, 'Good,' to his friends. 'Come with me,' he continued. 'We need that stuff in the gallery. I'll give you a hand with it.' The three of them walked round the tent, and into the doors that led to the screens passage, carrying their burden, leaving Imogen wondering what Mottle wanted with his very own Rosencrantz and Guildenstern. There was surely no part for last-minute extras in the play?

She walked slowly across Fountain Court to the common room. It was a fine evening, the moon pretending to be in a Japanese print, and a few stars pricking the paper-blue sky. Dennis and V-G were comfortably seated either side of a wholly unnecessary fire, with drinks in their hands. A glass was standing ready for her, and she joined them, glad of an interval in the calm company of ageing scholars before she had to plunge back again among the frenetic young.

'You know that young woman you were asking about, Imogen,' said V-G. 'I meant to tell you some time that

I saw her in very bad company yesterday. Wants watching, I fear.'

'What sort of company?'

'Obvious druggy. She was sitting with him in the Lion Yard shopping centre, holding his hand.'

'Love takes strange forms,' said Dennis.

'This form might mean trouble,' said V-G, 'and it didn't look at all like love's young dream. She was looking exceptionally glum, and he was snarling at her. I'm afraid I passed by on the other side.'

'Strange times we live in,' observed Dennis. 'Of course there were always young men who went slumming in the town for sweethearts; couldn't blame them when there were hardly any undergrad*uettes* in the place. But nice young women picking up rubbish men when they are surrounded by strong, handsome, healthy and clever ones . . .'

Imogen put this piece of gossip aside to be thought about later. A girl like Susan who didn't have a sheltered childhood might well know people who struck the ineffable V-G as trouble waiting to happen. But time was going by.

'I'd better take my seat,' Imogen said. 'You can take a little longer, but I'd better go.'

'See you over there,' said Dennis. 'And don't forget to remind me to pay you for the ticket.'

'It was free, Dennis,' said Imogen. 'I have friends in high places.'

The audience was arriving. The hall was filling up, and an excited buzz of voices filled it to the roof. Imogen went through to the marquee. There's a complete change in the atmosphere backstage when the audience has begun to assemble. Up till then it's a kind of game, a gamble of a kind.

Until a few hours beforehand it would be possible to cancel. One could refund people their ticket money. Until an hour beforehand the whole thing still seems a private concern of the people involved. Something could still be changed, fixed, improved. An understudy could be suddenly substituted, a stage-prop moved. The director could redirect. But once the audience assembles things have reached a different point. Like jumping off a diving board, everything is suddenly irrevocable, nothing can be taken back, everything is now too late to consider. A hand of fate hangs over the cast and their supporters; it will deal doom or glory.

Simon was giving a pep talk. 'Look, I know, everyone, how difficult this production has been for us. I know you will all do your best. And have no doubt, your best is pretty good, and it won't be your fault if not everything goes well. Do your best for me, and for each other. OK?' His team liked that: it was greeted with a brief ripple of applause.

Suddenly Nigel appeared, with a stranger beside him. 'Simon, this is a drama critic of *The Times*. He'd like to meet you.'

Simon shook hands, looking extremely miserable. 'I thought you were coming tomorrow night,' he said.

'We always make the first night if we can,' said the critic. 'I just wondered if you could tell me why you chose the Bad Quarto?' He had his notebook at the ready. 'I mean, it isn't usually done, is it? Doesn't it lose some of the best lines?'

Imogen saw Simon gulp. But he didn't say, 'Because it's the shortest version.' He rose to the occasion magnificently.

'It's the least literary, the least familiar version,' he said, 'and it's very actable. Those lines that everybody already knows by heart rather muffle the play, don't you think? And Shakespeare was a practical man of the stage. The Folio rather smells of the study to me.'

'That's very interesting,' was the reply. 'Mustn't keep you now, but would like to talk to you later.'

Simon nodded, and turned away.

Antonia stood in the door of the tent with a list in her hand. 'Horatio, Marcellus, Ghost: five minutes, please!'

Imogen went to her seat. She was at the back, as planned, on the dais and beside the kitchen doors, facing the screens passage. She was in a corner, but she had an unimpeded view. She could see Malcolm Gracie, standing at the front, keeping an eye on things. She noticed Samantha and Susan Inchman sitting together near the front. No sign of the undesirable boyfriend: they were sitting between James Shelford and the Master's secretary. Imogen looked around for the Master, and saw him arriving with Lady Buckmote, and taking front-row seats. She had no idea if he had come for pleasure. He would certainly have supported a college play, and perhaps he felt the Kyd Society were in his bailiwick since they were playing in St Agatha's hall. Dennis presented Imogen as she sat down with a programme and a box of chocolates. 'Those are for later,' he told her. 'Can't have extraneous rustle in a masterpiece.'

'Thank you, Dennis.'

'I am looking forward to this. Rumour has it we are in for a disaster!'

'Don't be too sure of that,' she said. She had still a very clear impression of Mottle. And that impression was still at odds with everything she had heard about him.

The lights went down, and the audience fell silent. A little stage smoke floated across the screen, and round the gallery. The

gallery, Imogen noticed, had been graced with a canvas
curtain, painted with a night sky. The curtain hung well
forward, leaving only some two feet of the gallery's depth
for ghosts or sentries. But Marcellus and Horatio entered at
ground level, and walked to and fro in front of the screen.

'Stand: who is that?'
'Tis I.'
'O, you come most carefully upon your watch . . .'

A few sentences, ringing not quite familiar, and then,
'Breake off your talk, see where it comes again . . .' and enter
the ghost. The ghost had presence enough to raise the hackles
on Imogen's scalp. He walked slowly across the gallery, in
front of the painted sky. He was tall, and dressed in black rags
and shining armour. He was wearing his beaver up. Wreathed
in stage mist though he was, Imogen recognised the ranting
tramp from the Market Square. This part at least was going to
be well played.
    'Thou hart a scholar, speak to it Horatio – looks it not like
the king?'
    Imogen shivered in her seat. *Hamlet* is an extraordinarily
good play; it grips and mystifies from the first scene. Somehow
in this brisk and truncated version Shakespeare's stagecraft
was what struck home. The audience was tense at once; either
because they were, as they ought to have been, concerned
about the honesty of the ghost, or because they were waiting
with suppressed excitement for Mottle's first entry as Hamlet.
And there he was! He was not, of course, a natural for Hamlet.
Stocky, healthy-looking, red-haired, corresponding to the
pensive prince only in being clad in black, and disappointing
everyone. Those who hoped for a fine performance would not

be much taken with this one – he was rather a monotone speaker. Those who had come to see a pratfall were likely also disappointed. Mottle's ineptness had an oddly convincing quality; the sense that he was reluctantly forcing the words out somehow seemed quite likely for the troubled prince.

> Him have I lost I must of force forgoe –
> These but the ornaments and sutes of woe . . .

There was a sudden timbre of grief in the young man's voice. Not at all in the controlled way in which a fine actor would have suggested it, but in an uncontrolled way, as though Mottle would rather have spoken woodenly and couldn't quite manage it. A deep hush of absorption sunk upon the audience. It included Imogen. Had she seen *Hamlet* since leaving school? Perhaps not. Or perhaps the stumbling and muted word-music of this version was made convincing by unfamiliarity? She watched fascinated while the ghost made his tremendous, blood-chilling speech. He prowled the parapet of the gallery; Horatio and friends crouched below, looking up, and Hamlet climbed the gallery to join him:

> 'Hamlet, if ever thou didst thy deare father love –'
> 'Oh, god.'
> 'Revenge his foule and most unnaturall murder.'
> 'Murder?'
> 'Yea, murder in the highest degree,
> As in the least tis bad,
> But mine most foul, beastly and unnaturall . . .'

They were creating an odd and wholly convincing effect. The wonderful performance of the ghost, broken-down great old thespian that he clearly was, and the stiff, reluctant response of Hamlet made the ghost seem untrustworthy and melodramatic, the prince a solid, reliable sort of young man in the grip of incredulity . . .

'Hmm,' said Dennis under his breath, beside her.

It became obvious, however, that Mottle didn't really have what he needed. He rose to the part only here and there. Short the Bad Quarto might be, and lacking in some of the heights, but it seemed to be dragged out by this performance. Mottle's idea of the things to emphasise was rather odd. For example he advanced to the front of the audience and declared woodenly and slowly the lines about the play that should have been spoken to Horatio:

> There is a play tonight wherine one scene they have
> Comes very near the murder of my father
> When thou shalt see that act afoot
> Mark thou the King, do but observe his looks,
> And if he does not bleach and change at that
> It is a damned ghost that we have seen . . .

And now the play-within-the-play was approaching. The cast assembled, and sat in front of the audience, making themselves part of the audience. The King and Queen on the right, Hamlet and Ophelia on the left.

'What does this mean, my Lord?' Ophelia asked.

'This is where the dumb-show ought to come,' said Dennis softly to Imogen.

And suddenly something was afoot. The painted sky in the gallery was rolled up; behind it was a vestigial stage set, not an orchard with a sleeping king, but an interior, with two upright wooden posts, and a mock-up window. The audience gasped, and an excited whispering began. It all went very fast. A young man appeared in modern dress, carrying a coil of bright blue climbing rope slung over his shoulder. He threw the coil to the floor, took up one end and tied it swiftly and expertly round one of the posts. Then he clipped the other end to his belt, climbed to the sill of the stage window, and jumped out. A sound of voices, clapping and laughing and shouting filled the hall from a recording in the gallery, as though from a crowd of onlookers outside. And without a second's pause, Venton-Gimps entered the gallery. Imogen, startled beyond measure, looked round at V-G still sitting the other side of Dennis; on the stage was an actor dressed like Venton-Gimps, yellow waistcoat, spotted cravat, who had entered the scene. He stepped to the centre stage, undid the knot round the post, and tugged the rope hard. The recorded crowd gasped, the rope flew out of the window, and a nasty soft thump was followed by silence, and then jumbled cries. The soundtrack faded, and the house lights went up.

Hamlet was standing centre stage below, and staring fixedly at the real-life Venton-Gimps. Everyone was looking in the same direction. The buzz of voices in the audience rose loudly. V-G stood up and shouted at Hamlet. He did not say, 'Lights, ho lights!' He said, 'How dare you! How dare you! What do you mean by this?'

Dennis said, 'Sit down, V-G, sit down, deal with it later.'

And for answer to V-G's question the house lights went down, the painted sky rolled down in front of the pictured tower room, and the player King and Queen entered and began the spoken play.

'What in hell was all that about?' called someone loudly from the middle of the hall, but the actors took no notice, and the play went smoothly on.

Smoothly on the stage, that is; various members of the audience rose and left. V-G went, noisily scraping his chair, and taking the door behind Imogen. In the front row the Master rose, and left, quietly decisive. Trouble, Imogen thought. What a prospect of trouble! The level of urgent and excited whispering in the audience reached a persistent high. As though the disciplined modern audience had been transformed into noisy groundlings. Imogen herself, of course, could not leave. She had to be there all through, until the last member of the public had left. She might have been the only person, apart from the critic from *The Times*, whose duties likewise detained him and enforced his attention, to notice a change of quality in the performance. Mottle's Hamlet was suddenly less awkward; he sounded almost decisive. He harangued his mother with an almost prurient glee; he smiled with grim triumph when he outwitted Rosencrantz and Guildenstern, and challenged Laertes with righteous dignity.

Imogen watched him with a combination of appall and admiration. He was playing Hamlet as triumphant. As a triumphant avenger. And it was at last very plain what this was all about. The prat Mottle thought that John Talentire's fall to his death had not been an accident. Mottle thought it had been murder. Murder not by a person or persons unknown, but by Professor Venton-Gimps.

9

My lord you playd in the Universitie.
That I did, my lord: and I was counted a good actor

I t seemed a long while before Fortinbras appeared, and the play was brought to a sombre ending. It played out to the distracting sound of excited voices outside the hall. Imogen was lost in thought. The whole of Cambridge had been buzzing with talk about John Talentire's self-inflicted disastrous death, this time last year. But in terms of the life of the university a year is a long time. One-third of the entire transit of a student generation, the equivalent of a quarter-century of a real life span. Tears had been shed, horror and sorrow expressed, a memorial service had been held, packed to the doors, in Great St Mary's, emergency teaching rosters for Talentire's supervisions had been organised, the inquest had found accidental death, with very severe remarks from the coroner about the risk-taking culture of the young . . . Life had moved on. Or Imogen thought it had.

When eventually the audience dispersed, and she was free to go, she went first into the marquee. *The Times* critic was still there, talking to Simon.

'Can you enlighten me as to what exactly that was about?' he was saying.

'I'd rather not say anything,' Simon said.

'Rather wise of you. Just as a matter of information: *has* anyone recently fallen out of a window?'

'Not recently,' said Simon, tight-lipped.

'OK. I thought I dimly remembered . . . never mind. The odd thing is that that whole palaver is actually rather authentic, isn't it? Using the play-within-the-play as Hamlet used it. A very clever twist. Better than a lot of modernisation I am condemned to sit through. I take it the actors in the dumb-show are or were entirely imaginary?'

Imogen saw Nigel pushing through the scrum to Simon's side. 'Of course,' he said.

'Well, I didn't think anybody could possibly be kitted out like that, these thirty years past,' said the critic. 'I was interested, too, in Hamlet being played as an obstinate, rather dogged sort of chap instead of a quivering, skinless one. Quite original.'

'It follows from the decision to use the Bad Quarto,' Simon said. 'It really does give a different picture.'

'Oh, quite. Rather difficult to do the endlessly undecided, delaying prince in a matter of two thousand lines. And by the by, what a coup for you to get Gadgby – thought the old boy was dead, actually. He was a great name in the seventies, best Shylock I ever saw. Must go – train to catch.'

Nigel followed him, asking for a copy of his piece when it was printed. 'You'll see it in *The Times*,' said the critic.

'I don't read *The Times*,' said Nigel tactlessly, sounding shocked at the mere suggestion.

'Well, there you are, then,' said the critic. 'And the *Sun* didn't send someone. Hard luck.'

Imogen looked round the marquee. The cast were all in impassioned conversation. Most had taken off their costumes, but their stage make-up had to wait for the washbasins and showers in their rooms. They had an eerie look to them, half in one world, half in another, like masked dancers. Imogen had always found masks rather sinister. Mottle was nowhere to be seen. The gist of the conversations Imogen was overhearing in fragments was people urgently asking each other who had known about the dumb-show. Nobody had known. Mottle had said there wouldn't be one, and made a secret of that very point.

'What have we done?' Fran was asking someone. 'Isn't it actionable?'

'We ourselves haven't done anything. Mottle did it. Let him pick up the tabs,' said Antonia. 'But *why* does he think pompous old V-G is homicidal?'

'Oh, I know why,' said Fran. 'Ask anyone in the English faculty.'

With a heavy heart, Imogen walked out of the fray to join Dennis in the senior common room.

The atmosphere there was just as fevered. Quite a few senior members had gathered, including several who had not been present at the play. And the Master was shouting at the bursar. Imogen had never heard him shout at anyone before, and she stood in the door, jaw-dropped. 'How in hell, Gracie, how in hell did we let that happen?' the Master was crying.

'We hired out the hall for three nights. I had no reason to think anything but *Hamlet* would go on. None at all.'

'Everybody knew there was something wonky about that production,' remarked Fairford, the fellow in economics, with ill-concealed glee. 'Talk of the town.'

Obviously Gracie felt pressured. 'Talk of the town that young Mottle had bought a leading role – yes,' he said. 'I hadn't heard anything else. Had you?'

'Had our supposedly devoted nurse?' said Fairford. 'Didn't you say she had introduced the gang of players?'

'Yes,' said Imogen, 'I did suggest to them that a college hall like ours – ours if you like – would be a good setting for Shakespeare. And no, I had no idea that anything like an attack on one of our fellows was planned.'

'Where is V-G now?' asked the Master, more calmly.

'Gone to ground. Up to his room to consult his lawyers,' said Malcolm Gracie.

'Can one consult a lawyer at half past ten at night?' asked Jeffrey, an engineering fellow.

'Depends how expensive the lawyer is,' said Remmer, who, as St Agatha's law don, presumably knew. 'He didn't ask me.'

'Well, if he had asked you, Remmer, what would you have told him?' asked Fairford.

'I'd have advised him to let the thing drop. To be content with cancelling the other performances.'

'The other performances will be all right,' said Imogen quietly. 'Mottle was in charge of just tonight's. The other two are back to Simon Malpas.'

'But as a matter of interest, Remmer,' Fairford persisted, 'however wise it might be to let it drop, does he have any alternative? I mean, what exactly has been perpetrated? It isn't libel, I take it, if it isn't written?'

'No, it's not libel. It must be slander.'

'But it wasn't spoken, either,' said the Master.

'It would be a particularly interesting case,' said Remmer. 'It amounts to slander – it has the effect of smirching someone's reputation.'

'Heaven protect us from being involved in a case that interests a lawyer!' wailed the Master.

'Heaven will sit on its hands as usual,' replied Remmer. 'But if V-G's lawyer is as good as he's pricey, he'll advise letting the whole thing drop. The thing is, one usually advises against suing people without any money, but Mottle's family are rolling in it.'

'It won't be money that motivates V-G,' said Dennis Dobbs. 'But he won't want to spend the rest of his life being thought of as a murderer.'

'I'm afraid he will so be thought of whether he sues or not,' said the Master. 'The lowest profile available will be best.'

'Tell you what, though, Remmer,' said Fairford, 'our beloved junior members being what they are, this will pack out V-G's lectures from here till the crack of doom.'

'There must be some university discipline that can be applied,' said Appleby.

'Not sure what it will be,' said the Master. 'But I'll ring Mottle's head of house in the morning. I'm going to bed now, my friends, and I suggest that we all sleep on this. Tomorrow is another day.'

As the company dispersed, Imogen and Dennis found themselves walking across the court with Malcolm Gracie. 'Well, at least we know why the young devil climbed in, Imogen, and gave you such a scare,' Malcolm said.

'He needed to see the inside of the room, to see—'

'Where the tying point for the safety rope would have been. Was. He needed that to be convincing.'

'To convince whom?' asked Imogen.

'A murderer. To convince *him* that Mottle knew what had happened, and how. You know, Imogen, it's natural for college fellows to think first about the college. It's natural for poor V-G to feel rage and alarm. But I think if I were Mr Mottle, I would lock my doors securely tonight and every night.'

'But, Malcolm, do you mean that you buy it? That you think there really was foul play?'

'I didn't think so till tonight,' said Gracie. 'Goodnight, Dobbs. Goodnight, Imogen.'

Imogen didn't sleep well that night. She found Fran in an excited state in her kitchen, telling Josh all about the night's spectacle. She extricated herself, pleading tiredness, and went up to bed with a mug of cocoa. She could hear their excited voices, behind the closed kitchen door, for quite a long time. But it was her racing thoughts that kept her awake.

Remember thee?
Yes, thou poor ghost . . .

ran on and on in her mind. But it was not Hamlet's father, the amazing performance of Gadgby, or any poor ghost from the cellarage, groaning, '*Remember me!*' that haunted her broken sleep. It was an image of John Talentire, walking smiling across Fountain Court, with a gaggle of adoring students in his train. His image walked past her without acknowledgement, just as she had complained to Dennis that the living man had done.

When college affairs became heated, or confrontational, which at St Agatha's they did only seldom, Imogen kept her head down. She had no standing in academic disputes, or the management of the college. She was in fact a fellow of the college, but that fellowship had been bestowed on her in a moment just like the present one, in which there was an agitation in the senior common room. The then dean – he had retired now – had remarked angrily that a proposal to suspend indefinitely the requirement that the students attend chapel once a term reduced the dean 'to the status of the college nurse'. He was not a popular man; the college had responded by elevating the nurse to the status of the dean – that is by making Imogen a fellow. She was not quite alone among college nurses in having been so honoured, but it was a very marked demonstration of the esteem in which she was held. However, she regarded it as a technical matter, the Cambridge equivalent of an OBE, and never used it in any way other than to take coffee in the senior common room if she felt like it, and dining in college at High Table once or twice a term. In no way did it encourage her to take sides in college disputes.

This time, however, she was in the thick of it. Whose idea had it been to suggest that the Kyd Society could use St Agatha's hall? Who had put them up to it? Imogen had. The Master called a meeting in his lodgings the following afternoon, and requested Imogen to be there. There would be no keeping a low profile over this.

The meeting did not include Venton-Gimps. Oddly, Imogen thought. Who did it concern more nearly than him? The Master had assembled the dean, the bursar, herself, Lady Buckmote, Remmer, and Mr Span, a lawyer from the London firm who dealt with the college affairs.

'Isn't V-G coming?' asked Remmer.

'He'll be along later,' said the Master. 'I thought we might like a bit of discussion first.'

Imogen took a seat in the back corner of the room: a window-seat overlooking Fountain Court, which was catching just a slant of late sunlight, and slipping into purple dusk. She felt a deep sadness. The Master was doing his duty to the college; putting its interests first. No doubt everyone would stand by V-G, if it could be done without damage to St Agatha's, but in a real crunch the college came first. The college was immortal, and of much more importance than the fate of any of its members. The meeting was clearly intended to brief the London lawyer about the situation. It began with Malcolm Gracie's report of the accident to John Talentire; the inquest's finding of accidental death. Then Imogen was asked to explain the situation of the Kyd Society, and why they had hired St Agatha's hall for the play. The Master gave a sharp and accurate résumé of what the dumb-show had consisted of, and of Venton-Gimps standing up and shouting.

'Unwise,' said Span.

'Very natural,' said Lady Buckmote.

'But confirming an identification that not everybody would otherwise perhaps have made,' said Span.

'I take it you consider he would be wise to keep a low profile?' asked the Master.

'He has a cause of action, certainly, if he wishes to take it,' said Span. 'But you want me to tell you, I take it, how this might impinge on the college. If Miss Quy's account is correct, then the college is an innocent party. Venton-Gimps could not pursue you. On the face of things he would have to sue the Kyd Society; and there are two reasons why that would be foolish. Reason one, we know they have no funds beyond the hundred thousand promised to them by Mottle, and their present debts account for much of that. Reason two, because, again, if Miss Quy's account is correct the Kyd Society knew no more about what was going to happen than the college did. Venton-Gimps had better sue Mottle himself if he wants any compensation.'

'But St Agatha's is in the clear?' asked Remmer.

'In my view, yes. But if a suit is to be brought against Mottle, I think you had better brief a QC to represent the college in court. In case of matters arising. Or someone challenging the facts as given us by Miss Quy.'

'I would lay down my life for the truth of evidence given by Miss Quy,' said the Master.

'Her good faith is not at issue. But her information might be subject to potential challenge. The law is an uncertain field.'

A feeling of relief spread through the room. The college would not be at risk; if there were a lawsuit they would take care to be represented. Everyone could sup up the Master's sherry and go to dinner at peace.

At this point Venton-Gimps entered the room. He was looking worn and grey, and almost unrecognisable: he was wearing a dark three-piece suit, and a conventional shirt and tie. All the flamboyance seemed to have been knocked out of him. 'Goodness me, Master, you have assembled quite a little cabal,' he said. 'There is no need, no need.'

'There is something to discuss, V-G,' said Remmer.

'I would like to assure you all,' said V-G, standing in the middle of the room, holding the sherry the Master had poured him in a slightly shaking hand, 'that I did not murder a colleague, and a fellow. I did not. I have an alibi; a perfect alibi, accepted by the police, by the coroner, by . . . I did not kill that wretch.'

'None of us thinks you did, V-G,' said Remmer. 'So certain are we of the falsehood of the accusation that we have been discussing your right to sue the slanderer.'

'I shan't sue him,' said V-G sadly. 'I am advised against it, and I think the advice is right. I must swallow my own bile, and keep mum.'

'Very wise, V-G,' said Span. 'You have been correctly advised.'

'However, isn't this pestilential slanderer an undergraduate? I would like to know, Master, friends, if there are statutes of the university to call in aid.'

'To do what?' asked Gracie. 'What do you want to do to him, V-G?'

'Remove him. Send him down.'

'I've been working on that all day,' said the Master. 'It's difficult. There doesn't seem to be a way to send down a member of one college for insulting a member of another.'

'Bringing the college into disrepute?' asked Lady Buckmote hopefully.

'Has he brought his own college into disrepute, though?' mused Remmer. 'I'm afraid I think not.'

'He has enraged his own college against him,' said the Master. 'They are considering sending him down.'

'The immediate question is shall we permit the play to go ahead tonight and tomorrow night?' said Fairford.

'We would just about be in time to stop it, if we hurry,' said Malcolm Gracie, looking at his watch. 'There's about an hour left before curtain up. But I don't advise it.'

'Why not, Gracie? We don't owe these scamps any consideration, do we?'

'Arguable. I believe they didn't know what was afoot. And then there is the matter of the audience; the tickets have sold out, and many people will be already on their way for the performance. I have received assurances about the conduct of tonight's performance; I shall stand in the gallery myself and physically prevent any attempt to stage a dumb-show. But the most powerful reason for my advice is that it will cause less stir to let it go forward than it will to cancel it.'

'I would prefer as little stir as possible,' said V-G.

'Very well. Let the play be,' said the Master, 'since that is the feeling of the meeting.'

'And find a way of making Mottle answer for himself,' said Remmer.

'If there is a way of calling that young man to account, we shall certainly do it,' said the Master.

'There must be something in the university statutes, surely,' offered Span, picking up his briefcase, as he took his leave.

'I've missed all the fun,' said Remmer sadly. 'I couldn't make it last night; my ticket is for tonight.'

Part three

IO

Come, the croking raven doth bellow for revenge

Imogen, it turned out, had not missed all the fun. First she had the pleasure of sitting through the second and third nights of *Hamlet*, in what she had come to see as the not-so-bad Quarto. It cast a new light; and Simon playing Hamlet was a good deal easier on the eye and ear than Martin Mottle. The missing dumb-show seemed not so glaring a lacuna; and Imogen, who had always thought of Hamlet as a bit of a wimp, was seeing that the question of the truthfulness of the ghost was far from an excuse for shirking a dangerous duty, but a real question. All quite interesting. But Imogen's real further fun occurred the following morning.

It took the very unexpected form of Josh, bursting into Imogen's room in college at ten in the morning, and demanding that she come with him at once. 'Fran sent me to fetch you,' he said.

'I'm on duty for another half an hour,' said Imogen, looking at her watch.

'It's urgent, Imo. Come now.'

And Imogen could gather from his tone that it really was urgent. She got up and put on her overcoat. 'What's it about, Josh?' she asked.

Josh took her by the elbow, and steered her rapidly across

the court, and through the gate. He had parked his car on double yellow lines, emergency lights flashing, right outside. 'Get in and I'll explain while we drive,' he said.

'Let me guess,' said Imogen, getting into the car. 'Something to do with Mr Mottle?'

'Oh, naturally. Exactly. The Kyd Society is not best pleased with him.'

'Didn't he pay?'

'He paid up as promised. Yesterday morning. But people are appalled to find they have been tricked into making allegations of murder. Just about everybody is facing disciplinary enquiries from their colleges, and the law students are raising their hackles with talk of suits for slander . . . So they asked Mottle to present himself to the committee and explain himself. And he wouldn't. He said he had kept his side of the bargain, and he didn't want anything more to do with them.'

'So what's the rush? And where are we going?'

'Well, it seems that someone in the Kyd Society also plays rugger. And happened to mention to a friend or two Mottle's unwillingness to show his face, and to cut a long story short, a rugger team has gone to fetch Mottle whether he likes it or not. Fran thought it could get ugly.'

'So am I supposed to practise first aid?'

'I think you are thought to be a calming influence and potent source of common sense.'

'God help us,' said Imogen.

Josh drove her through Newnham, and out towards Grantchester, turning in to the parking area for the sports pavilion of St Agatha's. They went in. A well-chosen place: it was out of sight and sound of anywhere, surrounded by soggy fields, private and at the moment unused by any sportsmen. The custom of the country was for sports to await the afternoon,

when presumably lectures and supervisions have been dutifully attended to in the morning. When Imogen entered the
clubroom was arranged for the intended kangaroo court: a
half-circle of chairs facing a single chair in the middle of the
room. The Kyd Society committee were all in attendance.
Mottle had not yet arrived.

'Miss Quy, thank you so much for coming,' said Nigel. 'We
need a dispassionate witness.'

'What you need most urgently of all,' said Imogen sternly,
'is a sensible adult to advise you very strongly against what you
are doing. You can't just "fetch" people. Aren't you in enough
trouble without facing charges for false arrest?'

'Too late!' said Fran. 'He's on his way.'

The room was very cold, but it was not only that which
made Imogen feel a sudden chill. She sat down in an end chair,
keeping her coat on.

There was a rumpus as Martin Mottle arrived. His escorts
burst through the doors, in a walking scrum with their captive
in the middle. He stopped short as he saw what awaited him,
and several brawny young men jostled him, pushing him
forward. Imogen, ever more deeply dismayed, recognised
Pete Varfell, St Agatha's Captain of Rugger, among the team.

'You can't do this, you know!' Mottle said. He sounded
rattled; his voice rose to a squeak.

'What exactly can't we do?' asked Varfell. 'As you see, we
are doing it.'

'It won't work,' said Mottle. 'I'm not having it.'

'Sit down in that chair, Martin,' said Simon Malpas.

'No, I bloody well won't!' said Martin.

There was a brief scuffle as he was lifted bodily forward,
over the back of the chair, and into it. He jumped up at once.
'Let me out of here!' he said.

'Let him go,' said Imogen.

'Let's have a bit of calm and common sense round here,' said Fran. 'We only want to ask Martin for an explanation. And he owes us that. Surely there's no need to get physical.'

'I don't owe you an explanation,' said Martin, suddenly sitting down.

'OK, friend,' said Varfell. 'Here you stay until Simon here says you can go. Or you have us to reckon with. Understand?' He loomed over Mottle, slightly tipping his chair backward.

'Oh, all right!' said Mottle. 'Pax.'

'We'll be just outside, Simon,' said Varfell, leading his troop out of the door.

There was a sudden heavy silence. Mottle looked round the circle of his inquisitors. He locked eyes with Imogen for a second. And it was Mottle who spoke first.

'We had an agreement,' he said wearily. 'Money, my money, in exchange for your co-operation. You co-operated. I paid. That's the end of it.'

'If only it was,' said Simon. 'But the trick you played has consequences. We are all more or less in trouble. And we haven't a clue what it was about. I can't say I like finding myself at once in hot water, and in the dark. How about anyone else?'

'All you have to say, you great booby,' said Mottle, 'is that you didn't know anything about it. Just stick strictly to that. It has the obvious merit of being true, and it keeps you all in the clear. That's *why* I didn't explain. And why I'm not going to explain now.'

'Oh, aren't you?' said Simon, who seemed to have assumed the director's part in the tribunal. 'In that case we shall be here a long time.'

Mottle looked at Imogen. 'Are you a party to this?' he asked.

'No,' said Fran hastily. 'I asked her to come.'

'In case I got hurt?' he asked. 'What is this?'

'I didn't think you would get hurt, Martin,' said Fran. 'But I thought it might help to keep the temperature down if Imo was here.'

'A sort of human thermostat, is she?' asked Mottle.

'Look, this mustn't get out of hand,' said Simon. 'Imogen said we were in enough trouble already, and so we are. But *why*, Martin? What were you playing at? We do seriously need to know.'

'Have it your own way. You all thought I was just an idiot wanting to play Hamlet, didn't you? And that suited me fine. You're a patronising bloody lot, you thespians, but promoting your play all round the town as a famous pratfall guaranteed a packed house. I needed that. I thought I was being so bad in rehearsals that you might twig it was being put on, but no. There was nothing I could do that made you think nobody could be so stupid as that. Simply nothing you thought me incapable of. You might have remembered that I got into Cambridge, same as you.'

'Fair enough, Martin. I'll put my hand up to that, and I'll apologise,' said Simon. 'But you shouldn't blame us. It was a jolly good performance as a duffer that you favoured us with.'

'Sorry, Martin,' said Fran. A chorus of agreement chimed with her apology.

'Yes, well,' said Mottle grudgingly.

Like a bloodhound refusing to leave the scent, Simon persisted, 'So what was going on?'

Mottle began to speak, rapidly, quietly. 'It's like this. A year ago, before most of you here came up, a friend of mine was killed. He fell to his death trying the jump called Harding's Folly.'

'John Talentire,' said Nigel. 'I heard about it.'

'*I* didn't hear about it for weeks,' said Mottle. 'I was climbing in the Andes, right out of touch. By the time I got back to Cambridge John was dead and buried and the inquest was over, and I couldn't find out a damn thing. I just met a brick wall everywhere.'

'What were you *trying* to find out?' asked Imogen.

'What had happened to John. He was my oldest friend.'

'Well, but . . . couldn't you just ask around?' asked Nigel.

'Oh, I asked all right. I could find that the inquest brought in "Death by misadventure" and I found a couple of people who had been there when it happened, both having obviously had rather a lot to drink. I heard what they had to say. It didn't add up to an explanation.'

'Your friend wouldn't be the first to fall to his death trying that jump,' observed Simon. 'It's notorious.'

'But John was using a safety rope. He might have been left dangling. He might have swung hard against the wall below the window, and been injured. But he shouldn't have fallen clear.'

'Look, we're sorry about this, Martin,' said Nigel. 'Hard luck. Nasty to lose a friend. But how does this get us to *Hamlet*?'

'I couldn't find out,' said Mottle, '*anything* except what was in the *Cambridge Evening News*. I could read a back number of that. It said that the inquest found John had tied a duff knot in his rope. It had slipped.'

'So?' asked Simon.

'No. No, he hadn't. No, it didn't. I wanted to read the transcript of the inquest, but you can't get them. It isn't like Hansard.'

'But isn't an inquest public?' asked Fran.

'Yes. You can attend it. You can take notes. But once it's over the record is private. For seventy-five years.'

'But what if a grieving relative wanted to check on something?' Fran asked.

'The coroner can release a transcript, or a bit of it, to a close relative, or someone closely concerned, at his absolute discretion. He wouldn't release anything to me. Not to a mere friend.'

'Hmm,' said Simon. The feeling of the meeting had changed. It was no longer confrontational, and Mottle was no longer in the hot seat, though he was the centre of everyone's attention. Outside on the playing field, the arresting party who had brought him there were kicking a ball around. Their random manly cries could be heard offstage, like gulls at a seaport.

'I tried everything I could think of,' Mottle went on. 'I asked John's father to ask for the inquest transcripts, but he was too distressed to do that. He wanted it left alone. Worse than that; he showed me the door, and he seems to have actually asked the coroner not to let me have a look. Well, someone did, and I think it must have been John's father. The coroner told me he wouldn't go against the family's wishes. I asked John's GP, but he wouldn't play either. So I was left with just a bloody stupid verdict, and no explanation. Then I happened to read *Hamlet*. It blew my mind. Could I sympathise with that guy!'

His audience were now spellbound and intent.

'He was in just the same fix as me; he needed to know what had really happened, and he was meeting a blank wall of obfuscation. And I thought his way of dealing with it was brilliant. And then I thought, well, I could do that too! That's where you came in. Thank you.'

'You seriously thought you could flush out a murderer by using the dumb-show?' Nigel's incredulity was audible.

'Well, I had worked out what must have happened. And I thought a mime of that might at least scare the murderer, and spoil his sleep. He would know that somebody *knew*. I got the agreement with you, and I enlisted a couple of climbing friends. And there you are.'

'Here we are,' echoed Simon. 'At least I cotton on.'

'Well, I don't,' said Nigel. 'Your bloody dumb-show depicts someone untying the knot in the safety rope. The coroner found that the knot was badly tied and slipped. I know which seems more likely, Martin.'

Mottle rose to his feet and began to pace the room. 'There's what could, possibly, have happened, and what couldn't possibly,' he said. 'I have known John, and climbed with him since I was fourteen. He was ten years older than me, and had a lot of experience. He offered to take me climbing with him, and the weather changed abruptly. We had to spend a night out on Scafell. We got down all right the next day. We helped each other. Since then I've climbed with him everywhere, all over the world. I've been roped up with John on plenty of tricky climbs. I've trusted my life to a knot that he tied. And I know, I just know, I absolutely know, that he didn't tie a silly knot. He simply *couldn't* have.'

'But this silly game you were playing has got us all in hot water,' said Nigel indignantly.

'Oh, rubbish, Nigel,' said Mottle. 'You didn't know a thing about it until it happened. That's your defence. As I said, it has the merit of being true.'

'Mightn't you yourself be in trouble?' asked Fran.

'What can they do to me?' asked Mottle contemptuously. 'Send me down? I'll just go to Harvard instead.'

Simon said, 'So Talentire didn't tie a duff knot. But it's a hell of a jump from that to thinking that it wasn't *any* kind of

accident; to thinking that somebody killed him, and it's another huge jump to dressing up someone to look like V-G.
Come on, Martin, spill the beans.'

'I've had enough of this,' said Martin. 'Stop bullying me.
Who in hell do you think you are?' His voice suddenly turned
tremulous. He angrily brushed the back of his hands across his
eyes, said, 'Oh, hell!' and turned away from them.

'I think that'll do, don't you, Simon?' said Imogen. 'Josh, get
Mr Mottle into your car, and let's take him home. Pronto.'

It turned out that taking Mottle home to Imogen's house was a
better idea than taking him back to his college. He was very
shaken by the morning's ordeal. His hands were trembling,
and his eyes were moist. Imogen prescribed a cup of hot sweet
tea, and two aspirins, and dispensed these in her breakfast
room. Josh, now fascinated by the whole *Hamlet* scene, stayed
around with Fran, and the four of them talked by the Aga,
which gently warmed the room, and Mottle gradually calmed
down and stopped shaking. Fran and Imogen talked quietly
together about Fran's research, leaving Mottle to his own
thoughts.

'S'pose I zipped up to the corner, Imogen, and fetched a
quick lunch for us all?' asked Josh in a while. Josh was always
punctually hungry.

'Yes, please, Josh. Bring fresh bread, and some deli. I've got
some salad,' Imogen said.

'I'd better go,' said Martin, getting to his feet.

'Not at all,' said Imogen. 'Stay to lunch. You'll feel better
with a bit of food inside you.'

Martin sat down again.

'Bring a can of soup, too, Josh,' said Imogen as he left.

'I do feel very odd. What's wrong with me?' said Martin.

'Shock, in a word,' said Imogen. 'Anger at being man-handled around. More than a little unresolved grief. Just ride yourself easy for a while. Stay here in the warm and eat a meal with us.'

'You're very kind,' said Martin.

'It's her stock-in-trade,' said Fran. 'She's notorious for it.'

'So how far do you reckon you got?' Josh asked Mottle over lunch. 'Did you flush out a murderer?'

'I scared him, all right,' said Mottle. 'Pinning it onto him is another matter. But there's some satisfaction in thinking of his sleepless nights.'

'You certainly upset old V-G,' said Fran. 'And why him, Martin? He's a harmless old git, isn't he?'

'It must have been him,' said Mottle. 'He's the only one whose room is near enough.'

But Fran deflected the conversation. 'You know what, Martin,' she said, 'you were aiming to cause your murderer sleepless nights. To let him know that somebody knew what he had done. Did it occur to you that you might be putting yourself in danger? That he might think it would be just as well to silence you for good?'

'Yes,' said Mottle. 'I did think of that. I'm very fit. I'm trained in karate. I carry a weapon, though please don't tell the police that. And I'm not going climbing in Cambridge till this is sorted. I can deal with Venton-Gimps, believe me!'

'But what motive did he have?' asked Imogen. 'Crimes tend to have motives, and serious crimes have weighty motives.'

'Oh, he had reason enough,' said Mottle. 'Plenty of reasons, I assure you. *Those* are easy to find out. No embargo on those. Those are published by the Cambridge University Press.'

I, Horatio, I'le take the Ghost's word
For more than all the coyne in Denmarke

It would have taken a lot to banish all this from Imogen's mind, but that is what happened. When she passed the porters' lodge that evening, the head porter intercepted her.

'Can you spare a minute, Miss Quy?' Mr Hughes led her through into his inner sanctum, a little room behind the porters' counter, with a board of keys, a few battered phone directories, and a run of volumes in, and about Cornish, for he was himself a scholar of sorts.

'One of the undergraduates has reported her room-mate going absent,' he told Imogen. 'Three nights now. I've left a note in the delinquent's room, and made a few enquiries, without result so far.'

'Who is it?' Imogen asked.

'Susan Inchman.'

'Ah.'

'I supposed you might perhaps know something.'

Imogen sighed. It wasn't, actually, unheard of at all for an undergraduate to simply disappear from the university during term. They had many motives for this irrational behaviour. Surely it was irrational to spend the latter years of their golden youth swotting desperately to get into Cambridge, and once there to abscond. But each term one or two people did it. Just now and then they were the true elite, so golden that they were actually disappointed at the company they found themselves in, or at the level of teaching they were getting. They took themselves off to Harvard, as Martin Mottle had threatened to do. Or they simply short-circuited their education, and launched themselves on the world without a degree. Most, but not all of them, informed the college what they were doing, and perhaps why. But frankly Susan might belong to another group, those who found the pressure too much, the competition too much, the contrast too much from being the cleverest in the class, heaped with praise by delighted and ambitious teachers, to being a dumb-dumb, floundering about in the supervision, outshone by their companions. Not everybody, in short, prospered at Cambridge, and this wasn't Imogen's field of responsibility.

'Well, lots of things could take someone off for three days. Of course she ought to have told someone, but she isn't much of a rule-keeper, I think.'

'Apparently not,' said Hughes. 'In my opinion, Miss Quy, a young person in her situation should be particularly careful to observe college regulations, not conspicuously lax about them.'

'In her situation, Mr Hughes?'

'One of these scholarship youngsters. Not up to the mark, and admitted for other reasons. Isn't she one of those?'

'I thought that was supposed to be strictly confidential, Mr Hughes.'

'Not much happens here that I don't get to know about, Miss Quy,' he said with tight-lipped satisfaction. 'Unless you happened to know what was what, I'm duty bound to tell her supervisor, and commence enquiries.'

'Yes, I think you should, Mr Hughes. She's a grown-up, for good or ill.'

Imogen left him, and sat in her office for the usual session, before going across to the Lodge for sherry with Lady Buckmote and the Master. She had a lot to tell them, to juice up the dry Amontillado. She would need to see if Samantha knew what Susan was up to, but tomorrow was another day.

'God help us!' said the Master, on hearing an account of Mottle being kidnapped and arraigned. 'He wasn't hurt, Imogen, was he?'

'Shaken and angry, rather.'

'I'm not surprised. And however much trouble he may have caused, this sort of thing can't be allowed. Are any of the perpetrators members of St Agatha's?'

'I'm afraid yes, Master. But I don't think we have to do anything unless Martin Mottle makes a complaint.'

'He's not in a very strong position to make complaints, is he?' said Lady Buckmote.

'He could go to the police. Think of the headlines!' said the Master.

'I don't think he'll go to the police,' said Imogen. 'But I rather changed my take on him. He does have a legitimate complaint.'

'What of?' asked the Master.

'A cover-up.'

'Oh, rubbish, Imogen! There was a nasty accident; the police investigated and ruled out foul play. There was an inquest which found misadventure. There absolutely hasn't been a cover-up. Just a simple disaster. A tragedy; but definitely the fault of the man who died. Jumping out of high windows just *is* dangerous. That's all there is to it.'

'I understand that the sense of a cover-up arises because Mr

Mottle can't see the inquest evidence. So he can't get any real account of what actually happened.'

'Why can't he?' asked Lady Buckmote.

'The coroner won't release the transcript. It's private for seventy-five years or something. And you know, he really is chewed up about it. I think it's real grief for his friend that is driving him.'

Sir William poured himself another sherry. He swirled the golden liquid gently round the glass. He had become abstracted from the scene. Lady Buckmote rose and refreshed her own glass and Imogen's. The window panes of rippled glass in the ancient casements of the room caught the purple dusk descending outside, and blazed briefly with the last gleam of the sun descending behind the gatehouse tower.

'Do you think it would comfort this unhappy young man if he could see the inquest evidence?' Sir William asked eventually.

'I don't know,' said Imogen. 'I can't say if it would convince him that there wasn't any foul play. I expect it would comfort him if it did.'

'It convinced everybody else,' the Master said. 'Including the man's father.'

'And Talentire senior is hard to convince that death was accidental when it comes to giving evidence in court,' added Lady Buckmote drily.

'Oh, but that fuss is about other people's children. Not his own,' said Imogen.

'What do I hear?' said Sir William. 'Cynicism from Imogen? My dear, we are getting to be bad for you, I'm afraid.'

'I don't think it's Cambridge, I think it's age and experience,' said Imogen, smiling. 'I'm very happy here. I seem to have found my place.'

'You do have a valued place among us,' the Master said. 'So if you have taken a liking to the pestiferous Mr Mottle, and if you think the inquest evidence would help . . .'

'It's entirely theoretical what I think,' Imogen reminded him.

'Oh, no it's not!' said the Master. 'We thought that inquest might reflect on the college in one or more of numerous ways, so we sent a stenographer to take it all down for us. We have a transcript in the safe. As long as you don't let it out of your sight, I don't see why we shouldn't let Mr Mottle see it. For his peace of mind, and everyone else's peace and quiet.'

'William, what about V-G?' asked Lady Buckmote. 'Might assistance to Mottle seem like a stabbing in the back to him?'

'I've known V-G for thirty years,' said the Master. 'Anything more preposterous than the idea that he could run up a flight of stairs and swiftly undo a knot in a thick rope I find it hard to imagine. He's so hopelessly clumsy he can't pick up a wine glass without spilling it. And for God's sake, Caroline, the man has a cast-iron alibi. I am taking it that the full account will squash any such rubbish. Let the boy read it, Imogen. But let's keep it confidential.'

The transcript was a thick file of neatly typewritten pages, in a stout ring binder with the label of the college office stuck slightly askew on the front. The weight of it tugged at the steering of Imogen's bicycle as she rode home with it in the handlebar basket, on a day with a brisk crosswind on the Lammas Land path. She had decided that she had better read it herself, or at least skip through it before exposing it to the not entirely predictable Martin. Some sixth sense of a precautionary nature made her withdraw to the armchair in her own bedroom to read it privately. Privately, she reflected as she settled down, pushing her shoes off her feet, curling her legs into the soft wide chair, propping the heavy file on the right arm, and adjusting the reading light, meant where Fran or Josh would not arrive and take an interest. She could hear Josh's choice of music playing in the flat above, not too loudly, but enough to make the house feel shared, rather than solitary.

If all this indicated that she expected bombshells of any kind in the file, she was disappointed. Her own evidence was accurately recorded. There was, naturally, medical evidence. An ambulance crew had arrived about seven minutes after the 999 call. They had found the deceased lying in Patten Alley, unconscious, apparently dead. A rope was attached to the belt round the body, and was coiled beside and across it. They had taken the body to Addenbrooke's where death was confirmed.

The casualty officer reported that the body had multiple injuries consistent with a fall from a considerable height. He gave it as his opinion that death had been instantaneous, and the cause of death had been fracture of the skull. Several other injuries sustained by the deceased would have been sufficient traumas to cause death, but he thought the massive fracture of the skull had been the proximate cause.

A police officer who had arrived at the same time as the ambulance gave his account. When he arrived a crowd of distressed onlookers was present. He had made them stand back, and he had inspected the scene. A man's body was lying on the ground in the middle of the alleyway, and there was an open window above the point where the corpse was lying, on the top floor of the tower in the corner of St Agatha's College. He did not know the name of the college building, nor of the tower. As soon as his colleagues had arrived, very shortly after his own arrival, he had cordoned off the alleyway, and taken names and addresses so that witness statements could be obtained at a later date.

A more senior police officer testified that he had been called to the scene, at about nine-twenty p.m. He had effected entry to the college, where the porters were unaware that anything untoward had occurred, and on raising the alarm had been escorted to the tower room. The room was found to be empty, with the window standing open, and unlatched. There was nothing of any significance visible in the room, but he had ordered it to be sealed, so that fingerprints could be taken later. A search of the other rooms on the staircase had found two of the rooms leading off it to be empty and a first-floor room, where a Mr Potts, on being roused, had reported seeing Talentire running up the stairs some time earlier.

'Did you in fact take fingerprints from the tower room?' the coroner had asked.

'We did. The deceased's own fingerprints were found on one of the upright beams in the room. I can offer the court a floor-plan and a photograph. There were also his fingerprints on the window catch, along with those of several other people. Most of those have been matched with college servants. A few fibres from the climbing rope found with the body were recovered from the upright beam in the room, and also from the lower sill of the window, over which it had been drawn when the deceased fell. However, the witness statements taken the following day did not suggest foul play of any kind, and an exhaustive search for the unmatched fingerprints was not undertaken.'

The inquest had moved on to those witness statements.

The picture Imogen had formed from college gossip unrolled in the transcript, the details filled in, but the overall picture unsurprising. There had been a riotous drinking party, going on all afternoon, at the Pickerel. The drinkers had been celebrating an achievement, the successful climb the previous night by one Perkinson of a drainpipe on the side of Caius, followed by jumping the famous gap across the Senate House Passage, and making a safe descent. There had been much boasting and challenging, and talk of which was the most dangerous climb in Cambridge, and by and by, how the Senate House Passage compared in difficulty with Harding's Folly.

The problem with this as a narrative account was that witnesses overlapped each other, and were not heard in strict sequence. There were the usual minor contradictions. Imogen got out her notebook, and set herself the task of taking 'case notes' on all this, quietly piecing it together as she read, working towards a coherent account.

In the pub the jolly drinkers had complained to each other bitterly about Harding's Folly. Even the best of them, the ones who had climbed every other height in the city, had not managed a total triumph, because Harding's Folly was inaccessible. One or two of them had tried drainpipes and handholds, but it was agreed to be impossible to reach from outside. Imogen made a mental note to chalk one up to Martin Mottle. It had emerged as they boasted and drank that John Talentire had access to Harding's Folly – full-time, unimpeded access. He had the room from which the jump had to be made. He had not been extremely willing to co-operate. He had given it as his opinion – all witnesses agreed about this – that it was dangerous enough to be foolish to risk oneself on. It would be as dangerous as a chunk of Swiss Alp, but not as exhilarating. Predictably someone called him a coward. He had not risen to that, but told the man to stuff it. Someone in the company had begun to collect money to place bets on the jump – the money to go to charity if anyone present would try it. The money mounted alarmingly in the hat, until about a hundred and twenty pounds was staked. Several young men and one young woman offered to jump, and John Talentire eventually said, 'Oh, all right then.'

A brief argument followed, in which Talentire made it very plain that he would jump himself; he absolutely would not open the door of his room to let anyone else jump. Himself, or no one. The kitty to the Save the Children fund. Agreed? That or nothing.

What followed, Imogen pieced together with particular care. The party had left the pub, and trooped up the road to St Agatha's. There they had split; John Talentire had dashed through the college gate, and everyone else had trooped a little further up the hill, and into the passageway where they would have a good view. Some of them still had beer mugs in their hands, and they were rather noisy, to the annoyance of several St Agatha's students who had leaned out of study windows to yell at them to piss off and shut up. Somehow news had got about; people who opened their windows to object to the noise were soon joining the crowd in the lane. It took Talentire some time. 'Finding his rope, I suppose,' one witness had offered. Evidently the rope was not really in the spirit of the thing.

At last the tower room window was pushed open, and Talentire appeared, to look down on a sea of upturned faces. The crowd below him had parted, moving to left and right; the best view was not immediately beneath the jump, but a little way either side of it. Just as well, Imogen thought, or more lives would have been lost. Silence had fallen.

'Everyone held their breath,' the witness reported. 'Like in church.'

Talentire crouched in the window opening, and then jumped, sailing over the gap above them, and landing lightly on his feet, knees bending immediately, like a cat. Below him, came the opening instants of a cheer, which died instantly. He stood upright, on the very edge of the library roof, and raised an arm as if to salute his audience. He was turning to look down. And then he suddenly lost his balance. He pitched forward, and fell. Wincing, Imogen read accounts of the sound his body made on the pavement, and the whispering sound of the rope, coiling down on top of him. He fell to cries of horror and dismay, and then to a long stunned silence before someone came to his senses and called the police.

The coroner had taken a great deal of evidence on the question whether anybody had accompanied John Talentire up to his room, and been with him when he jumped. It seemed not. The college porter remembered him running through the gate, without so much as a good evening, and was sure that he had been alone, and not closely followed by anyone. 'We keep an eye on coming and going after dark,' he had said. 'Just in case, you might say.'

The coroner had turned his attention to the question whether there had been anybody inside the college who might have accidentally witnessed anything to the point. It seemed not. The jump had happened a little after nine o'clock: the police had logged the 999 call at nine eighteen. Most of the dons had adjourned to the senior common room for dessert and port. Most of the students were still in their own common room, or had wandered back to their rooms. There were only three undergraduate rooms on the tower staircase; one belonged to Felix Potts, who had been trying to write an essay. He had put his head out of his room door to protest as someone thundered up the stairs, making a hell of a racket, seen that the offender was Talentire, a senior member, and beaten a hasty retreat. A second room belonged to a student who had slept through the crisis. The third belonged to a student who was playing darts in the junior common room, and remained oblivious of the whole drama till the following morning. Two fellows of the college had rooms on the tower staircase: one was Professor Appleby, who had been attending a meeting of the Royal Society in London, and the other was Venton-Gimps.

He seemed a little uneasy about it, thought Imogen, reading his verbatim evidence, but he was definite that he had not been anywhere near his room at the time in question. It was a teaching room, not a college set, and he had gone home to his flat in Chesterton after hall dinner, in time to hear the news at nine o'clock. A neighbour had called to give him a parcel she had taken in for him, because it wouldn't go through his letterbox, and she had confirmed that she had heard the professor come in at eight thirty. She could hear his footfalls on the floor above her own flat, although all the flats were close-carpeted. She had rung on the professor's doorbell, and she had seen him for the few seconds it took to greet him and hand him his parcel. It was always happening. The professor ordered a lot of books from Amazon, and the letterboxes were ridiculously small . . .

Imogen carefully finished her note-taking, and sat in thought. How sad this was – how silly and arbitrary. Accidental death in young manhood was such a disaster that it seemed insultingly absurd for it to have no serious cause but only folly and carelessness. She wondered if it was really wise or kind to let Mottle see this stuff. How could it help reconcile him? How could it do other than pain him? And yet it seemed the only thing now that could in any way help lay it all to rest –

unless Mottle was right, and Venton-Gimps in an access of fury tried to murder Talentire! Well, no, now she came to think of it, the inquest evidence should at least convince Mottle that V-G was in the clear. He should see it.

12

But, Hamlet, this is onely fantasie,
And for my love, forget these idle fits . . .

'I 've brought you something to read, in exchange,' said
Martin Mottle, arriving at Imogen's front door. She had
arranged for him to come and read in her sitting room, since
she had promised not to let the transcript out of sight. The
little table in the back half of the room had a comfortable chair
pulled up to it, the inquest transcript and her own notes on it
lying ready. She had provided a plate of biscuits, and a smell of
coffee, good coffee from the shop in King Street, drifted
enticingly from the kitchen. Imogen was close to identifying
Martin as the site of a painful wound, albeit a mental one,
which needed comfort.

When the coffee was made and poured, she picked up the
book he had brought for her, and sat in her armchair at the
other end of the room to read it.

'There's no hurry,' he said. 'You can keep that.'

But reading gave Imogen cover to keep an eye on her guest.
The slender volume he had brought her was indeed published
by Cambridge University Press. It was the twenty-third annual
Ansome Memorial Lecture, delivered in the Mill Lane lecture
rooms two years back, by John Talentire. His title was: 'The
Shakespeare Controversy'. Imogen began to read.

It had been quite some lecture. It started by filling Imogen in very comprehensively on the state of Shakespeare studies two years ago. The idea that there was any particular merit in the works of Shakespeare, was, according to the prevailing school of thought, an artificial creation, put up by British imperialists, white supremacists and male chauvinists, because it privileged the culture of the 'master-race' over all others, and underpinned the imperialist agenda. If Shakespeare was the greatest writer of all time, then he could justify the forced teaching of English all over the empire, and by implication the subordination of authentic native cultures everywhere. Since Shakespeare was a man, and feminist orthodoxy ordained that no man could understand a woman or represent any female character truthfully and fairly, it followed that the worship of Shakespeare was also part of a conspiracy to justify the marginalisation of women and the rejection of women writers from the canon of English studies. The word 'bardolatry' was liberally sprinkled throughout such expressions of opinion; which reached the pinnacle of absurdity, in John Talentire's view, in an article published in the proceedings of the Higher Falls University by one Venton-Gimps, who he admitted with regret was a fellow of his own college. This article put forward the view that everyone would be better off studying Aphra Behn.

Ignoring a groan from Martin, Imogen read on. John Talentire conceded at once that objectivity in the judgement of works of literature was problematic. However, this did not mean that any opinion, however vacuous, ill-informed, prejudiced and inattentive to the text, was as good as any other. In particular a universal relativism should not by any respectable person be made the occasion to base judgement on a priori theoretical systems which dictated, ahead of any encounter with the play, or poem or novel itself what its worth must be – or more often could not be. In his opinion many of the judgements masquerading as being part of 'theory of literature' were political, based on class envy, and appealing strongly because they relieved scholars of the labour-intensive need to read poems, plays and novels, and to read attentively and with an open mind.

Next he offered to give the benefit of the doubt to his colleague.

Let us suppose for a moment that the man actually has read the plays of Shakespeare, or seen them on the stage. Let us suppose that it is his sincere judgement that they are not particularly good. Now let us consider what qualities are required to have come to this judgement in good faith. Firstly, perhaps primarily, the man must be spectacularly deaf to the beauties of Shakespeare's language, immune to the appeal of precisely and beautifully articulated meaning. Then, I should think, he would have to be completely uninterested in the varieties of human character, in moral dilemmas of any kind. He must on the other hand be very ready to fall in with fashionable thinking of the present day, especially if it is politically correct and, indeed, largely political. He must be unresponsive to the usual human emotions, to the famous pity and fear aroused by tragedy, and he is probably hard to make laugh if he finds absolutely nothing to admire in the comedies. Here I will concede that many of Shakespeare's jokes are now obscure and require some time immersed in the footnotes of a good edition to elucidate them. One might hope that a scholar ensconced in a Cambridge college would find the necessary time, but perhaps he was very busy in the pursuit of strange waistcoats.

'Oh, *really!*' exclaimed Imogen under her breath. Surely that was way over the top. It should have been edited out of the printed edition; perhaps the editor did not realise it was a direct allusion to a particular real person.

Further, this person must be unable to distinguish between works of art created in the sixteenth and very early seventeenth century, and accretions of later critics and worshippers. Was Shakespeare to blame for plaster models of Anne Hathaway's cottage on sale in Stratford-upon-Avon? Does the bad taste of the souvenir market subtract a single tittle from any of his works? *How* does it do so? I am afraid to say that I think the use of the disdainful references to bardolatry in works of criticism has a very unpleasant overtone. A contempt for the masses is clearly informing it. Now you might innocently suppose, ladies and gentlemen, that contempt for the masses was incompatible with a Marxist outlook on the world; but you would be wrong, at least where academic Marxists are concerned. Safely en-sconced in seats of learning in the West, they have long contrived to combine theoretical admiration for the proletariat with elite disdain for the masses. I regret to tell you that I think that one of the things wrong with Shakespeare in the minds of these learned gentlemen is precisely that he is loved by count-less ordinary people, and read in almost every language on the face of the globe. What everybody can understand and enjoy, like a production of *Twelfth Night*, or *Macbeth*, is clearly inferior to *Abdelazar*, or *The Dutch Lover*, which most of us have never heard of.

This is criticism in the guise of priesthood. It has two very undesirable results. It makes impressionable undergraduates imagine they can score by making clever derisive remarks about a very great dramatist; and it makes clever people assume that only those who cannot see what's good about Shakespeare would admire Aphra Behn, who was actually an interesting and highly innovative writer, well worth the disinterested attention of those of us who *can* see what's good about Shakespeare, even though yellow waistcoats rank in our minds with cross-gartered hose . . .

Imogen looked up to find Martin looking at her expectantly.

'You wonder how all that went over? Gales of laughter, stamping, and when he finished a ten-minute ovation. That's how.'

'And you think it gave Venton-Gimps a motive for murder?'

'Well, don't you think so? He's just destroyed in that lecture. I'm amazed he had the effrontery to stay on in Cambridge after that. As a matter of fact,' he continued, shaking his head slightly, 'I don't think John should have done it. It went too far. He shouldn't have made it so personal. It was bound to leave Venton-Gimps with a grudge against him. People began to laugh in the Gimps lectures, and even laugh at him in the street. Of course he had a motive.'

'Talking of what shouldn't have been done,' said Imogen, 'I don't think CUP should have published this verbatim. Shouldn't they have edited it?'

'Well, John was dead before they got the proofs to him.'

'So no second thoughts?'

'Not that the printed text caused the bother. It came long after the event as far as reputations were concerned.'

'There's a lot more of this,' said Imogen. 'I'd like to read the rest.'

'Oh, keep it. That's fine. As long as you like.'

'And your reading? How did you get on?'

Martin shook his head. 'Not very well. May I stay a bit

longer and read it through again? And did anyone say I mustn't make some notes on it?'

'Yes, you can stay. And no, nobody told me you weren't to make notes. Is there something there that's helpful?'

'Not a thing,' he said sadly. 'It all still swings on the idea that John tied a stupid knot. And they didn't hear any evidence from any of his climbing friends. Not a squeak from an NC anywhere in it.'

'What's an NC?'

'A night climber.'

'I thought a night climber would not attempt with a rope anything he would not attempt without one.'

Martin fixed her with a steady considering stare. 'You've been doing some homework,' he said.

'I've been trying to understand you. I know you think John Talentire couldn't have tied the wrong knot; but you would be surprised, Martin, you really would, how often people do things they couldn't have done. They couldn't have mistaken the dose for their medication, doubled it or forgotten it. They just *wouldn't* have. Not according to their best friends. People just aren't reliable. The fact is you can't be certain of what you are so certain of. You need to back off, and calm down. Before I find myself visiting you in a mental ward.'

Martin greeted this in silence. Then: 'I'll show you if you like,' he said. 'I'll need some things.'

'What sort of things?'

Martin looked round the room. His eye lighted on a little nest of tables.

'Those, for a start,' he said. 'And then a weight and some string.' Carefully he put two of the tables on the floor in the middle of the room, on their sides, so that they made a pair of vertical surfaces, facing each other. 'This is Patten Alley,' he said indicating the space between them.

Just at that moment Fran and Josh came in. Fran put her head round the living room door, with the words, 'Coffee, Imo?' on her lips. 'What's going on?' she said as she saw them kneeling beside the upset tables. 'Is this a private fight, or can anyone join in?'

'Oh, join by all means,' said Martin. Imogen got up and quietly closed the transcript he had left open on her dining table, and put it in her bureau, out of sight. The newcomers' attention was on Martin, anyway. 'I need some string and a weight,' he said.

But when Imogen produced a roll of string he rejected it. It was the stiff, strong, hairy kind that she used to tie up parcels.

'Have you got anything softer?' he asked. 'And we need to find the right kind of weight.'

'It would be easier to help if we knew what you were trying to do, Martin,' said Fran.

He sat back on his heels and looked up at her. 'I'm trying to demonstrate what would actually happen to someone on the end of a rope if a knot slipped,' he said.

'Oh, right,' said Fran. 'What about Mr Noah? Would he do?' She ran up the stairs, and returned a minute later holding the little wooden figure from her ark.

'Perfect,' said Martin.

'Something to resemble rope on that scale?' said Josh. 'Knitting wool, Imo?'

A rummage in Imogen's workbox produced something better: an off-cut of the sort of twisted cotton cord used for piping. Imogen liked to finish her patchwork cushions nicely.

'Right,' said Martin. He tied one end of the cord round Mr Noah's waist.

'You'll need this, next,' said Imogen. She produced the mug tree from her kitchen, denuded of mugs.

'What's that for?' asked Josh.

'A pretend post to tie a rope to,' said Imogen.

'Look,' said Martin. He had placed the mug tree on a pile of books, seized randomly from Imogen's shelves, and wound the free end of Mr Noah's rope lightly round the upright rod. 'This is what is supposed to have happened. This table is the wall of the college building, the other the New Library. OK? The rope is tied to a post in the college tower room.'

Suddenly they were all intent on the game. The little figure in Martin's hand, on the end of its rope, was carried across the gap between the tables, and left standing on the rim of the further one. The cord bridged the gap.

'He jumped, and he landed,' Martin said. 'Then he is supposed to have toppled over for no special reason . . .' He flicked the little figure with his finger. It fell, swung against the other table, with an audible tap, at first tightening the lightly tied cord and then pulling it loose, and landing at the foot of the drop right against the pretend college wall.

'That is what would happen if things went as they are supposed to have done,' he said. 'However badly you tied a rope, it would have to be tugged a *bit* to come loose. While your weight was undoing it you would dangle on the end of it. You would swing back against the wall you have jumped from. See . . .' He mimed the jump and the fall again.

'Now look at this,' he said. Nothing in his performance as Hamlet had held the audience as he held them now. He returned the figure to balance above the gap between the tables. He untied the knot in the safety rope completely, and then gave it a very gentle tug. The figure toppled at once, but this time did not swing against the opposite wall, but fell in the middle of the space. It lay face upward, its folksy painted face staring up at them benignly.

'John was found lying in the middle of Patten Alley,' Martin said quietly. 'Not at the foot of the wall. Isn't that so, Imogen?'

'But Imogen would have been looking to see how the man was, how badly injured, not looking exactly how he was placed,' protested Fran.

Imogen considered. 'No; Martin is right. He was lying in the middle of the lane,' said Imogen. She remembered perfectly the blood pooling behind Talentire's head. His head was lying in the central gulley that drained the alley, still paved as it had been in the Middle Ages, with the gutter in the middle, not at the edges. She hadn't appreciated that it could matter – but she was quite sure of it.

In the next half-hour it became apparent, as the demonstration was repeated again and again by each and every one of them, that Martin was right. However badly Talentire was supposed to have tied his knot, any resistance at all on the rope would have swung him back against the college wall. He should have landed at the foot of the wall. Only if the rope was completely loose when he fell could any of them get Mr Noah to land in the central gutter of the alley, well away from either wall.

At last Josh said, 'Well, he just didn't tie the rope at all. That's the only explanation.'

But Imogen jibbed at that. 'He went back to his locker for the rope. That's the other side of the college, and it took him some minutes, even at a run. Why go back for a rope if you're not going to use it?'

'For effect?'

'It would have the opposite effect, though,' said Fran. 'The gawping crowd would have been more impressed if he did it without a rope.'

The sun, which had been shining through the window all morning, had sneaked away, and the room felt cold. Imogen felt chilled to the bone. Martin was right, he had to be right.

John Talentire had been done to death by a third party. It *had* been murder.

13

Who hath murdred him? Speake, I'le not
Be juggled with, for he is murdred

Martin departed to attend a lecture by twelve, and Fran put Noah back in the ark, and Imogen righted her coffee tables and replaced the mugs on the mug tree. Then she wandered out into her little back garden, deep in thought. So Martin was right about murder; did that mean he was also right about motives and the perpetrator? Somehow it didn't seem so to Imogen; the thing was off-key. The *tonality* of venomous discussion in the English faculty and actual cold-blooded killing seemed too disjointed to Imogen. Well, though, it couldn't have been cold-blooded, it must have been opportunist and impulsive, because nobody could have foreseen the turn the talk in the Pickerel would take, or actually formulated a plan that depended on bets being laid, and Talentire being willing to take them on. The whole thing depended on Talentire having a deadly enemy who was at hand.

So had Martin made out a case that that enemy was Venton-Gimps? Certainly, because his room was just below the tower room, if he had been there, he could have heard, or even through an open door have seen Talentire galloping up the stairs with a coil of rope. It was just barely possible to imagine him galvanised into action, and leaping up the stairs behind

Talentire . . . He seemed to have a pretty good alibi; but then if he could perform murder he could perhaps contrive alibis. Perhaps that helpful neighbour was a little bit muddly? Imogen found herself mildly embarrassed by her own train of thought. It really does seem impertinent to consider whether someone one knows is a murderer. Just as she found the church language at funerals, confidently asking for the deceased to be let off their sins. One knows perfectly well that nobody is perfect, and perfectly well that real people do kill; but somehow it seems quite uncivilised to talk of it. Imogen's sixth sense was very finely honed, however, and she knew the fellows of her college rather well. Instinctively, reading V-G's evidence to the coroner's court she knew he had been ill at ease. Something about that alibi had been troublesome at the time. But surely he couldn't have faked it?

Samantha, whom Imogen consulted the next morning about Susan, was very uneasy about it. 'She just said, "I'm off," Miss Quy. She didn't say where, and she didn't say why.'

'Did she take her things?'

'She didn't have a lot of things. She took a rucksack. Her Ipod. That was the only thing of value I ever saw her with. I had to lug the books she had out of the college library back myself.'

'And no hint at all where she went?'

'Didn't she go home to her foster-mother? She used to speak kindly about her. Now I come to think about it she was very restless the night before she left; tossing and turning about, and getting up for a glass of water. I was a bit cross, because it woke me a couple of times.'

'Didn't you ask her what it was about?'

'Well, I did, but she didn't tell me.'

'Did you think she was fed up with Cambridge?'

'It was a bit sudden if it was that,' the girl said.

Imogen was made uneasy by this conversation, as she tended to be when a discrepancy opened up between her own impression of somebody and the effect they were having on others. She had been unhappy about that word 'prat' applied to Martin Mottle, for example, and she had been right. And now there was a similar gap between her recollection of Susan getting help, cleaning up after Samantha, and expressing scorn for the immaturity of other undergraduates, and the idea of her simply copping out and leaving Cambridge without a word.

When Susan Inchman had been missing without explanation for a working week, the college instituted what Malcolm Gracie called a 'DSMS': a discreet search for a missing student. Long experience of the vagaries of students had made the college careful about this, and wary of too heavy-handed a reaction. Nearly always the student had just decided to run away, drop out, go abroad. They were fully entitled to do so, and under no enforceable duty to tell anyone. Often their parents didn't know what was going on, but students were, after all, legal adults. A student had been known to be enraged at being reported to the home base, and full of dignity and talk of rights of privacy. The only sanction available to the college was to expel runaways, but this statement did not cover the true situation. However discreetly, senior members did care about the young people they taught, and felt human anxiety about them when it seemed called for. And of course a disappeared person was a source of anxiety, a vanished student would certainly have been reported to the police soon enough if they vanished when living at home.

A DSMS usually involved a confabulation between a tutor, the bursar, Imogen, and any known close friends of the missing. Very often indeed it also involved the Master's wife, who functioned as a sort of godmother-in-general to the college in general. The confabulation about Susan led to a decision to contact her next of kin in the college records, her adoptive mother, and to Lady Buckmote's firmly expressed opinion that it would be better done face to face than by an unexpected phone call. Naturally this led to her being co-opted to drive across the country to Swindon to carry out the interview, and as she usually did she in turn co-opted Imogen to share the driving. That would be tomorrow; in the meantime Imogen mused on what little she knew about Susan. Susan had been capable and sensible over the affair with Samantha. Yet Samantha had been worried about her. Something Samantha had said, when talking to Imogen that first time, hovered just outside recollection . . . that was it! Samantha hadn't known Susan long, because she had been moved from an earlier room-share with someone who couldn't stand her. Now who was that? Imogen looked up the file.

Alison Worley. Alison had rejected Susan. When her office hours closed Imogen went in search of Alison, and found her in her room, working.

'*She* was all right,' said Alison readily enough when Imogen asked about Susan. 'It was that terrible friend of hers that got up my nose. Literally, Miss Quy. He stank.'

'A smelly friend? Called?'

'Dave.'

'And did you have to see much of him?'

'He was here a lot. She was always wanting him to kip on the floor here overnight. Really bullying me. "He isn't in a condition to go . . . hasn't got anywhere to sleep . . . don't like him sleeping rough . . ." that line. And I really didn't like sleeping with him in the room. I didn't feel safe.'

'So what condition was he in when this happened?'

'Drunk sometimes. And he took . . . stuff. I couldn't imagine why she put up with him, to be honest. He was always hanging around, whingeing and sponging off her. And leaving his needles on the floor where I might have stepped on them. And he was really unwashed. She would take all his clothes off him and take them down to the laundry to put them through the washing machines, and leave him under her duvet till she got his things dry again. But he wouldn't stay put; he'd get up and walk around, and I would come back and find him starkers. A horrible sight, Miss Quy. Bruises and needle holes all over him. He would just stand there and leer at me.'

'Lord!' said Imogen, genuinely appalled. 'Did you tell anyone in college about all this?'

'Didn't want to get anyone into more trouble,' said Alison, 'who was plainly in a lot of trouble already. I just asked to be moved, and in their wisdom they moved her. What's up?'

'I don't know. She has left college without explanation. We would like to know why.'

'I don't *think* she would have run off with Dave,' said Alison. 'She seemed sort of angry with him a lot of the time; at the end of her tether, kind of. As who wouldn't be? Now you come to mention it, I haven't seen him hanging about here recently. I think she might have given him the push.'

'As who wouldn't have?' asked Imogen.

'You said it,' said Alison.

'Thanks,' said Imogen, leaving Alison to her work.

It's a somewhat dreary drive between Cambridge and Oxford, involving the transit of thirteen roundabouts in Milton Keynes. The ring roads round Oxford rival the M25 in nastiness, and it's only on the stretch between Oxford and Swindon that the road becomes tolerable and tolerably interesting. But by then the two friends were muted; the task ahead of them, bringing alarming news to an unprepared and unknown person, loomed over them.

'At this stage I rather wonder . . .' said Lady Buckmote, as they drove past the turn-off for Faringdon.

'If it was me, I'd rather be told face to face,' replied Imogen.

Mary Ollery saw them as trouble the moment they opened her garden gate and found her clipping a hedge. Her house was one of those pleasant, spacious council houses built in the thirties with a slightly garden-city design. It had a gable end facing the street with one slope longer than the other; metal window frames painted white, and a shallow porch round the front door. The generous front garden was rather scruffy, but had space for dogs and toddlers to move around. A broken bicycle lay on its side on the path. Those were the days, Imogen thought, as Lady B. lifted the latch and walked into the garden, when houses were provided to decent working families, deliberately pleasant and sufficient. Replacing slum dwellings with new and nastier slums had not yet been envisaged.

Mrs Ollery looked up in alarm as they entered her garden. She was a plump, grey-haired woman, flushed with the effort she was making to clip her hedge with weighty, ancient-looking shears. 'Now what?' she said. 'He's been indoors all week with a broken leg, so you're probably barking up the wrong tree.'

'Who has?' asked Lady Buckmote. Her obvious bafflement produced a change in their welcome.

'You're not after Denny? You're not social workers?'

'Not as such,' said Imogen.

'And it's Susan we've come about,' added Lady B.

Mary Ollery carefully put down her shears, and turned on them an expression of bleak dread.

'Something's happened to Susan?' she asked.

'We don't know. That's what we've come to find out,' said Lady Buckmote.

'She's at college in Cambridge,' said Mary Ollery.

'Not for the last few days,' said Imogen. 'We were hoping you might know where she might be.'

'You'd better come in.' Mrs Ollery led the way indoors. Imogen picked up the garden shears, and carried them indoors with her.

Inside it was a shabby, comfortably untidy house. The door opened directly into a front room where the lad named Denny was sitting on a nearly collapsed sofa, with his leg in plaster propped up straight in front of him, watching ice-hockey on the box.

'Come through,' said Mary Ollery. The back room was quiet. There was a dining table in it, and a number of loaded sagging bookshelves. The mantelpiece was crowded with photographs of children and young people, in sporting uniform, in academic dress, in ballet gear. 'My family,' she said. 'Sit down and tell me who you are.'

Her visitors obeyed. She drew back a chair opposite them, and sat down, but then at once jumped up again. 'I'll put the kettle on,' she said. She walked through to the kitchen that opened out from the room they were sitting in. 'Denny's eaten all the biscuits,' she observed.

She fussed around for some time, bringing tea in tough-looking mugs, and finding a pair of broken Garibaldi biscuits on a saucer. Putting off the bad news as long as possible, thought Imogen.

When at last Mary Ollery sat down she said, 'Not in college, you say? Susan is the last of my children I would expect to give trouble.'

'She hasn't been giving trouble,' said Imogen gently. 'But she might be in trouble.'

'Same thing,' observed Mrs Ollery crisply.

'Perhaps it is,' said Imogen.

'You could tell us it isn't any business of ours,' said Lady B. 'Your Susan is an adult. She can leave the college if she wants to. But we would rather like to know why she left us – if there is something we could put right; something that would help her complete her studies.'

'I don't know where she is,' said Mrs Ollery. There were tears in her eyes. She rubbed them away and faced her visitors. 'You know, it's the hardest thing you could imagine to survive a bad start in life. Most of my children don't really manage it. They're always wobbly.'

'You speak of children you have fostered?' asked Lady B.

'Yes.'

'Many children?'

'More than a dozen by now. Denny is the latest. Stepfather beat up the poor little sod.'

'But Susan wasn't fostered – you adopted her?' asked Imogen.

'Yes, I did. But I fostered her first. Then I cottoned on to how bright she is, and I coached her a bit, and when she got to sixteen and social services washed their hands of her, I adopted her, and got her into the sixth-form college.'

'She didn't take your name, though?'

'She didn't have to! She thought it would seem like dumping

her blood-mother. She was very attached to her, in spite of . . .'
The sentence tailed away.

'In spite of?' Imogen prompted.

'Having been taken from her. Having been put into care.'

'Where is that real mother now? Do you know? Might
Susan be with her?'

Mrs Ollery shook her head. 'She killed herself. I've often
wondered if she had known that Susan got to Cambridge . . . if
she had known maybe she wouldn't have thought things so
black . . . But there you are. She never knew.'

'Her death must have upset Susan a good deal. Was it
recent?' asked Imogen.

'No. Five years ago. I thought Susan had put it all behind
her, and was set fair for a fine degree and a good job. And now
this.'

'Well, we don't know what "this" is yet,' said Lady B.

'What about her father?' asked Imogen. 'Might she be with
him?'

'Oh, no. He is long dead. He died of one of those sudden
awful things – meningitis, was it? That was when Susan was
only three. She can't remember him.'

'Poor child,' said Lady B.

'I can't go chasing after her,' said Mrs Ollery, 'I've got
Denny to look after. She would know that. But she does know
she was the one I really loved. And she hasn't come home, or
even rung up, and that isn't kind of her! It's really too bad!'
She was fighting back tears again.

Imogen said, 'Perhaps she doesn't expect you to know she
had gone missing. Not just yet. So perhaps she expects to turn
up again before anyone tells you about it. That could be why
she hasn't been in touch.'

Mrs Ollery looked doubtful. 'Well, perhaps,' she said. 'She

doesn't write much in the term, being so busy. She maybe didn't think I would get worried just yet. I am now, though.'

'We could do a certain amount of chasing after,' said Lady B. 'In an unofficial kind of way. If we knew where to start. And we could report her as a missing person. The police would help, I think, wouldn't they?'

Imogen shook her head. She knew, as it happened, how many Cambridge people were on the missing persons' register with the Salvation Army and other charities and how difficult it was to find someone who didn't want to be found. 'If it wasn't for looking after Denny,' she said, 'and you were free to look, where would you look for her?'

'I'd look in Cambridge, or in Richmond,' said Mrs Ollery.

'Why Richmond?' asked Lady B.

'It's where her mother used to live. But I don't know. Something must have happened to make her run off, and I don't know what it is.'

'You don't know the name of her boyfriend, do you?' asked Imogen. 'It might be a help if we could find him.'

Mrs Ollery shook her head. 'I didn't know she had one,' she said. 'Though of course, it's natural that she would. Just she didn't say.'

'Did she come home last vacation?' asked Imogen.

'Yes, she did for a bit. But it wasn't easy for her to study with Denny around. He played up; didn't like sharing the lime-light.'

'So where did she go?'

'Bournemouth. She got a live-in job waitressing at a hotel. So she said. It was only for three weeks. She said she could study in her time off.'

'And then?'

'She came home to pick up her things, and take me out to

the cinema; then she went back to Cambridge, and then you know as much as I do.'

'If that was just the beginning of this term, it wasn't long ago, was it? Did she seem all right?'

'She was just fine. Much better than last year. She was a bit shaky and upset last year; something had put her off her stride. She didn't want to talk about it, and it passed. Last time I saw her everything was fine. Apart from Denny getting at her, that is. Mostly she's very kind to the new children I'm looking after. She knows what they've been through. But she was trying to work, you see.'

'We'll make some enquiries,' said Lady B., getting up. 'Could you promise to let us know if she phones or writes?'

'You won't have shopped her to the police, will you?' said Mary Ollery. 'Only I couldn't have anything to do with your enquiries if you're going to do that. She's very sensitive about that. They all are.'

'We have even less chance of finding her if we don't report her missing,' said Imogen.

'Just the same, I'd rather you didn't,' said Mrs Ollery.

'OK, then,' said Lady B. 'We'll leave it like this. We will try to find out anything we can without reporting her. We'll give it another week. If she gets in touch with you during that week, you'll let us know. If nothing has happened in a week, we'll report her missing. We would have to some time, you know,' she added gently.

Mrs Ollery thought about it. 'All right then,' she said. 'That seems about the best we can do, really.'

'You wouldn't have an address for her in Richmond?' Imogen asked.

'That was years ago,' said Mrs Ollery. 'Before she was taken into care. But I think the address is in the adoption file. I'll look it out for you.'

'One last thing, Mrs Ollery,' said Imogen, as they were leaving, in possession of the address. 'Did Susan have trouble with her temper? Was she easily made angry?'

'She was a termagant when I first had her,' said Mrs Ollery. 'But she calmed down quite a bit as she got older. Who told you about that?'

'A fellow student. Was this a real problem, do you think, or just something that she could deal with?'

'It was a problem to her, yes. It's like I say, Miss Quy, kids in care are damaged goods. They all bear the marks of it. But it's not so much what they do as what has been done to them. That's my view, anyway.'

14

The time is out of ioynt; Oh cursed spite
That ever I was born to put it right

Back home in Cambridge, Imogen sat and mused on what could be done towards finding Susan. It seemed much more urgent since talking to Mrs Ollery. Somehow Imogen began to wonder if Susan was in danger of some kind. Perhaps the dodgy boyfriend kept even dodgier company.

The best lead was surely that boyfriend, the malodorous Dave, and since he had been hanging around Susan here in Cambridge, it seemed possible that here in Cambridge was where he might be found. And from the description he was a drug-addict. Imogen knew her limitations looking for someone like that.

There are places in Cambridge that people who have lived there all their lives know nothing about. There are damp little clumps of foliage, scrappy woodland along the river behind streets in Newnham, half-shelters under bridges, back yards with a little cover, bin stores where a bin might be emptied, laid on its side and crawled into, vacant garages with dodgy locks, changing lockers at the swimming pool standing unused for half the year; there are garden sheds at the far end of the gardens from the houses, there are car parks where one can break into a car to sleep, even a few organised shelters. And all this goes on pretty well out of sight. It isn't college Cambridge where these holes in the structure are found – college Cambridge is well patrolled by college porters; this is town territory. Cambridge is cold in winter, and sleeping rough there is harsh and dangerous; in summer it's survivable. Each fair on Midsummer Common leaves a group or two of sturdy disreputable men and women, with mongrel dogs, sitting round illegal fires on the grass, putting up shell tents, begging from passersby on the paths, being reported again and again, and eventually moving on.

Imogen was not particularly well up on scenes such as these. But she knew who to ask. So the morning after her return from the visit to Mrs Ollery she set out in search of Mick. Mick and his friends used to be found very early in the morning lolling on a park bench on Lammas Land, ankle-deep in litter and empty bottles: a mess not down to the city council, but entirely of their own making. When his friends shambled off, Mick would fish in his plastic shopping bag, and bring out a copy of the Greek Testament, kept precariously clean in a wrap of newspaper, and begin to read. Imogen thought he might be around at this time of year; every year in the autumn he committed a series of trivial offences and got sent to prison for the coldest weather. But he should be out now. Imogen did not go in search of him empty-handed; she racked her memory for his earlier requests and loaded her shopping bag with unhealthy eating: good cheese, chocolate brazils, peanut butter and a bottle of Baileys. Cholesterol didn't seem the most urgent thing to worry about with Mick.

It took her several hours to find him; eventually she ran him to earth in the Lammas Land, sitting on the edge of the paddling pool, still empty because out of season. He had taken off his shoes and socks, and was dangling his bare feet in the dry. He appeared to be talking to a responsive blackbird on a nearby branch. As Imogen sat down beside him, he said, 'I don't know what he thinks he's got to sing about!'

'Life not treating you well?' asked Imogen.

'Sure, the top of the morning to ye!' said Mick in stage Irish. 'And what would a beautiful young whore like you want with the likes of me this sunny morning?'

'I have come to ask a favour, Mick,' said Imogen, coming clean at once. Obviously Mick was not in the best of moods.

Imogen began to unpack the shopping bag. 'I thought I remembered you liked these,' she said, showing him the chocolate brazils.

'Bribery, is it?' he said.

'Fair exchange,' she said.

'What is it, then?' he said. 'No picking locks this time, mind.'

'Nothing of the kind. I need a bit of help finding someone.'

'It's the poll-eess you need for that,' he said.

'Could you ask around for me?'

'Who is it you're after?' he said.

'I don't have much to go on, I'm afraid. A lost young man on drugs. Called Dave. Has or had a girlfriend in the college.'

'Better ask her, then,' said Mick, gazing askance at Imogen. He had a surprisingly alert expression when one caught him eye to eye.

'She's gone missing. It's her I'm after, really, but of course it might help if we found him.'

'You're not thinking of reporting them to the police? This isn't a chargeable matter?'

Mick had lost the Irish voice now, and was speaking in what might have been his natural voice, years ago when he was respectable. A student or professor of Greek, presumably. Or a spoiled priest. Imogen had never asked.

'No, just a college matter. Looking after students, whether they like it or not. It's mostly not. But we would like to know why the girl has gone missing; and her boyfriend seems the best lead. You wouldn't be sneaking or shopping anyone.'

'Dave, you say? And on drugs?'

'I understand he injected something. Lots of needle holes.'

'Trash,' said Mick unexpectedly. 'Trash do that. Then they'll do anything, right down to beating up their own kind. If I put you on the right track, nobody gets to know who fingered him, right?'

'Of course not,' said Imogen. 'And whether you can help or not, drop round for a hot meal some time?'

'Maybe when I'm feeling better,' said Mick.

Since that seemed to be all she could do at the present, Imogen left him with the goodies, and trotted home.

Home seemed unusually unsatisfying. Neither Fran nor Josh were around to share a coffee and a chat; there was rather too much housework to do to seem tempting – Imogen hated to start a task without sufficient time to finish it. Instead she took her notebook, her famous case-notes, to the breakfast room table, where she sat to write down diligently everything she knew about Susan Inchman. It hardly filled half a page. Another visit to Mary Ollery? But the week they had promised was still on its first day. Had Mary Ollery said anything that Imogen could follow up? Yes; she had given them the old address in Richmond. Imogen did not know Richmond, but she thought it was not far from Kew. A trip to Kew seemed suddenly a very good idea; her friend Shirl had asked her several times to go with her, and Imogen had not found the time. She went to her telephone, and rang Shirley.

Both friends were good at gardening, and Imogen could not imagine why she had left it so late in life to see Kew.

Admittedly it wasn't lilac time, but the Pagoda tree was more interesting than any amount of lilac would have been. And Imogen was staggered by the beauty of the great palm house, rising like a schematic cloud above its reflecting pool, and wonderfully jungly inside. The two friends basked in the moist warmth of the interior, climbed the spiral steps to all the galleries, read all the labels, and then wandered away down a wide avenue towards the river and a long prospect of Syon House. Completely delicious. They ate a picnic lunch under a huge holm-oak, and then wandered arm in arm happily back to the car. At this point Imogen broke the news to Shirl that she would like to dash down the road to look for a house in Richmond.

'Parking is hell, there,' said Shirl, but they found a space, fortunately, in the car park on Paradise Road. A bit of asking the way from shoppers in the main street, and they walked through an alleyway lined with expensive shops, and found themselves on Richmond Green.

'You could do a quick tour of architecture here, without moving from the spot,' remarked Shirl. 'Look, a fifteenth- or sixteenth-century palace frontage; lots of early Georgian terraces, a row of Victorian villas, an Edwardian theatre, and those not very impressive 1960s town houses. The lot. Now what are we looking for?'

It turned out that what they were looking for was one of the nicest houses on the Green – a lovely section of Georgian terrace. And Imogen was considerably taken aback. However long ago it was that Susan's family had lived here, it must always have been millionaires' row. A staggering combination of wealth and good taste and convenience. Not a flaw to it except for the aircraft overhead. Shirl started to ask what was the point of the quest, and her voice was blocked out entirely by the roar of a 707 descending to Heathrow.

'It's all right,' said Imogen flippantly as the sound receded, 'it's one of ours.'

'You're not old enough,' said Shirl firmly.

Imogen did not reply. She was staring at the house, musing on the social fall represented by starting from here, and landing up in care adopted by Mrs Ollery. Not that Mrs Ollery didn't have a heart of gold, but still . . .

A woman emerged from the door they were looking at, and came down the steps towards them. 'Can I help you?' she asked crisply. The question had the unmistakable tone of one repelling boarders.

'I had a friend who lived here once,' said Imogen, lying cheerfully.

She found herself being looked over shrewdly by the house-holder, and she returned the attention. A woman of fifty, or so. Very well dressed in a country fashion. Obviously suspicious.

'And who would that have been?' she asked.

'Mrs Inchman,' Imogen tried.

'You knew Valerie Inchman? That's a while back. And such a tragedy. A disaster, really, though it took a few thousand off the price of the house for us. It was still notorious when we bought it.'

'A tragedy?' asked Shirl, bewildered. Imogen had not briefed her.

'Most of the neighbours wouldn't believe she'd done it, at first,' the woman went on. 'That was before she was convicted. But then of course, she hadn't a friend in the world. The knives were really out, then. But if you're a friend of hers you know all this. Loyal of you.'

Imogen blushed. Subterfuge felt very shabby, faced with

this. 'No, I'm afraid I don't,' said Imogen. 'I've been out of the country. I was hoping to get back in touch.'

'You're too late, I'm afraid. She's dead now, I've been told. It's the children I was sorry for,' the woman continued. 'Poor little mites. But what can one do? Now if you'll excuse me – you don't look as if you were up to no good, and I've got a meeting in twenty minutes . . .' She retreated up her grand steps, framed by their elegant railings, and closed the beautifully proportioned door behind her.

'Imogen,' said Shirl firmly, 'you've got a lot of explaining to do.'

The explanation took them most of the way round the North Circular Road to Brent Cross. And it was full of holes, of course. What Imogen didn't know greatly outweighed what she did. Research would be called for. Shirl, who had once lived in Twickenham, suggested the *Ric and Twic*, otherwise known as the *Richmond and Twickenham Times*.

But the Cambridge University Library did not keep a run of the *Ric and Twic*; and Imogen did not have time for at least a couple of weeks to get to the newspaper library at Colindale, or even back to Richmond, where a phone call had told her a run of back numbers on microfiche could be found in the Central Library, and so the whole matter was on hold.

When the week's truce agreed with Mrs Ollery was up, Imogen did just briefly consult her friend Mike Parsons, now an inspector, on the subject of missing persons, but she was quickly made aware of the facts of life in that quarter: missing students needed to be missing for some time before an enquiry was mounted by the police, unless there was some definite sign of foul play; otherwise there would be no police time for anything else, so unreliable and irresponsible were the young of today.

'I realise you're not liking the smell of this, Imo,' Mike told her over a coffee at Starbucks. 'But we would need something to go on. The police take an interest only if there are fears for the missing person's safety. Alarmed friends or family with whom she usually kept regularly in touch would be listened to. If there's nobody with whom they kept regularly in touch . . .' He shrugged eloquently. He carried on for some time about how Cambridge University life was not everyone's cup of tea, and he couldn't blame them if they absented themselves for visits to the real world, or even if they never came back. But he promised to log Susan Inchman on the local list of missing persons, and let Imogen know if anything turned up.

Walking back from Starbucks something occurred to Imogen that she could do. On getting home she rang Mrs Ollery, to find out if Susan had been in touch yet. She had not. Mrs Ollery sounded deeply depressed. 'It's only Denny that's keeping me afloat,' she told Imogen. 'Little perisher gets into a scrape every day. I've got to keep on top of things. And I'm beginning to worry about Susan, really worry. Something's got to be badly wrong if she hasn't been in touch all this time. It isn't like her.'

'Might it be time to ask for help from one of the missing persons' agencies?' Imogen asked.

'No, I wouldn't do that. She'd never forgive me. I've just got to wait for her to get in touch.'

Imogen expressed sympathy.

She waited for a quiet moment in an empty house to take up her case-notes again, and simply *think*. Her training had made her good at systematic note-taking, and she found the activity an aid to clear thinking about many matters, most of them non-medical. Or perhaps most matters were medical in a way, if they yielded insights to close observation, to a diagnostic curiosity. Imogen turned the Susan page in her book and began to write down everything she knew about the death of John Talentire. That was a long task, and took her most of the evening. But it did enable her to identify little snags in the story where something struck her as a bit odd. There was Venton-Gimps's alibi, over which he had made such a song-and-dance at that college meeting; it was rock-solid, surely, and yet he seemed to need to make a point of it. Was there anything odd about that? Imogen was not quite sure.

What she was sure about was that there was something odd about someone else, that someone being Duncan Talentire–Talentire senior. According to Martin Mottle he had been approached for help getting a transcript of the inquest, and had declined to help. Imogen sat at her fireside, thinking about that. Talentire junior had been a friend of Martin's since boyhood. They had survived a night out on the fells together, and then they had climbed together in many parts of the world. Didn't a father usually know his son's best friend? At least somewhat? Why wasn't Talentire senior touched and concerned at Martin's grief for a loss they both shared? Why wouldn't he help? Well, perhaps he found the whole subject unbearable. Just wanted to put it behind him. But he must have felt this very strongly if he had actually asked the coroner to withhold the transcript from Martin, as Martin thought he had. It occurred to Imogen that what she and the Master had done had defeated this express wish.

But the Master had acted out of concern to put the poor young man's mind at rest. A kindly intention. It hadn't worked, of course, just made things even harder for Martin to accept; but one was to understand that no such kindly impulse towards his son's friend had weighed with Duncan Talentire. Was this odd? But human nature was so quirky, so unpredictable, so murky when in the deep water of loss and grief, that nothing could be deduced about it by a stranger. Imogen abandoned that train of thought. Something was snagging in her mind about that conversation in Richmond, something that had surprised her slightly at the time. But she could not recall what it was. She hadn't liked the snooty woman, nor had she believed her when she had said it was the children she was sorry for.

Just then the key turned in the front door, and admitted Josh and Fran, both freezing cold, having walked from the Green Man in Grantchester, leaving Josh's car in the car park, because they had met up with a crowd of the Kyd Society, and had had rather too many drinks for safety. They were just what Imogen needed to take her mind off its worry-groove. She offered hot chocolate, with a tot of rum to warm them up, and soon they were settled comfortably in the sagging arm-chairs in the living room, with the gas-fire turned up full on.

Nothing much missed Fran's sharp eyes, and she saw that Imogen's notebook was on the coffee table. 'More detection?' she asked. 'Have we got anywhere towards pinning it all on the dreadful Mr Venton-Gimps?'

'No. Don't believe it had anything to do with him.'

'Shucks. You mean the Kyd Society went through all that palaver for nothing?'

'Nothing except for a hundred thousand pounds,' said Imogen drily.

'Point,' conceded Fran. 'Do we know what Martin Mottle is currently thinking?'

'I don't,' said Imogen.

'Well, let's hope it doesn't involve any more tricksy stuff for us,' said Fran. 'Simon is thinking of trying to get a quick production in early next year, to try to repair the Kyd Society's reputation.'

'But what repair is needed?' asked Imogen. 'Didn't you get a lovely write-up in *The Times?*'

'It wasn't bad,' said Fran. 'But it wasn't a review of Simon. Mostly about Gadgby, as I remember. And by the way, what has happened to him?'

With a sinking heart Imogen realised that she didn't know, and hadn't wondered, and ought to find out. Another request for help from Mike?

15

Doe you not come your tardy sonne to chide
That I thus long have let revenge slippe by?

Imogen did not usually encounter Professor Appleby; indeed she had not talked to him since talking over one of his students who had inhaled an allegedly secret substance and needed sending into A & E. So she was mildly surprised when he dropped in on her during office hours one morning shortly after her trip to Richmond.

'I wonder if you have noticed that Duncan Talentire is dining in college as the Master's guest tomorrow night,' he said. 'Softening us up, obviously.'

'To give him the Postgate?'

'Yes. And I got the impression you were very interested in all this.'

'Yes, I am. Perhaps I will put my name down to dine in. But then again, perhaps I won't. I have after all seen Talentire around from time to time.'

'What I thought you might like to do,' he said, 'was attend a little *conversazione* I have arranged in my room tomorrow night at six. I have invited the senior law fellow, and both the medical fellows, and a friend of mine who works in paediatrics, and a local solicitor who deals in family law cases. I'm sorry it's such short notice; we wanted to get our ideas sorted before being confronted by Talentire.'

'I can come; I will gladly come. Thank you for thinking of me.'

'Drinks at six then,' he said, departing.

Dr Appleby's rooms were rather splendid. His sitting room had a low plastered ceiling crossed by a massive beam carved with oak and vine leaves. There was a vast fireplace with an elaborate Elizabethan surround and overmantel, and a log fire burning cheerfully between wrought fire-irons. The sofas and chairs were upholstered in dark red, and an ancient oak table stood under the window overlooking Fountain Court, laid with glasses and bowls of nuts, and bottles of wine with the corks ready drawn. There were some good paintings on the walls, and the dark bookcases contained a fine collection of books on art and architecture. Imogen arrived first by just a few seconds, and as the others assembled and chose what to drink and where to sit, Imogen weighed them up.

Robert Remmer, the fellow in law, she already knew; and Peter Mons, one of St Agatha's medical fellows she knew slightly. He was a rowing man, seldom ate at High Table, and Imogen had very little contact with him beyond the occasional discussion of crucial injuries like sprained wrists or knees that might hobble an oarsman. The other fellow in medicine, John Lund, she had seen even less of. He was only partly based in the college, and worked a good deal in a London hospital. Appleby introduced Laura Neild, the solicitor, and Barry Collard, the paediatrician, and there followed an awkward silence.

'Thank you all for coming. Where to begin?' said Appleby.

'Well, it's your wicket, Alan,' said Peter Mons.

'Very well. You see, I have been taking an interest in the science that lies behind expert medical evidence in a number of legal trials,' Appleby began. 'At first I was intrigued by cases involving SIDS; cot death so-called. I was involved many years ago in a research project to try to establish whether chemicals present in foam cot mattresses could be responsible for some of these tragedies. I have been following the law reports on cot death cases ever since. Then my attention was drawn to cases involving shaken-baby syndrome.'

'These are two rather different types of occurrence,' said Peter Mons.

'They have much in common,' Appleby answered.

'Nevertheless, for the sake of clarity it would help to look at them one at a time,' Mons said.

'Then let's talk about shaken-baby syndrome,' said Appleby, mildly surprising Imogen. She had naturally thought it was cot death cases that had been troubling him. 'I've been reading up on that more recently,' he added.

'What do you want to know about them?' asked Peter Mons.

'Any conviction for assault or murder in such a case would have to rely on expert medical witness,' said Appleby.

'Or on a witness to the assault, or on the confession of the accused,' said Laura Neild.

'Of course. But take a case in which the parent or carer vigorously denies harming the child, there are no independent witnesses, and a medical witness tells the court *what must have happened*. I would like to try to reach an understanding of what degree of certainty a disinterested person could have available in such a case.'

'Well, these are muddy waters,' said Barry Collard. 'We would be talking about a baby brought into hospital with

subdural hacmatomas, or retinal bleeding. The current orthodoxy—'

'A subdural haematoma is what, exactly?' asked Laura
Neild.

'A closed-head injury: a blood-clot between the brain and
the skull. Very dangerous. The current orthodoxy is that
babies do not suffer such haematomas or retinal bleeding
by accident, unless in a severe accident. So if the account
of the person bringing the baby into hospital was of a fall from
a considerable height – greater than one storey of a house – or
involvement in a car accident, with the car travelling at speed,
then the injury would be treated as an accident. But if the baby
is supposed to have fallen only a short way – off a sofa or out of
a cot, for instance – then the alleged cause of its injuries would
be thought improbable. Non-accidental trauma would be
suspected.'

Laura Neild said, 'Something like this happens, not every
day, but fairly frequently. The consequences are very grave.
The social services are immediately involved, and parents find
themselves facing the loss of the child, or even charges of
assault, and with no right to ask for a second medical opinion.'

'The consequences of returning a baby to the care of an
abusing parent would be even graver,' said Barry Collard.

'So the law and the social services put the safety of the child
above all other considerations. Is that wrong?' asked John
Lund.

'And while a child is in the care of the hospital, or of the
health authority, there is no responsibility to the parents,'
added Laura Neild.

'Once these allegations are made, parents, and the baby
come to that, are at the mercy of the expert witnesses. The
people who know what must have happened,' said Appleby.

'There are controversies, however,' said Barry Collard. 'In reality, forensic medicine is very difficult. It is one thing to diagnose an injury, and say what the consequences for the patient are likely to be; quite another to observe the condition of this baby now, and reasoning backward deduce that the cause must have been non-accidental. The received opinion is that only prolonged shaking of a healthy baby could produce retinal bleeding. So much force is required that only violent accidents or violent assault could account for it. I must say that I think this is probably correct. But how could it be verified?'

'You could take a healthy baby and shake it violently for three or four minutes, and then inspect the damage that has been done,' said Mons drily.

A silence in the room followed this remark.

'You could rely on evidence of the damage sustained by children when there has been a witness to the assault,' said Remmer, speaking for the first time.

'There are very seldom witnesses. People don't batter their children with witnesses present,' said Barry Collard. 'But children in our society spend most of their time with a single adult looking after them. Anything that might happen to them, accidental or not, is likely to happen with only one person present and no independent witness.'

'The intellectual apparatus involved in asserting that violence must have been used against these babies is as follows, if I have understood correctly,' said Appleby. 'Please correct me if I am wrong. It is being assumed that alternative explanations are not available. Injury to the baby's skull during birth, for instance. It is acknowledged that subdural haematomas can occur during delivery. But it is asserted that such an injury always leads to immediate unconsciousness. No lucid interval before the symptoms show up can happen. So a baby who seems awake, and normally reactive on the delivery table has not suffered a haematoma during the birth, and any such must have been caused by a later injury. Further such haematomas never bleed again spontaneously in infants, although it is known that they do so in adults. Where is the evidence for these beliefs? Where are the medical papers I could read?'

Another silence. 'Supposing we carried out the verification process suggested by Mons here,' said Barry Collard. 'It would be definitive only if we could also assume that all babies are the same; that there are no predisposing weaknesses which made one baby more likely to suffer grave consequences from slight injury than another baby.'

'Well, at least we can be certain of that,' said Peter Mons. 'Babies are not all the same, any more than adults are.'

'There could be conditions not yet diagnosed, which pre-disposed a baby to retinal bleeds, for instance, on a very slight trigger?' said Appleby.

'What you are calling the intellectual apparatus doesn't allow for that, the way people are trained at present. Once the question has been raised,' Laura Neild observed, 'any other symptoms are interpreted not as indications of particular vulnerability, but as signs of previous abuse.'

'To know whether they were really that, however, one would have to screen large numbers of healthy and uninjured babies,' said Appleby. 'Am I right?'

'Look, Appleby, this is all very fine and good,' said Barry Collard. 'But it is absolutely right to put the safety of babies ahead of the interests of their parents. Suppose that you think a child has probably been injured by a parent or a carer; obviously you act on that probability. You have to.'

'But that wouldn't do in a court of law,' said Remmer. 'It isn't enough to say that something criminal probably happened. You have to show it beyond all reasonable doubt. From what I hear you all saying, there seems to be a good deal of reasonable doubt. It may be all right to remove a baby to a children's home on the balance of probabilities; it isn't all right to send the parents to prison on that basis. There has to be a proper level of proof.'

Laura Neild said quietly, 'Children are separated from their parents every day on a balance of probabilities. Putting the interests of children first sounds quite right on first hearing. But it puts parents in a very difficult position. I wish it could be remembered that justice is whole cloth; justice for one member of a family cannot be obtained by gross injustice to another member. Families are more interdependent and more fragile than that.'

'There is a very serious difficulty interpreting probability in the courts,' said Peter Mons. 'Juries don't understand it, and very often neither do judges. For example, supposing three children in one thousand have a condition that predisposes them to injury from slight causes: thin skull, or brittle bone syndrome or something. You can have a witness telling the court that the chances of accident causing an injury in this case they are hearing are 997 to 3 against. But that is quite wrong. If the child in the case does have the predisposition, then the chance that it was injured by accident is *much* higher; and if it does not have a predisposing weakness, then the chances that it was injured by accident are unaffected by the presence in the wider population of other babies who do.'

Robert Remmer said, 'I think the real problem here is that medicine and law are very different cultures. They have different ideas of what constitutes certainty. The degree of certainty required in a court of law is not often obtainable in medicine, and waiting for it before taking action would leave patients dying in every ward. But when the man in court says he is absolutely certain of something, the court hears him saying that he is certain in a legal sense – beyond all possible doubt.'

'The man in court may say that he is certain of something when he knows perfectly well that some of his colleagues disagree with him,' remarked Laura Neild. 'And of course if there is a medical controversy in the background, then the fact that this witness takes one view where another might take a different one falls very far short of the degree of certainty required.'

'It's up to counsel for the other side to find and call the other witness,' said Remmer.

'If he knows enough to be aware of the controversy,' remarked Peter Mons. 'You're looking agitated, Appleby. Is this discussion giving you what you wanted? There are many other aspects we could explore.'

'I take it that what this is really about is a certain candidate for the Postgate?' said Remmer. 'A person whose evidence has secured convictions which are being overturned wholesale on appeal.'

'Ah, yes,' said Mons. 'But you should remember that when a verdict is overthrown on appeal, and the conviction is held to be unsafe, that is just what it means and no more. It doesn't mean that the accused didn't do it. It may simply mean that the charge wasn't proven.'

'The conviction is overthrown,' said Laura Neild. 'But many people, including the social services, are deeply suspicious. The child will be on the at-risk register; it may be in care and not be returned to its parents' custody. A place of safety order will hover over the family like the sword of Damocles; the truth is once these charges are made there can be no acquittal. The suffering and distress involved are horrendous.'

'The suffering of helpless tiny children being battered by an adult is also horrendous,' said Barry Collard. 'And it must be deterred.'

'I shouldn't think dozens of convictions for cruelty to children have deterred anyone,' said Laura. 'Most often I think cruelty cases involve people at the end of their tether, incapable of thinking what they are doing, and probably ignorant of how dangerous it is to shake a child. We would all do better to think of support for parents, than to pursue allegations based on iffy science.'

'That's it!' said Appleby. 'That's what I am after: is this science iffy, as Laura puts it?'

'Well, say a baby has retinal bleeding,' said Collard. 'A doctor could perfectly honestly go into court and tell the jury that such a thing could have been caused by violent shaking, and that his colleagues would agree with him on that.'

'But that's exactly the problem: could he tell the court that retinal bleeding can *only* be caused by violent shaking; that it is known that no other situation ever gives rise to it?' said Appleby.

'No; that would be going too far in the present state of knowledge,' said Mons.

'That is what I thought,' said Appleby sadly.

'Well, cheer up then, old chap,' said Mons. 'The feeling of the meeting is that you are right.'

'I didn't want to be right,' said Appleby. 'It would seem that certainty is as hard to find in medical science as it notoriously is in English literature. We must go down to dinner. But many thanks to you all.'

As they went down the stairs, Imogen said quietly to him, 'Doubt grows with knowledge.'

'Yes,' he said. 'Yes. Whose saying is that? Some scientist?'
'Goethe,' she told him.

Imogen was sitting far down the table that night. Duncan
Talentire was on the Master's right, and various members of
the selection committee for the Postgate were at the top of the
table. Lady Buckmote, whom Imogen had expected to be
there, since she was certainly very interested in the Postgate
appointment, was not present. It seemed she had flu and was
keeping to her bed. Imogen gratefully sat out of earshot of all
that, and gossiped with Malcolm Gracie and a couple of
research fellows about this and that, mostly that – i.e. rowing,
and the possible fortunes of the St Agatha's boat in the Lents.
    John Percy, a research fellow in computers, who rowed in
one of the college boats, was complaining about the presence
of canal boats on the river; they were encroaching all along the
stretch of the Cam opposite the boathouses, and especially if
they were double moored, or wide boats, they constricted
space available for eights to pass each other on the water.
Imogen said that some of the boats were handsome, but John
Percy objected to them whatever they looked like. Whatever
the conversation was like at the top of the table, down here it
was all peaceful and friendly. Imogen resolved to go home
when the table got up, instead of going through to the
combination room for dessert and port. From time to time
she glanced up the table, past the austerely beautiful silver
candlesticks, the golden glow that the candle flames cast over
the polished mahogany table, and all the paraphernalia of
college dining, to let her gaze rest thoughtfully on Duncan
Talentire.
    He was energetically discussing something or other. Why,
Imogen wondered again, had he not helped Martin Mottle?

Surely that was odd of him. But her contribution was needed now to a discussion of wrist injuries; they plagued oarsmen who also spent a lot of time at keyboards. John Percy lamented the deep past, when rowers were lazy scholars who put college glory well above the personal glory involved in getting a decent degree. 'Now everyone hopes to be good at everything,' he said. 'It sprains their brains as well as their wrists.'

Malcolm Gracie recalled a time when a certain Oxford college had toughened up its law degree, and people had asked, 'What will the oarsmen read now?'

'How deplorable,' said Robert Remmer, overhearing from a few places up the table. 'Now if they had thought of toughening the English degree . . .'

At this interesting moment the Master stood, and led his guests along the table towards the combination room, and the reshuffled grouping that would partake of dessert. In the throng that moved from the table and into the passageway, the Master stopped beside Imogen, and introduced her to Duncan Talentire.

'Our invaluable college nurse, Duncan. She also happens to be a friend of someone you must know – Martin Mottle.'

A cloud crossed Talentire's face. 'Do you have any influence on that young man?' he asked.

'Not someone much susceptible of being influenced, I think,' said Imogen.

'If you have any sway over him,' Talentire continued, 'do try to dissuade him from this crazed obsession with John's death. Get him to leave it alone, for everyone's sake.'

Very boldly, Imogen said, 'Is there nothing in anything he says?'

They were holding up progress from the hall, and many people were in earshot.

'Miss Quy,' said Talentire, 'I know who murdered my son; I know how and I know why, and nothing but further harm can result from pursuing the matter.'

With that he moved on, following the Master's lean figure in its billowing gown across the court to his glass of fine port, and leaving consternation behind him.

16

Zowndes, do you thinke I am easier to be pla'yd on then a pipe?

Imogen detached herself from the buzzing conversation that broke out as fellows spilled out into the court. 'I thought it was an accident! Found to be!' someone was saying.

'But what about the notorious *Hamlet*?' came the reply.

'I say, could he really mean that he thinks Venton-Gimps is a killer?'

'He can't do! Do get a move on, it's freezing out here.'

Imogen turned as she stepped under the arch of the college gate, and looked back at the little procession moving across the far side of the court from the hall door to the door of the combination room. She remembered the terrible night when a body had floated to the surface of the fountain pool as they made just such a familiar transit. She had an awful sense of something rotten coming to the surface now; not in the fountain but in the deeps of her own mind. In detective stories, of which Imogen was an occasional reader, there was usually a sense of triumph as all the mysterious pieces fell together and the truth emerged. In real life it was a sickening feeling. She had to pull herself together to ride her bike home safely.

How welcome it was, as she wheeled her bike down the path behind the houses, and into the tiny back garden, where a late thrush was singing finely, to see lights on in the kitchen, and realise that Fran or Josh were home! They both were, gossiping as usual mildly together about their respective days like an elderly married pair, and making a lethal bedtime snack of frittata with sausage and potato. Imogen, with a college dinner inside her, declined a wodge of frittata, and accepted a glass of wine; she never drank more than a glass at High Table if she was on her bike. Cyclists in Cambridge needed their wits about them to avoid myopic car drivers, although it was at least equally true that a motorist in Cambridge needed pin-sharp night vision and quick reactions to avoid suicidal cyclists wearing dark garments, carrying no lights, and riding through the red at traffic lights. A second glass of wine now was welcome.

'How's the murder investigation going, Imo?' Fran asked.

'There isn't one, as far as I know. I have been worrying about a missing student. That's not likely to be murder, God willing.'

'So how's St Agatha's? Trolleying along as usual? Is the ineffable V-G in trouble again?'

'Not as far as I know.'

'Well, have you heard that his lectures are packed out to the doors? Everyone wants to hear the local murderer,' said Fran.

'That's probably what he did it for,' said Josh. 'Boring lecturer – desperate for an audience – kills colleague – packs lecture room. Evil triumphs.'

'You know that has got to be a farrago,' said Fran. 'V-G would have neither the guts, nor the speed on his feet, nor the imagination to foresee the good it would do him. I'm sorry, Josh. It would be excellent fun if he really had killed on a point of scholarship; but I don't believe it. Anyway, incredible as it seems, his preposterous views about Shakespeare are in the majority; he really didn't have a casus belli.'

'Being laughed at in public does make people fearfully angry,' said Josh, cutting himself another hunk of bread. 'In fact nothing upsets people as much as a bit of unfairness; like one's own lectures suddenly half empty and the other chap's packed to the doors. And that's how it was with him and Talentire, before the fall.'

'And Martin Mottle seemed so certain of the fact; and V-G seemed so uneasy about his own alibi,' said Imogen, musing.

'Cool it,' said Fran. 'When I asked if he was in trouble again, I only meant was he forgetting his own supervisions, or keeping people waiting for ages at his door.'

'Oh,' said Imogen. 'But actually there's something else on my mind tonight. I'd like to know about someone who served a prison sentence, someone who lived in Richmond. And I can't find the time to get down to the library there to look for the newspaper reports.'

'You mightn't need to,' said Josh. 'What was he called? I'll Google him.'

'He's a she. Don't know the first name. Surname was Inchman.'

'OK. Give us a mo,' said Josh, running up the stairs to his study.

He returned very quickly, descending more slowly, and rejoined them with his hand full of printout. 'Inchman,' he said. 'An Armenian version of the Yeti. A young man called Andy posting stuff about a maths problem. A kind of knife. A woman called Valerie Inchman sent to prison for life in 1990.' He handed Imogen the paper in his hands.

'Does it say what she had done?' Imogen asked.

'Oh, yes. It was murder.'

'Who had she killed?' asked Fran, coming to lean over Imogen's shoulder and read the page in her hands.

'Two of her children,' said Imogen faintly.

'Shook the little beggars to death,' said Josh cheerfully. 'Case of first baby's death reopened when second one died. Degree of force equivalent to a car crash at thirty-five miles an hour at least, or dropping the mites from a two- or three-storey building.'

'She deserves all she got then, doesn't she?' said Fran.

'Who said all that? About the force used, the car crash?' Imogen asked Josh.

'Doesn't say. It's a sort of digest of judges' summing-ups that I found it in. Hang about; here . . .' He pointed to a paragraph well down his tightly spaced printout: ' "The medical evidence we have heard attests to the degree of force required . . ." Do you want me to try to find out who the expert witness was?'

'I think I already know,' said Imogen very quietly.

'What's this?' asked Fran. 'Imogen's famous intuition now amounts to second sight!'

'It isn't intuition,' said Imogen. 'It's a sort of dark understanding.'

Although ridiculous things happen every day, it is a habit of human expectation that they shall not do so. We do not expect to bump into old school friends in crowded streets in Rome, learn an unusual new word and find it three times in *The Times* the following day, or discover a long-lost relative by falling into conversation with a stranger on a train. And Imogen did not expect unconnected murders to form clusters, although Malcolm Gracie, whose subject was economics, kindly explained to her over coffee the next morning how a random distribution could include clusters which stood in no need of explanation, being truly random.

That afternoon Dennis, typically, expatiated on the words of Aristotle, who had apparently stated that one should prefer the probable impossible to the improbable possible. To neither of these friends had Imogen confided the reason for her sudden interest in probability. What in the end did this amount to? A college fellow had been done to death at a time when an undergraduate college member was in residence whose mother had been convicted of murder. A faint connection with two murders at one time was unlikely, certainly. Surely for most of the long years of college history there had been nobody in residence in any way connected with a murder. There was the strange incident a few years back of the poor young man dying in the Wyndham case; but all that was well downstream now. John Talentire's death, on the other hand, had been brought uncomfortably back into the present by Martin Mottle.

And all day, as she went about her duties, that dark understanding lay in her mind like a premonition of disaster. She had, by careful introspection, recalled when she herself had last seen Susan: it was at the first night of *Hamlet*. But why would that have mattered? Susan couldn't have been in the tower at the relevant time, because none of the residents had mentioned her. And she couldn't have had a supervision with Venton-Gimps, since he was picking up parcels from a neighbour at the time . . . And then suddenly she realised what was chancy about Venton-Gimps's alibi: it proved he wasn't in his room at the crucial time, but perhaps he *should have been*; what if he *should have been there?*

That at least was easy to check up on. Imogen wandered down to the college office, and enquired for last year's teaching schedules. A bit of scrabbling about in the filing cupboards in the basements produced them. And there it was. Venton-Gimps was supposed to be taking a supervision on the day John Talentire died. It was at six, and it was with three students, one of whom was Susan Inchman, and another of whom was Alison Worley. Six was too early in the evening. Talentire's fall had been a little after nine. But Alison's room was not far from the college office. Imogen climbed up the flight of stairs and knocked on Alison's door.

Alison was at her desk, working with loud music playing. She turned it down on seeing Imogen.

'I just wondered, Alison, can you remember last year? Your supervisions with Dr Venton-Gimps were at six?'

'Should have been is the word,' said Alison. 'He was always moving it later or earlier.'

'The night Dr Talentire died?'

'He moved us from before hall dinner at six to after hall dinner at eight thirty. I was cross because there was a disco that evening. We all thought it was a bit steep. I cancelled a date. And then he didn't turn up.'

'You were there and the supervisor wasn't?'

'Yes. I got browned off after twenty minutes, and I left.'

'You all left?'

'I got pissed off first. The others were still waiting when I left.'

'Thank you, Alison.'

Imogen left in a sombre mood. There was no escaping it; Susan was a loose cannon, and finding her was urgently necessary. And she knew already that the police would not be worried.

Somehow she thought it might be nice to have somebody with her on such a quest. And who would help her? Lady B.

was laid up with flu; Fran or Josh would both be willing, but were both busy; Dennis was as likely to need help as to be a help; Malcolm Gracie, who was chivalrous and kind, would have limited time available; Imogen would have to fall back as she had often done before on Shirl, her sewing circle friend, a friend from schooldays, willing and practical and down to earth. She would ask Shirl. But meantime, before going home for the day, she would go across to the Master's Lodging and see how Lady B. was doing.

She found her sitting up beside a fire in the small sitting room, with the Master sitting reading in the opposite chair. Caroline Buckmote was looking pale and drawn, but her temperature had come down, and she seemed to be doing the right thing, taking it easy and keeping warm. The conversation naturally turned at once to the bombshell that Duncan Talentire had dropped of last night.

'I distinctly heard him say that he knew who had murdered his son,' said the Master. 'He did, didn't he, Imogen?'

'Yes, he did,' Imogen agreed.

'*Murdered* his son,' the Master repeated, in distressed tones. 'And it happened on college property!'

'Well, where it happened is hardly the worst thing about it, William,' protested Lady B. 'It's a dreadful thing to happen anywhere.'

'Of course, of course it is,' said the Master. 'But if it had to happen I'd just as soon it had happened anywhere else. It was bad enough when it seemed to have been an accident.'

'It still might have been an accident,' said Lady B. crisply. 'The police and the coroner thought so, and still think so. It's only various madmen alleging otherwise.'

'Imogen doesn't think so,' said the Master, eyeing Imogen as he spoke.

'I'm afraid not,' Imogen admitted.

A little while later, as she walked through the porters' lodge on her way home, Mr Hughes, the head porter, beckoned her. 'There has been a disreputable person asking for you,' he said.

'Oh? What sort of person?' asked Imogen.

'A person of extremely shabby and dirty attire, unshaven and unwashed, and well-spoken with it,' said the porter. 'I refused him permission to wander into the college looking for you. I rang your office but you were not there.'

'I was visiting the Master's wife,' said Imogen.

'The person left you a message,' the porter continued.

'Good. I'll be glad to see it,' said Imogen.

'It was not a written message, just a spoken one. He said to tell you to try the boats.'

'Ah,' said Imogen. 'Thank you, Mr Hughes.'

Shirley and Imogen tackled the towpath on their bikes. Shirley was just as interested as Imogen had been in the boats which had somehow infiltrated Cambridge, creeping along the river banks like an invasive form of natural life. The line-up began along Midsummer Common: *Unthinkable, Costabomb, Flowing English, Norfolk Lass, Gonzoogler, Ratty and Mole, Out of Phase, Athene Noctua* . . .

'Rather better than house names, aren't they?' said Shirl. They rode on. When there was some sign of habitation on a boat – a bicycle chained up nearby, a spinning wind-generator, cabin doors open – Imogen stopped, and tapped on the roof to draw attention. Each time someone appeared she asked for a girl called Susan, and her boyfriend. Nobody knew a thing. Pursed lips and shaken heads were all that she could evoke.

After a few such duff tries she changed tack. She began to preface the query with the remark that Susan was not in trouble; it was just that she had a message for her and was hoping to deliver it that afternoon. 'Can't help, mate,' was still the only response. They rode all the way to the Pike and Eel without finding any information. But there their luck changed a bit. They stopped for a drink in the pub garden, and Imogen recognised one of the other drinkers as Gray, the man who had shown her and Dennis round his boat weeks ago.

Gray wrinkled his brow when Imogen posed her question. 'Nice-looking girl with wrecked-up-looking boyfriend? Don't think so. There aren't that many decent-looking girls on the boats, and I know them all. All the ones that clean up in the morning and go off to work. There's an association of boat-dwellers. We get to know what's going on. Stick up for each other.'

'Aren't there incomers? Visiting boats?'

'Yes. Plenty. Mostly in summer. We'd pass the time of day with those. Tell them where the shit station is, and where they can get a drink. If the lass you're looking for is on one of those, heaven only knows . . .'

Imogen gave up. They did ride further, all the way down to Baitsbite Lock. But without result, so they turned and rode back to Cambridge. Upstream of the Green Dragon Bridge the line of boats stretched along the path again. *Unthinkable, Costabomb, Flowing English, Norfolk Lass, Gonzoogler, Ratty and Mole, Out of Phase, Athene Noctua* . . .

Imogen stopped abruptly, and got off her bike at Cutter Ferry Bridge, surprising Shirley, who drew ahead, and then wheeled round to rejoin her.

'*Swan of Avon,*' said Imogen. 'When I was here with Dennis there was one called *Swan of Avon*! Did you see it?'

'Don't think so. Neat name. No, Imogen, I don't think we saw that one.'

'So she could be on that.'

'Well, if you say so. I suppose.'

'Look, Shirley, I'm going back to see if I can talk to Gray again. Do you want to split and go your own way?'

'I think I must, alas,' said Shirley. 'I'm having my hair done at two.'

Imogen sped back towards the Pike and Eel, and met Gray coming towards her over the Green Dragon Bridge.

'Hello again?' he said.

'A boat called *Swan of Avon*, Gray. Used to be here. Isn't now. Whose is it?'

Gray leaned against the railing of the bridge, and contemplated her in silence for a moment. 'It's the nature of boats,' he said. 'Here today, gone tomorrow. If you want a fixed address you live in a house.'

'Yes. But that particular boat – what do you know about it?'

'Not a lot,' said Gray. 'Belongs to a wild old geezer, talks to himself. Harmless, though.'

'Well, put it this way. I'm looking for someone—'

'You said. Girl with boyfriend.'

'And I get a tip-off that I should try the boats. You tell me, and so have several other boat-people that you can't think who I mean; but one of the boats that used to be here – just one, mind you – isn't here now. So how would I find it?'

'You'd follow it down river,' he said.

'So you do know something about it. You know it's gone downstream.'

At this Gray looked at her pityingly. 'Yes, that I do know.

Upstream is, you might say, a cul-de-sac. You can go easily as far as Jesus Lock. Then if you can get permission, in theory you can go to the head of navigation, which is Newnham Pool, right along the Backs, right through the punts. Discouraged, naturally. But above the Mill dam you cannot go. So, yes, I do know it went downstream. OK?'

'So downstream, where could it go?'

'Anywhere. Look, come back to my boat with me, and I'll show you a map.'

It was only a step back to *Wild Thyme*. Graham unlocked the back door, and led Imogen into the cabin. There he took down a heavy tome called *Bradley's Inland Waterways*, and unfolded a map that was stuck inside the back cover.

'We're here,' Gray said, stabbing at the map with a stubby finger. 'Downstream to Baitsbite Lock. Below that lock, to Bottisham Lock. Down to the confluence with the Great Ouse. There's a nice pub there – middle of nowhere – called the Fish and Duck.'

'That's at Little Thetford,' Imogen said. 'I've been there.'

'Well, on the Great Ouse you could turn right, and go down past Ely, and by Denver Sluice to the sea, or up the Lark, or the Wissey, or Brandon Creek. Or you could turn left and go upstream: Earith and St Ives, and up to Bedford. Or you could go through the Middle Level Ditches through Whittlesey, and to the Nene, and from there you could go downstream towards the Wash, or upstream and lock up onto the Grand Union Canal; and from there—'

'But you couldn't go to any of these places *fast*?'

'Not fast, no. There's a speed limit of about four miles an hour, and a practical limit of maybe seven miles an hour, and there are locks; they take twenty minutes or so if they are for you, and more if they are against.'

'So if I jumped into my car, and drove around . . .'

'I would say you can't find a boat in a car,' said Gray. 'There's miles of waterway nowhere near any road, and across the Fen you can't even see the water, or anything on it, because it's between high banks. You could set a watch at locks, but these days not so many of them have keepers. Mostly the boaters work the locks themselves. You need a boat to catch a boat, I would say. And if the one you were after kept moving, all the hours of daylight and some of the darkness, you wouldn't easily catch up.'

Imogen winced. 'A boat to catch a boat?' she said.

'Not this one, I'm afraid. It belongs to my son, and he comes home from work to sleep in it every night. You can hire boats at Ely or March, week at a time.'

'But if I started as far downstream as that, I would have to look up towards Cambridge as well as down in all the directions you mentioned; this seems impossible to me, Gray.'

'Tough, admittedly.' But he was looking at her shrewdly. 'Look,' he said at last. 'I haven't a clue who might have been on the old geezer's boat. But if his is the one you want, he will be inside this circle, somewhere.'

Gray ran his finger round an area of the map, encircling the Fish and Duck, and a few miles of waterway all round it. '*Swan of Avon* is a slow old thing,' he said. 'A really old boat; on a wooden, one-time-working hull. Grotty old engine, always breaking down. He upped his mooring spikes and went down two days ago. Forty miles is the outside he could do. Much less, more likely, unless he was running away from something.' Once again he was looking at her assessingly.

'And you don't think I could hire or borrow a boat anywhere in Cambridge?'

'I didn't say that. There's various people here short of a quid or two. I could ask around. Let you know. You'd need to make it worth while. Couple of hundred should get you afloat for a day or two.'

'Thanks, Gray. I'd better think about that,' Imogen said.

17

O, fie, Horatio, and if thou shouldst die,
What a scandale wouldst thou leave behinde?

Sitting in her comfortable kitchen, Imogen thought. And what she was thinking about was money. The truth was that her finances had not recovered from that impulsive purchase of *The Night Climbers*. Imogen was modestly paid by St Agatha's. She owned her house, a legacy from her parents, and had a small holding of savings certificates. She had taken the view that she would rather have a restricted salary and lots of free time than a full-time job and more money. This was a life-style choice she seldom regretted. But the twenty minutes she had just spent with the Yellow Pages, ringing round to price the cost of hiring a boat, had left her all too aware that the decision to live on the breadline had a downside.

'Oh, come on, Imogen!' she admonished herself. The breadline? She remembered with a rueful smile a conversation between her father and the Welsh farmer's wife with whom they used to spend their summers. Imogen's father had complained of being hard up.

'*Mr Quy!*' the farmer's wife had said. 'What is the price of a large loaf?' Imogen's father, of course, had not known. Imogen had seldom seen him so badly wrong-footed. But it put the 'poverty' of the prosperous in perspective. Just the same, Imogen could not afford to hire a boat. They came by the week only, and even off-season they would cost four hundred pounds a week. Eager though Imogen was to find Susan Inchman, this was seeming impossible. And after all, she didn't *know* that Susan was on a boat, that was just a hint from Mick. And she didn't *know* that if she hired a boat, and got Josh perhaps to help her navigate it, she would in fact be able to find *Swan of Avon*. And if Susan was on a boat, and Imogen could find *Swan of Avon*, it remained only a guess that it was the right boat. That was a lot of speculation to get heavily in debt for.

Unhappily, Imogen got up and phoned Mrs Ollery again. And against the odds, there was some news. Susan had, at last, phoned home. She had refused to say where she was, and had told her adoptive mother, very fiercely, not to look for her. 'She says she's all right and not to worry,' said Mrs Ollery.

'But she can't be all right, really, can she?' said Imogen softly.

'I told her to get right back to college, and be grateful,' Mrs Ollery said. 'And she said she couldn't do that, not never, that was all over, and not to worry.'

'But you are worrying, no doubt,' said Imogen.

'Not as much as before she rang, to be honest,' Mrs Ollery said. 'I was afraid she might be dead. And alive is better than dead, whatever she's up to. And at least she realised I would be out of my mind with worry and she phoned. She's a grown-up, Miss Quy. I would leave her to her own devices now, and I wish you and that Lady what's-her-name would do so too.'

'We'll think about it,' said Imogen.

'If you go after her now, it's over my dead body,' said Mrs Ollery. 'I've asked you not to, and I won't help you a step further. Sorry. Perhaps you mean well, but my Susan has had a lot to put up with from bossy-boots people, all her life.'

'As I said, I'll think about it,' said Imogen. Then, not wanting to leave a hostile tinge in the air, she said, 'How's Denny?'

'Not too happy,' said Mrs Ollery. 'He pinched a pair of trainers, much too expensive for me to buy for him, and now there's a curfew on him. He's got to be in by nine, and he can't go out with his mates. I've got a very cross boy here.'

Imogen expressed sympathy, and rang off. 'What's the price of a pair of trainers?' she wondered. What's the price of a bit of self-respect for unlucky youngsters like Denny? And then, naturally, she wondered what could make a girl who had clambered out of such a morass, and got as far as Cambridge, throw it all away? 'It's got to be something to do with that boyfriend, hasn't it?' she asked herself.

Very unwillingly, but knowing that Mike Parsons' trust was too valuable to mess about with, she then rang the police station to tell him that Susan had phoned home. 'Won't say where she is, though,' she told him.

'Oh, OK. That's family quarrel stuff, then,' he said. 'I'll take her off the missing persons' register.'

'Oh, but I'm not sure she's really all right . . .'

'My dear Imogen, I know you like being a little friend to all the world, and I love you for it. But unless this girl has broken the law, she's a free agent. And it isn't against the law to scarper from a Cambridge college.'

'I think she has broken the law, Mike.'

'Oh? What do you reckon she's been up to?'

'It's just a hunch. I'll tell you if I happen across a scrap of evidence.' But that was not very likely, if the girl was really 'on the boats', and the boats were beyond Imogen's means.

However much Imogen might have decided to forgo a better paid position, it's not pleasant to be stopped from what one might otherwise do by simple lack of means. It's actually somewhat humiliating. Who could you confide in? Anyone you confide in might think you were touching them for a loan.

Luck, however, can quickly change. Around mid-morning Imogen's phone rang. It was Gray. 'If you can get down here right away, I've got a lift for you. Far as the Fish and Duck. If that helps. Stout shoes, anorak. OK?'

Imogen, dressed as he suggested, rode off on her bike within ten minutes.

The lift was a boat called *Jason*. It belonged to a water-borne software engineer called Alan, who was meeting his girlfriend down river, and needed a helping hand with the locks on the way down. Imogen was on a steep learning curve. River locks, she learned, are electrically controlled. You can wind the gear only slowly, however much hurry you may be in. Baitsbite Lock when they reached it was empty, and they needed it to be full. Alan closed the bottom gate, leaning his backside on the balance beam, and walking backward. Then Imogen, with a windlass in her hand, wound the top gate upwards, letting water pour into the lock, and fill it, fast at first with lots of turbulence, then slowly. It seemed an incredible length of time before the upper gate was raised high enough to allow the boat to pass beneath it into the lock. Alan eased the boat into the lock, and the whole process was repeated in reverse, lowering the gate, raising paddles, waiting while the boat sank gently to the lower level, and the bottom gates could be opened.

In a while Imogen found herself enjoying this; it was gentle, steady work in the open air. Frightfully good for you; no wonder boat-people were robustly healthy. As a way of running away it seemed painful. Far too slow. But as the boat chugged gently on below the lock, following a river lined with sallows and hawthorn hedges on the towpath side, and past green fields with grazing cows on the other bank, a river full of reflected sky, and lined with bulrush and arrowhead, and one or two lily-pads, Imogen changed her mind. The very slowness of the boat suggested that any pursuit would soon overtake you. Soon a hue and cry would be far ahead. And the towpath was not a road; you could not give chase in a car. Only a bike would do. Imogen's own bike was lying on its side on the roof of Alan's boat. Along the peaceful reaches of the river, here and there were wonderful hiding places, little inlets with one or two boats in them; patches of woodland where someone had tied up alongside a battered shed under the trees, and where a whirligig on a mast was spinning and making electricity. Many of these moorings, Imogen noticed, were inaccessible except by water.

A sense of peace descended into Imogen's anxious mind, and calmed her. There was a lot to look at: she saw swans nesting among riverside rush-beds, and a crested grebe diving a little way ahead. A mile or so further a kingfisher left a perch as they approached, and blazed away upstream, a tiny horizontal spark. The pace of the boat was not quite like any other Imogen knew. A little faster than walking; to keep up along the towpath would entail a brisk trot. Much slower than any other motorised transport. A pace just right to let the scenery spool past, always changing, but changing slowly enough to allow for detailed observation. The diesel engine made a pleasantly rural sort of chug. After a while Imogen realised it reminded her of the sound of the tractor on a farm. Many people fail to see the beauty of the Fenland landscapes. A lot of it consists of sky. The river appreciated the sky, Imogen decided, answering it cloud for cloud, and depth for height.

Alan was a man of few words. However, after Bottisham Lock, when the river mysteriously raised itself above the land on either side, and began to run in high banks, he did ask Imogen which boat she was looking for.

'*Swan of Avon.*'

'Ah. Belongs to a madman, that one.'

'Well, it's really a person I'm looking for. Might be on that boat, might be on another.'

'Hmm. It's easy just to duck out of sight on a boat if you don't want to be seen,' Alan said. He didn't ask what this was all about, and Imogen was grateful. About Fenland waterways he was more talkative. Imogen learned that the river they were cruising on had once been level with the land. But the great Dutch engineers who drained the Fens had not realised that peat would shrink once it dried out. The land had dropped by feet and feet, until the drains were aerial, the banks were made higher and higher, and the land-water had to be pumped up into them.

'Must have been nice when the pumps were windmills,' he offered. 'Must have looked like a Rembrandt landscape.'

'How is it powered now?'

'Diesel. There's still a steam pump at Stretham, but it's just a museum.'

'When will we reach the Fish and Duck?'

'Fivish. Sixish. Whenever.'

Imogen was going to have a problem getting home. She hoped the lights on her bike were in good nick. And all the time she looked carefully at every boat they passed; she could not remember much about *Swan of Avon*. After all, when she had seen it first she had no particular reason to notice that boat rather than any other boat.

It was dusk before they reached the Fish and Duck. It stood on a tongue of land at the confluence, where the Cam joined the Great Ouse. There were boats tied up all along the bank there, and Alan brought his boat smoothly alongside another one and tied up to the boat rather than to the bank.

'Mightn't this boat-owner mind?' asked Imogen.

'Belongs to Harry. He won't mind,' said Alan. 'Here's where I leave you. Many thanks.' He lifted Imogen's bike off the boat roof, and over the companion boat, and put it on the bank.

Imogen realised that he was impatient to lock up and go and find his girlfriend in the pub. But the pub was a possible source of information. 'Let me buy you a drink,' she said. 'Least I can do.'

The pub was busy, and the company was mixed. It was full of rather scruffy people, wearing sensible all-weather clothes. Alan's girlfriend stood out: she was a slender blonde wearing a pinstriped dark grey suit, and carrying a briefcase. Imogen bought a round of drinks, and took the opportunity to ask the barmaid about *Swan of Avon*. Her reaction was to raise her voice above the hubbub and yell: '*Swan of Avon*. Anyone know where he went?'

'Didn't come down past me,' said a fellow who was propping up the bar.

'Where are you tied up, then?' the barmaid asked.

'Ely. Just beyond the railway bridge. I didn't see him come down. Didn't pass him on the way up here. Who wants to know?'

'I do,' said Imogen.

'And what's it to do with?'

'I heard he had passengers. And I'm looking for someone who might be with him.'

'Yes, well. I wouldn't like to say. You might be trouble for someone, for all I know. In fact, I shouldn't really have been so sure he didn't come down past me in the night. Can't see what a boat is when it's dark, can you?'

'Can you move at night?' Imogen asked, surprised.

'If you've got lights, you can,' he said. 'Now if you'll excuse me . . .'

It didn't seem likely that Imogen would get much more low-down from him. She returned to Alan's table, where he was deep in conversation with his girl, and put the drinks on the table.

'Nothing for you?' Alan asked.

'No, I'd better be going. Many thanks.'

'Sorry it wasn't much help,' he said.

'It was fun,' said Imogen.

She moved to the pub door, and standing in the porch contemplated her long ride home, after dark, and on roads unfamiliar to her. Then she took out her mobile phone, and, sighing at the thought of the expense, she rang the familiar number for a Cambridge taxi. 'One of those big ones,' she said, 'I've got a bike with me.'

She sat down at a garden table outside the pub, somehow not fancying the warm rowdy interior. She was warmly wrapped up, and quite happy to wait under the stars.

While she was waiting someone came out of the pub and stood, hands in pockets, looking around. He came over to her. 'Was it you what was asking about old Swanny?' he said.

'Yes.'

'You don't mean trouble, do you? Don't look like a copper.'

'I'm not a copper,' said Imogen.

'Thought not. He came past here three days ago, and he went upstream. If I know him, he'll be tied where there's a pub. Earith maybe; or St Ives, or Godmanchester. Don't think he'll have got much further in that old tub of his.'

'Thank you,' said Imogen.

'Yeah, well,' said her informant.

Imogen got home very late, and the taxi fare was a palpable fraction of the boat hire she had baulked at. Fran and Josh were already in bed, and the house was dark and quiet. Imogen went wearily to her bed. There was, however, just a gleam of daylight. Pubs in Earith or St Ives or Godmanchester (did she remember from her schooldays that local people called it *Gumster*?) were all within reach by road.

A bright morning followed, and it was a day when Imogen's surgery hours were four thirty to six. After breakfast she drove off in her little car resolved to give this quest just one more try. All the reasons she had given herself for not spending money on boat hire were still valid. But after all, an excursion out of the city would be fun. She started by driving to Earith. There was a little boat-basin there, but not the boat she wanted. Then to St Ives. St Ives had a big marina, but she had no luck. The manager had neither seen nor heard of any such boat as *Swan of Avon*. He suggested the town quay. One or two boats were tied up just below the bridge, a pretty bridge with a little chapel on it for pilgrims. Imogen was told that you couldn't tie there for long.

'I think he was here, though,' a boat-owner told her. 'He was looking to stay a few days and he got moved on. Try a bit upstream; Hemingford Grey or Hemingford Abbots.'

Imogen drove to Hemingford Grey. The road ran through

the village and came to a stop at the river bank. A pretty place: there was a cluster of houses, a thatched cottage, a fine Georgian house, and a view of the church with its truncated tower. Imogen had been here before, she realised, when her father took her to see the oldest house in England, which must be somewhere along there on the left. Across from the village the further bank was a pretty green water-meadow. On this bank the towpath led onwards. Imogen locked her car, and set out on foot. Soon she passed the house she remembered; a notice at the garden gate invited visitors, but Imogen went on until the path came out onto a meadow where a low embankment had been built to contain winter flooding. Against this bank there were several boats tied up, three fibreglass cruisers of various degrees of marine swank, and one narrow boat. *Swan of Avon*, at last.

Imogen walked along the bank for the length of the boat, looking carefully. There was no sign of anyone on it. It was a rather untidy boat, having a load of coal sacks on the roof, and worn paintwork. A brass tiller and tiller-pin had once given a touch of class, but were now tarnished and dull. There was a gang-plank propped up from bank to rear deck; not much rear deck, as the boat had traditional lines. The river sparkled serenely, a few cows grazed in the field beyond the bank, and the church tower dominated the bend in the river just behind. A thatched boathouse leaned somewhat ominously at the water's edge beside the church. A scene of perfect, English rural peace. There was even a lark trilling overhead.

Imogen stood, hesitant. That dark understanding that had seeped into the back of her mind seemed melodramatic, and preposterous. She felt foolish. But then she pulled herself together. She really did need to find Susan; and Susan might be on this boat. If she wasn't, the sooner Imogen eliminated the possibility and looked elsewhere, the better. She leaned over, and with a clenched fist she knocked on the side of the boat. 'Anyone there?' she called. Expecting the answer no, or rather, no answer. When nothing happened for a couple of minutes, she knocked and called again.

And then the hatch at the back of the boat was slid back, and the ghost of Hamlet's father rose slowly and majestically into view.

18

The poysned instrument within my hand?
Then venome to thy venome, die, damned villain!

'Mr Gadgby,' Imogen exclaimed.

'Who wants me?' he said. 'Can't you people leave an old man in peace?'

'I'm not "you people",' said Imogen. 'I'm the college nurse at St Agatha's. An admirer of yours. Imogen Quy.'

'You aren't from the welfare?' he asked suspiciously.

'Not in any shape or form. I thought you might be able to help me.'

'You'd better come in then,' he said. His head disappeared down the hatch, and he unbolted the doors from within. Imogen clambered aboard, and down three wooden steps into the cabin. The cabin had a musty sweet smell, a reek of stale food and cannabis. It was wildly untidy. There was a sink piled with dirty dishes, and a counter covered with supermarket plastic bags, not unloaded. Imogen gagged, but her host led the way through to another cabin, beyond a compartment smelling of Racusan, and she found herself in the central part of the boat. And this cabin was clean and tidy. It had a little stove, a chair and a built in sofa, and it was lined all round the lower part of the walls with shelves of books. The contrast was dazzling. One could see at once what Hamlet's father cared about in life, and what he didn't. He gestured Imogen towards the sofa, and she sat down there while he took the chair.

He didn't look like a man who cared for food; he was skinny, and unhealthy-looking. He wasn't so much dirty as unkempt. He was staring at her now with red-rimmed eyes. 'Yes, I have seen you before,' he said. 'In the green room for that play. Did you see what *The Times* said about my performance?' He got up, and wavered down the boat to a rack of newspapers, from which he extracted a copy of *The Times*, folded to show the theatre review.

'Yes, I did see that,' Imogen told him.

'Congratulates them on getting me. Fine performance,' he said. 'Want a drink?'

'Rather early in the day for me, thank you,' said Imogen.

' 'Tisn't for me,' he said, reaching down beside his chair and bringing up a bottle of Napoleon brandy, from which he took a generous swig.

It said it all. No wonder he was leery of 'the welfare'. No wonder his friends were leery of giving out information on his whereabouts. And a boat was perfect for him; he could slip from one area to another as soon as anyone started talking about a care home. She glanced along his rows of books. Probably not very many, but fully as many as could be got into the narrow cabin. *Concordance to Shakespeare*. Bradley's *Characters of Shakespeare*, a long run of *Arden* editions. Imogen recognised these titles easily because they were on her own shelves, where most of her father's books still remained. The library of an educated man forty years back . . .

She braced herself for the question she had to ask.

'Mr Gadgby, I'm looking for someone who might have hitched a lift on a boat. A young woman and her boyfriend.'

He fixed a steady appraising gaze on her.

'And since your boat left Cambridge at about the right time, I just wondered . . .'

'A young woman and her boyfriend? No.'

'Oh. I'm sorry then, I needn't have troubled you. I'll leave you in peace. Unless you have seen them on someone else's boat? It's important; I really do need to find them.'

'No. Haven't heard anything.'

'OK, then. I'll leave you in peace.'

'On your way, then,' he said, standing up. He was tall; his tousled head only just cleared the cabin roof, and he loomed over Imogen. The boat shifted slightly as he moved. It wasn't solid ground. 'A young woman and her boyfriend, no,' he said. 'A young woman and her brother, yes.'

'Oh, God,' said Imogen. 'Oh, God.'

His beady eyes never left her face.

'Where are they now?' she asked.

'Don't know.'

'You don't know at all?'

'Nope. They had a quarrel. Nasty one. Nothing to do with me; you needn't ask me what it was about, I didn't listen, I went for a walk. I don't like shouting and upsets. Next morning he got up very early, and went off, and when she woke up and found he'd gone she threw a fit, and went screaming after him. That's all I know.'

'Thank you, Mr Gadgby. Before I go, is there anything I can do for you?'

'Like what?' he said.

'Clean up the galley for you?'

'*She* was always on about that,' he said. 'You women are all alike. I thought you were the welfare in one form or another.'

'Fund some groceries?'

'If you give me money I'll spend it all on drink,' he said, smiling. 'Bye-bye.'

Imogen climbed off his boat, and walked back to her car with a chill at her heart. The derelict young man was Susan's brother, not a bizarrely chosen boyfriend. That explained a lot; did it explain everything? It was fairly baffling to know what to do next. She mused on it as she drove back to Cambridge. In one way this was just a question of finding a missing student and persuading her to return. But it was also about Martin Mottle's angry certainties. Obviously, to do nothing was one option; just await developments.

But the developments didn't wait. When Imogen walked in through her front door, Fran was waiting for her. She came through from the back of the house, to meet Imogen in the hall.

'Imo, something's happened. Something awful has happened. Someone has tried to kill Martin Mottle!'

Imogen stepped into her sitting room with her coat still on, and sat down.

'Take it slowly, Fran. Is he all right?'

'No; he's in Addenbrooke's. I don't know what happened, and I don't know how hurt he is. A friend at his college rang me up to tell me about it, all agog. It seems there was a struggle in the front court, and a gunshot, and a lot of blood, and paramedics and a lot of drama. Then ambulances. That's all I know.'

'God help us,' said Imogen.

'He doesn't have brothers or sisters, and his mother's dead and his father is in South America somewhere,' added Fran miserably. 'Who is there to make sure he's all right?'

Imogen weighed it up. Had Martin been a member of St Agatha's she could clearly have gone into A & E and done a bit of talking. As it was she would be pushing her luck. But she found that she minded desperately if Martin Mottle was hurt. Luck was there to be pushed.

'Fran, are you calm enough to drive me to Addenbrooke's? I'm feeling a bit shaken myself.'

There was rush-hour traffic all along the Hills Road, and Fran talked all the way. She told Imogen she hadn't really believed it, when they had mentioned to Martin the chance that if he was right he was at risk. It had had that improbable, storybook feel. It didn't now.

'So there really was a murder,' Fran kept saying. 'There really was someone who would be out to get him after that dumb-show. And I just thought he was a bit fanatical, you know? Poor, poor Martin . . .'

'In a way he got what he wanted,' said Imogen drily. 'Let's hope there wasn't too high a price to pay.'

The A & E department was in chaos. But once Imogen talked her way past reception her luck proved good. Two of the nurses on duty had trained with her, when a few years back she had trained in A & E. She had soon found the endless succession of crises too tough for her – she couldn't keep detached. Now far from wishing to fend her off, Gwen cried, 'Thank God! Another pair of hands! Just hold this for me, Imo,' and thrust into her hands a drip line to be held aloft while they moved a bed further back in the department, and into a curtained lobby. At first glance Imogen thought the patient on the bed was someone she had never seen before. Then she recognised the desperate addict who had been evicted from the Fellows' Garden a few weeks back. 'Of course,' she murmured to herself. 'Of course.'

'He'll be all right for the moment,' Gwen said.

'What's happened to him?'

'Gunshot wound to the leg. More or less kneecapped him. They'll have to operate to get the bullet out. We need to admit him, when we can find a bed.'

'He's very calm. Have you doped him?'

'We haven't. He's up to the eyebrows with whatever he takes himself.'

Imogen said, 'Can I help with anything?'

'Just lurk around for a few minutes, would you? We don't often get a stab wound and a gunshot wound admitted simultaneously. We'll have the police under our feet any minute.'

'I actually came about Martin Mottle.'

'He's the stab wound. We'll have to admit him too. Over there, if you want to hold his hand. In fact, keep an eye on him, could you, while I deal with the hysterical young woman outside.'

Imogen entered the curtained compartment in which Martin Mottle, deathly pale, was lying. He had been stabbed in the shoulder, and in the upper arm. He was bandaged, and hooked up to a drip. He greeted her with a faint smile.

'Oh, thank God you're here,' he said. 'They keep telling me I'll live, but they won't tell me if *he* will live. I aimed low down,' he added, 'but I didn't see what happened. I haven't killed anyone, have I? Please tell me I haven't killed him.'

'You haven't killed him. He'll live.' Imogen let this sink in, and then said, 'I thought you *wanted* to get the man to attack you. Wasn't it part of the plan?'

'It wasn't the right man,' said Mottle sadly.

'Oh, but I think it was,' said Imogen. 'And do keep calm.' She reached out to hold his wrist and take his pulse. It was raised, but not as much as she had expected. There is no end to the amazing resilience of the healthy young.

Beyond the gently swaying curtain there was an increasing commotion. Gwen suddenly put her head into the compartment.

'Imo, I'm so sorry, we do need help. We've got a serious incident: an accident on the M11. They're bringing in a lot of casualties, and I don't know when anyone will get round to finding beds in the wards for these two. Can you keep an eye on blood pressure and such for a while? Can you manage to monitor both of them?'

Imogen had hardly had time to say yes, when they whisked the curtains aside, and trolleyed Martin along to the very last compartment, where they hitched him up to the blood-pressure monitor. Seconds later Martin's victim was wheeled alongside, and with him came a tear-stained Susan Inchman, who collapsed onto the bedside chair, and grabbed his hand. She looked with dazed incomprehension at Mottle lying nearby, while Gwen showed Imogen briefly how the up-to-the-minute machine spewed printout. 'We've only got one of these to spare,' she said. 'They'll have to share it. There's the emergency bell, Imo, if you need it. Sorry to do this to you.'

Imogen had forgotten the strange rhythm of work in casualty. There is a fast and professional reaction to crisis, followed by an extended slowness; once it's not a life-threatening emergency the patient simply waits and waits. Waits for the result of tests, waits for a bed, waits for permission to leave. Their families arrive. There are people waiting on rows of chairs in mute anxiety and distress for hours. And this is what happened now. Dramatic though stab wounds and gunshot wounds might be, they were not as urgent as accidents on the M11. And there didn't seem to be any beds available.

At ten o'clock the orderlies came for Martin, and wheeled him away to have his wounds stitched up. A little before midnight a tired junior doctor told Imogen that Mottle would be kept in casualty overnight, and admitted to a ward in the morning. He suggested she go home. Imogen looked around for Susan; she would have taken the girl home with her for a comfortable bed, and a little kindness. But Susan had quietly disappeared.

Just for confirmation, as she left, Imogen read the admission ticket on the young man's bed. *David Inchman.* Just so.

19

Let there a scaffold be rearde up in the market place,
And let the State of the world be there;
Where you shall heare such a sad story tolde
That never mortall man could more unfold.

Imogen got herself up to Addenbrooke's fairly early the next morning. Martin was now in a male surgical ward, where Imogen also found Dave Inchman. They were in adjacent beds, or rather Martin was in an extra bed, under the window, pushed in alongside Dave – presumably the only place available. Susan was there again, holding her brother's hand, and with a blank expression on her face that Imogen read as shock. She walked down the ward and got permission to make a cup of tea in the nurses' room, and bring it to Susan.

When she returned there was someone there: Martin had a visitor. The visitor stood at the foot of the bed, and Martin was smiling sheepishly at him. Duncan Talentire.

'What in hell have you been up to, Martin?' the great man said. 'Your father rang me in a panic from Bogotá, and asked me to get over here and find out how you are.'

'I'll be all right,' said Martin. 'It wasn't a very competent attack. But I'm afraid I am in trouble. I defended myself with a gun I shouldn't have had.'

'Fool,' said Talentire crisply.

'He did have a knife,' said Martin.

'Were you being mugged?'

At that Dave turned his head, and said, 'You lay off my sister, or I'll do it again. Better, next time!'

Susan Inchman said, 'I told you it wouldn't help, Dave.'

Talentire said, 'Is there anybody here who can tell me what in hell this is about?'

Imogen wondered for a second if she should embark on a story of guesses and maybes, but Susan spoke up. 'I was badly bothered,' she said. 'And Dave thought he could scare him off.'

'The Bad Quarto bothered you? The *Hamlet?*' asked Mottle. 'Why? I wasn't trying to bother *you.*'

'Oh, weren't you, though?' said Susan. 'Got it right, though, didn't you?'

'Do you want to tell us what happened, Susan?' said Imogen gently. 'What happened the night John Talentire died?'

'I might as well,' the girl said. 'I'll be telling the police any minute now. Well, I had a late supervision with that shit Venton-Gimps. And he didn't show up. It wasn't the first time, he was always bumping us. We were waiting on that freezing cold staircase, and he hadn't even unlocked his oak so we could wait in the warm. There were three of us, but the others gave up and went for a drink. I hung around because I was so angry I thought a drink would choke me. So I was stood there when John Talentire came galloping up the stairs with a coil of rope over his shoulder. He came right past me, and I followed him a bit behind. I stood in the door of his room and I watched what he was doing, tying up his rope, and standing on his window-sill.' She stopped. She was shaking.

'And I thought, It's not fair, it's not fair, look at him – handsome and healthy and famous and clever and brave, stupid brave, and I bet his father's proud of him – and my poor Dave wrecked up and miserable, because of that same father, and I wondered how *he* would feel if there was a funny death in *his* family. . . So I just walked into the room while John was standing on the window-sill. I untied the rope. And then I watched. And when he landed on the roof the other side, I just gave the rope a little pull – ever so gentle – and he toppled and fell. I thought I'd got away with it. I thought I'd evened the score and I could just get on with life, and then I saw that play. So I hopped it.'

An appalled silence greeted this. Silent tears were flowing down Susan's face.

Then Dave said, 'She's lying. She's just trying to cover for me.'

'Don't, Dave!' wailed Susan.

'Why not?' he said. 'What have I got to lose compared to you? I was dunning her for money,' he went on. 'I needed money for my fix. And she wouldn't give me any, and she said she had to go to her class or what. So I followed her up those stairs, and kept on at her while she waited. And this Charlie came galloping past us, and Susan said, "Do you know who that is?" And I said, "Oh is it?" and I followed him into the room, and I undid his rope and tugged him off his perch. Got my own back. Susan was still down the stairs. Didn't know a thing about it till I told her later that I done it.'

'He's lying,' said Susan.

Duncan Talentire said, quite coolly, 'If you both stick to those stories, absolutely, without any deviation, they will find it remarkably difficult to convict either of you.'

Martin Mottle cried, 'Duncan, what are you doing? Are you trying to *help* John's murderers get away with it?'

Talentire said, 'I've had enough, Martin. I'm tired of chains of consequences running on for years. I'm tired of unlooked-for collateral damage. John's death was collateral damage. If anything could bring him back to us . . . but I don't want his death used to inflict further harm. I did ask you to leave it be. You ignored me; and now look what has happened.'

'You said it was an accident.'

'No; I told you that the coroner concluded it was an accident. Do you take me for a fool, Martin? I know the names of many people who have a grudge against me; and I saw the name Inchman in a college brochure. I thought, Well, at least one of them has surmounted the disaster, and made it to Cambridge. Then John came to grief. And it could have been an accident. I would rather have left it at that. I would rather not have heard what I have just heard. What I would dearly like to do is to unhitch the past from the future, and let life go on unhampered. For everyone.'

Susan said, quietly, 'I bet you would! I wouldn't have your conscience for anything. You stand up in court and tell a jury it's millions to one against what really happened. Someone gets sent to prison, and the kids get taken into care. Do you know that's called "a place of safety"? Don't make me laugh! A place where they take your clothes and leave you in a cold room all day to punish you for something. A place where the little kids' bottoms are for rent to local bigwigs, and they dumb you down with drugs and get you hooked. Then when you're sixteen they throw you out. Place of safety, my arse!'

'I'm sorry,' said Talentire. 'Not all children's homes are like that. Not many are. You were unlucky. But at least you are both alive, not like your two little brothers.'

'Not like our mother, either. She couldn't cope with it; she topped herself. And whose smart talk got an innocent woman sent to jail? No wonder you'd like to stop the consequences. Well, you're several consequences too late!'

Then suddenly Dave said, 'Hang about, Susie. Hang about. She wasn't innocent, you silly cow. I saw her, didn't I? I saw her do it!'

'No, Dave, you can't have . . .' Susan tailed off into silence.

'I did, too,' Dave said sulkily.

Duncan Talentire said, 'David, exactly *what* did you see your mother do?'

'Little tyke wouldn't stop crying,' said Dave. 'It went on and on. And our mum had a horrible temper. She was shouting at him, and stamping round the room. He went on screaming. So she put a pillow on his face, and leaned on it. I saw her. She had me in the same room, in a playpen.'

'No, David,' said Talentire softly. 'It wasn't a cot death case. Your baby brother wasn't smothered. It was shaken-baby syndrome. I was sure, all those years ago, what caused such injuries. Now we are less sure.'

'But I saw her . . .'

'How old were you? Three? Four?'

'Three and a bit.'

'I think probably someone told you about it later. Getting the story wrong. And you saw it in the mind's eye. That's what you remember.'

Dave looked at him with tearful eyes. 'Are you telling me it never happened?' he said. 'You're a bastard.'

'I was very sure of myself at the time,' said Talentire sadly. 'But there's nothing here now but uncertainty.'

Then, turning to Martin he said, 'Had enough, Martin? Is this enough for you? Will you let it go? Or do you want it to go on?'

Martin said, 'Look, Dave, if you and I both say we were

fighting over a rude remark – I insulted you and that's what made you go for me – then they probably won't be reopening stuff about John's death.'

'Why should I?' Dave said.

'Well, you'll be lying about why you and I were fighting, or you'll be lying about who pulled John's rope. Straight choice.'

'The rope bit wouldn't be lying,' said Dave valiantly. 'But whatever you say, mate.'

'Well, make up your minds quickly,' said Duncan Talentire. 'There are a couple of policemen walking down the ward just now, notebooks at the ready.'

Hurrying behind the policemen came a nurse, to clear the ward of visitors.

20

For I'le have a sute of sables. Jesus, two months dead,
And not forgotten yet?

After all the excitement, getting back to normal was gritty and uncomfortable, like putting on a wet swimsuit for a second dip. Imogen was restless, and full of a feeling that there were things she ought to be doing, though she couldn't think exactly what they were. She certainly ought to see the Master, and put him in the picture. Shortly.

The Master was available before dinner in hall that same evening, and so Imogen found herself once more in his sitting room, a drink in her hand and a dish of nuts at her elbow, telling her tale to the Master, and to Lady Buckmote. As she had expected it to do, her story agitated and upset her audience.

'So am I to understand that John Talentire's death *was* murder, beyond a doubt, and nothing is likely to be done about it, because there will be a conspiracy to ignore the matter?' said the Master. 'What an atrocious situation!'

'I rather think that Talentire senior is right about it, on a practical level,' said Lady B. 'And who has more right than he to forswear revenge?'

'Well, I'm sorry about his guilty conscience,' said the Master, 'but what about justice? Surely murder ought not to go unpunished!'

'Would it entertain you to secure a trial in which both Inchmans are acquitted because there isn't enough evidence as to which of them it was?'

'And where does this leave the college?' cried the Master. 'Are we to have a student who might have murdered someone *on these premises*, but whom we cannot expel, having no official grounds against her? This is an intolerable situation!'

Lady Buckmote said, 'You could ask her to leave, William. She might agree to go.'

'Oh, might . . . she might agree; chance would be a fine thing,' he said. 'I'll need to think hard about this.'

'Poor John Talentire,' said Lady Buckmote. 'I never liked him much, but he didn't deserve to die so that someone could get at his father. In no way fair.'

Is murder ever fair? Imogen wondered. The word 'murderer' has a diabolical image; how often, if one only knew, did it refer to marred and damaged people like Dave Inchman? He could have done it, although in her heart of hearts she thought the deed was Susan's, and Susan seemed perfectly in control of herself; except, of course, for that temper. What was it Mary Ollery had said about the slim chances of recovering from a disastrous childhood? A bad childhood, a late rescue, an inherited filthy temper? But that applied just as much to Dave, except that nobody had rescued him. No one had any time for Dave except his sister. And somewhere in the back of her mind, of unidentified origin, she had the idea that Dave might not be any good at untying knots.

Dutifully, Imogen cycled over to Addenbrooke's that evening to visit. Martin had been moved into a private room; Dave was where he had been in the morning. Dave was alone, with his leg in plaster and held in a hoist. He didn't know, or so he said, where Susan was.

'Ask her to get in touch, will you, Dave?' Imogen left her phone number on his bedside table.

Then she went upstairs to find Martin Mottle. 'So which particular set of lies got propounded to the police, Martin?' she asked him.

'Oh, the milder set. We both swore we had been pissed as newts and fighting over something I called him. I insulted him; he went for me with a knife; I defended myself with a gun. Hermetically sealed incident, nothing to do with anything else.'

'Well, perhaps that was best, overall,' said Imogen.

'I hadn't the heart to go against Duncan. It isn't justice for John, though,' he said quietly. His eyes brimmed with tears.

'You are a loving and a faithful friend, Martin, aren't you?' said Imogen. 'I like you for that.'

'That's what John was to me,' said Mottle. 'Duncan just wants it left alone. But I won't forget. I'll think of something else.'

'Well, not something too dramatic, Martin,' said Imogen. 'Please.'

Seeing Professor Appleby was also on Imogen's job list. She visited him in his rooms before hall dinner, and told him at some length that she thought Talentire was now very penitent about over-confident diagnoses in the past, and she told him how she knew.

'Fascinating!' he said. 'Tragic, really. What a punishment for getting something wrong!'

'Perhaps he *was* wrong,' said Imogen carefully. 'But also, perhaps he was right. I think, if you don't mind my saying so, that we might easily commit, ourselves, the very thing you have against Talentire: being sure of something beyond what can be known for sure.'

Dr Appleby considered. 'I stand rebuked,' he said. 'You are quite right, Imogen. It's devilishly hard not to run ahead of the proof. That's what makes science hard.'

'I think it might make any subject hard, if one pursued it with proper rigour,' Imogen said.

'You're a loss to scholarship,' he told her. 'I am right that you never took a degree? Can I talk you into throwing up nursing and studying chemistry?'

'I have such an interesting life as it is,' said Imogen.

'Pity. Now I come to think of it, if I caused the college to lose your services, I would be deeply unpopular. Might even find myself competing with V-G as the least liked don in the place. Well, in view of what you have told me I shall be inclined to modify my position on the Postgate, if it comes up again. I don't think it will though. The grapevine informs me that Talentire will be offered a very lucrative post at Princeton. Nice change of scene for him, surely?'

'So you don't think we shall have him in college, after all?'

'Probably not. Princeton pays very well, I'm told.'

'So have you thought of someone else to put forward?'

'I'm working on it,' he said.

When something has been on one's mind for a long time it can be hard to step back from it. Imogen asked Mike Parsons, her police inspector friend, out for a drink at the Anchor to pump him a bit. He told her quite readily what was happening. 'We've laid charges. Assault and illegal possession of a weapon against Inchman; assault and illegal possession of a firearm against Mottle. The magistrate will send it up to the crown court. Needs a longer sentence than a magistrate can impose.'

'What will they get?'

'Mottle is a first offence. Suspended sentence of about a year, I should think. Inchman will go to prison; he's got a string of minor offences behind him.'

'What happens to addicts in prison? Will he get methadone? He'll have a desperate time, otherwise.'

'Don't ask me that sort of stuff, Imogen. I don't know. Do you want me to tip you the wink when the cases are heard?'

'Yes, please, Mike. That would be kind.'

But shortly Imogen had something else to think about. Dennis Dobbs seemed, not quite ill, but strangely passive. When she returned his copy of *What Happened in Hamlet* she brought with her a copy of the programme at the Globe.

'We could take the coach from Drummer Street to the Embankment,' she suggested, 'and if we made it a matinée we could get comfortably back to Cambridge by mid-evening. Would you like that, Dennis?'

He smiled at her seraphically. 'Some time, Imo. Some time.' She heard the unspoken 'not now' very clearly. 'I've never quite worked out why you're so nice to me,' he added.

'I don't have a reason,' she told him. 'I just like you.'

'Mad,' he said softly. 'Utterly mad. Tell you what, Imo. Let me know if you hear what's happening to that Malpas fellow, will you?'

'Of course, Dennis. You can trust me for all the gossip. You know that.'

By and by, Imogen found herself sitting in the public gallery of the Crown Court – a brash new building opposite the Grafton Centre – to hear Dave Inchman stand trial on a charge of ABH. Actual bodily harm, the judge decoded it. Martin in the

witness box was an amazing phenomenon. He said he had
been drinking in the Green Man at Grantchester, and he had
'taken against' a fellow drinker. He had made remarks about
people in smelly clothes, and when the object of his scorn . . .

'Do you see the person in question in this court?' the
prosecuting lawyer asked.

'Yes, he's in dock. He told me to stuff it, and I called him
some names.'

'Insulting names?'

'I think I called him a mother-fucking bastard. Then he
followed me out into the car park, and he went for me.'

'He went for you?'

'I brushed him aside. Well, I slapped his face, actually.'

'Then what happened?'

'He showed me he had a knife. And I said he was too feeble a
wimp to use it. Then he lost his rag and stabbed me. I got really
scared then, and so I got out my gun and shot at him. I didn't
mean to hit him, but my aim was lousy, what with blood
pouring from my shoulder.'

The magistrate said, 'So basically you are telling the court
that you fired in self-defence?'

'I did rather provoke him,' said Mottle, smiling sweetly.

A lot of talk followed about Martin's gun. Martin said he
owned the gun for use in some of the wild mountain country in
which he went climbing. 'There are places in South America
where bandits are an everyday occurrence,' he told the magistrate. 'And our gear is valuable. We have to be armed. It isn't
illegal in most of the world,' he added.

'This hardly explains why you were carrying a loaded
firearm in the car park at Grantchester,' said the judge
severely.

'Of course not,' said Martin. 'It was an oversight. At the last minute I realised it was raining, and I took my all-weather jacket. The gun had been left in the pocket.'

Imogen listened and looked lost in amazement. This was lying as an art form: extended, narrative, 3D long-distance lying. The boy was a brilliant actor, a great loss to the profession. He could put Simon Malpas to shame.

When the defence lawyer called Dave to the stand he just muttered, barely audibly, hanging his head. 'It's like he said,' he mumbled, indicating Martin. 'He said I stank,' he added morosely.

Dave too had a lawyer. Quite a smooth-talking one. 'My client was provoked, sorely provoked,' he offered.

'We've heard a fancy story about why the witness was carrying a gun,' the judge said. 'Do we have an account of why the defendant was carrying a knife?'

'You gotta have one,' said Dave. He flashed the judge a face full of fright. 'It's dangerous sleeping rough. Nasty. You gotta have a knife or a dog.'

Imogen suddenly spotted Susan, sitting opposite her in the visitors' gallery, biting her nails.

The whole business seemed to move in slow motion. Statement for the prosecution, statement for the defence. The jury retired to consider. Seeing Mike among the police officers in the hallway, Imogen asked him about Martin Mottle.

'That case was heard yesterday,' Mike said. 'Sorry, Imogen, the previous case dropped out and I didn't have time to warn you. You didn't miss much; he pleaded guilty and so no witnesses and no jury.'

'But what happened?'

'Oh, usual harangue by judge. Need to deter carrying firearms. Should have known better being as how he's a rich lad . . . previous good character . . . one year in prison suspended for a year. Fine of one thousand pounds, and the confiscation of the weapon. Pretty much what I told you would happen.'

There was a stir as the jury returned to the court, and the audience took their seats in the gallery again. The jury found Dave guilty of ABH, and of carrying an illegal weapon, with a recommendation to mercy on the grounds of provocation.

This judge too was inclined to pontificate. 'I would normally be inclined to send you to prison,' he said. 'But we have a probation report informing us that a place has been secured for you in a private residential de-toxification unit in Leicestershire. We take into account that you have now spent five weeks in custody, awaiting trial. We therefore sentence you to two years in prison, suspended, on condition that you attend that clinic and complete the course of treatment there.'

He called the next case.

Imogen left with several others, and in the lobby outside she found people milling about. Susan was standing beside Dave, who seemed distressed. 'It doesn't work, Susie,' he was saying. 'I've tried that sort of thing.'

'This one worked for a friend of mine,' said Mottle, who was standing within earshot. 'Give it a serious try, friend.'

'Is it you that's paying for it?' asked Susan. 'Is it you that paid that swanky lawyer?'

'Nope,' said Mottle. 'Why should I? Little rat tried to kill me.'

'You're an awful liar, though,' said Susan.

'Do you think so?' he said cheerfully. 'I thought I was a rather good one.'

They all watched him walk away, his lawyer striding beside him.

'Susan, do you need help getting Dave to Leicestershire?' asked Imogen.

'No, thanks. I'm taking him for a hot meal, and then social services are getting him there. Delivered to the door.'

'And what about you? What are you thinking of doing?'

'I'm through with Cambridge, Miss Quy. Just not my kind of thing. I'm going to look for a down-market sort of place. And I won't be doing English, either. I'm going to change to law.'

'In my opinion you need psychiatric help, Susan,' said Imogen. 'I'm going to insist for your own safety and that of others that you get it.'

'You can't insist,' said Susan. 'You can't make me do anything.'

'I might have more leverage than you think,' said Imogen quietly. 'Duncan Talentire told you that if you and Dave both stuck to your stories about his son's death, neither of you could be convicted. But I think he was wrong. The case could be reopened. And I think if someone asked Dave to untie a climber's knot in a thick rope, taking only seconds to do it, it might become clear who could and who could not have committed murder.'

Susan stared at her. Fascinated at a phenomenon she had heard of but never seen before, Imogen watched the colour drain from her face.

'Get help, and let me know who is treating you, Susan,' Imogen said.

As she walked away towards her bus stop, she found Mike Parsons at her shoulder. 'All's well then?' she asked him. 'Two more cases to add to the cleared-up files.'

'Funny thing, though,' Mike said. 'When there's a fight or an affray there are nearly always witnesses, sometimes dozens

of witnesses, all upset and eager to give evidence. This time
nobody saw a thing. Not one person saw it happen. Odd,
don't you think?'

Imogen came back from court to find her house full of happy
people. A meeting of the Kyd Society was in session, and they
were on various highs. The treasurer reported that all claims
against them had been settled, and there was even ten thousand pounds of Mottle's money towards drama productions
next year. What was really causing rejoicing, however, was
Simon's news: he had landed a job in a theatrical agency, not
as an actor, but as a producer. And his wonderful Ophelia,
Amy, had a part in a play at a festival in Southwold. 'It's a
start,' he kept saying. 'Watch this space.'

'To be honest,' he told Imogen confidingly, sitting in her
favourite armchair, legs extended halfway across the rug, 'I'm
glad to be deflected. I got a fright this summer, when I saw
what had become of poor old Gadgby. You sort of think that if
only you are good enough, it will all work out. You'll be rich
and famous; well, famous and solvent, anyway. But then you
see that being absolutely marvellous didn't keep him in parts.
Didn't keep him off Skid Row. I honestly couldn't claim to be
better than him, or even as good. So perhaps a bit of producing and arts admin will be a better way to go.'

'I expect you're right, Simon,' said Imogen, though she felt a
touch of sadness at it: at the edge taken off ambition in this
hard world.

'I need to be solvent,' he added. 'Amy wants children, and
we'll need child-care so she can work.'

Imogen slipped away, and rode her bike round to Dennis to
bring him the promised news. He was fast asleep in his

armchair. She sat down opposite him, and studied him. He was drawn and grey; his hands on the book held open on his lap were as foxed as old paper. And Imogen had medical knowledge. Dennis was not for long, she saw. Best be kind to him as much as possible. Best not to wake him now.

It was a week later, drawing near to the end of term, that Malcolm Gracie dropped in to Imogen's office.

'A conundrum for you,' he said. 'Can you see any reason why the college should refuse to allow a private party to take place on the Mound?'

'On the Mound? Why the Mound?' Imogen was baffled. The Mound was just that – a huge, tall, man-made, pudding-shaped heap of earth, which had once been the motte of an ancient castle, and now stood in the middle of the St Agatha's Fellows' Garden, with a spiral path up it to the top. Dennis would have insisted that it was a helical path . . . At the top was a level circle of ground, with a bench or two, and a lovely prospect over Cambridge.

'I would have said, "for the view", since he says his own college is too low-lying, except that the party is proposed for ten p.m. A generous fee is offered,' Malcolm expatiated. 'The proposer wanted the tower room, but I absolutely and resolutely declined that.'

'This is Martin Mottle, no doubt,' said Imogen.

'Yes, indeed. But can you see what kind of mischief might be afoot this time?'

'I'm glad to hear that Mr Mottle is enough recovered to get up the Mound at all,' said Imogen. 'As for what he's up to, Malcolm, I can't imagine. But then, none of us could imagine what he was up to last time.'

'So shall I take his pieces of silver and we'll see? I have made it plain to him that I shall attend, as a condition of permission, and he says, that's a good idea, and that you will be invited too.'

'I haven't been invited yet,' Imogen said.

'Well, I haven't given permission yet,' said Malcolm. 'But I rather think I will risk it.'

Imogen considered Malcolm Gracie. Had he acquired a soft spot for the incorrigible Martin Mottle? Or was he a natural risk-taker, free of the suffocating safety-first blanket that enveloped so many of the academics she worked among? She smiled serenely at him.

'Malcolm, have you ever read *Gaudy Night?*' she asked him.

'Yes, as a matter of fact.'

'And did you think it ridiculous, wildly idealistic?'

'For portraying academic life as a noble quest for truth, you mean? Yes and no. No, of course academic life isn't some latter-day chivalric quest. But, yes, I have known one or two scholars like that.'

'Yet another indefinite answer,' said Imogen.

'About truth,' Malcolm said reflectively. 'It's a fine thing to be in quest of. It's when you think you've got it that the trouble starts.'

21

Last night of al,
When yonder starre that's westward from the pole
Had made his course to illumine that part of heaven,
Where now it burns, the bell then towling one . . .

There was never any shortage of boring tasks in Imogen's office. Filing, archiving records for the students who graduated last year and disappeared into the maelstrom of life, auditing the medicine cabinet, disinfecting things . . . After her evening 'surgery' on the night of Mottle's party, Imogen kept herself busy till nine forty-five without the least difficulty, and then put on a reasonably smart black sweater, and a silk skirt, though she wondered as she did so why she was bothering with that. Nobody, surely, in the darkness, would be able to see what anyone else was wearing.

She crossed the Fountain Court and went under the elaborately decorated Elizabethan archway that led to the Fellows' Garden. Only part of this ancient garden was actually reserved for fellows; most of it, including the Mound, was available to all. Mottle was in luck with the day he had chosen: it was a fine summer night, with no moon, and so the stars were brightly visible. So also was a line of flares, driven into the ground alongside the path ascending the Mound, and lighting the way. They looked charming; as though someone had cast a necklace of sparks round the prominence in the ground. There were people around, moving shadows, voices in the dark.

At the foot of the Mound, beside the first of his flares, Imogen encountered Martin Mottle himself, looking slightly ghoulish, as people tend to if you light their faces from below. He had attracted a crowd of curious undergraduates, and was making them welcome. 'Go up; go on up,' he was saying. 'Everyone welcome.'

To Imogen he said, 'Don't worry, Imogen.'

She wasn't worried. The night was soft and enticing, the lights delicious, the trees in the garden contriving to show themselves as vestigially darker shapes against a dark sky. The whole scene had an ethereal unreality about it, like a stage set. More like *A Midsummer Night's Dream* than like *Hamlet*, Imogen thought, she hoped irrelevantly.

When she reached the level space on top of the Mound she found by the flickering light of the torches people she knew. Malcolm Gracie, there as promised. The Master and Lady Buckmote, seated on one of the benches. 'I hope you are wrapped up warmly,' Imogen said sternly to the Master.

'A string vest, a flannel shirt, two waistcoats and an over-coat,' he said. 'And I've brought my hip-flask just in case.'

'You may have a gold star for prudence, Master,' Imogen said.

The Master's hip-flask however was not going to be needed, for here were a bevy of girls bringing drinks on trays round the company. 'Champagne or Pimm's or orange juice?' Imogen heard them asking. Trays with little bowls of strawberries were also appearing. The self-invited seemed bashful at first, but not for long. A very jolly party was soon going strong. The company seemed to include most of the

Kyd Society. Surely that pair embracing over there were Simon and Amy?

'What's all this about, do you know?' Imogen heard someone ask.

'Ours not to reason why,' came the reply.

Imogen found if she avoided looking directly at the flares her eyes accustomed themselves to the darkness, and she could actually see better. Below them under the stars the city of Cambridge lay spread out, made of shadows. If you knew the panorama in daylight you could distinguish the shapes of gables, pediments, lanterns and towers, like the trees visible mostly as an interruption in the scatter of stars.

And here came Martin Mottle, ascending the path, bringing someone with him: Duncan Talentire. Talentire was visibly reluctant. 'Night revels are not my kind of thing!' Imogen heard him say.

'Oh, Martin, now what?' Imogen said to herself.

Martin said, 'We need the lights out now. Not on the path; just where we are here.' The girls who had been plying everyone with drinks obeyed him; one by one the flares were hooded and expired. The great clock in the Fountain Court behind them struck the half-hour, sonorously self-important.

And suddenly there was a gasp. Everyone's attention was bent on the scene below them, where a spot of bright light had appeared. Imogen blinked incredulously at it, but it was indeed as she thought, the figure of a young man, illuminated and standing upright – *oh, surely not!* – on the topmost narrow pinnacle of the New Tower of St John's. The figure stood perfectly still, picked out by a beam of light from somewhere below.

An excited babble of voices broke out all around her, and then faltered, and fell silent. Another spot of light, another figure had appeared, and then another and another. All over the roofscape of Cambridge young men had ascended to the highest points, and were standing in immediate danger of death, bathed in pools of light. On the Great Gate at Trinity, and on the Wren Library, on the two visible corner spires of King's, on the lantern at Clare, on the roof of the city hall, on the porters' lodge at King's, on the Senate House, on the Pepys Library at Magdalene, and more and more, standing in the dark sky, on further ledges and points that Imogen could not identify, perhaps two dozen of the immortal young appeared in beams of light. They were as unlikely and beautiful as angels, and it made your flesh creep with fear for them to see it.

While everyone was staring and holding their breath, Martin Mottle said, 'This is a tribute from the night climbers. Homage to John Talentire.'

And as he spoke the lights began to falter and go out, the roofscapes were returned to darkness, and the descent of the night climbers to safety – please, God! – would be wrapped in obscurity. There was a long minute of awed hush on the Mound, before the clamour of voices began again. The sound of police sirens beginning to wail in every corner of the city reached them. The flares were being relit. Duncan Talentire and Martin Mottle passed Imogen, their arms round each other's shoulders, like father and son, as they walked away together through the pools of light and shadow on the descending path.

'Will that be that, do you think?' the Master asked Imogen. 'Will the man let his friend rest in peace, now?'

'I think so,' said Imogen. But her face was wet with tears,

and so she slipped away between the shrubs that the gardeners had planted on the western slopes of the Mound, and went down on an unlit minor path, to be, for a few moments at least, alone and unseen.

22

He is dead and gone, Lady, he is dead and gone,
At his head a grasse green turffe,
At his heeles a stone.

Eighteen months later Malcolm Gracie asked Imogen to
accompany him on a short walking tour in the Lake
District. There was a lot of water under the bridge by then.
Martin Mottle had, in spite of all the distractions, achieved a
first-class degree, and gone to work in his father's firm. The Kyd
Society was under new management now. It no longer met in
Imogen's front room, but had new premises, and was putting on
a production of *The Duchess of Malfi.* Duncan Talentire had
been offered the Postgate, but had declined it, and the college
was still looking for a suitable person for it. They had success-
fully appointed a new fellow in English, a young woman whose
special interest was Defoe, a writer who seemed acceptable to
both traditional and new-style critics. She was a bright and
practical young woman, who liked the college room she had
been offered – the tower room – and understood perfectly the
need to keep it locked when she wasn't there.

Venton-Gimps's reputation as a murderer had lost nothing
in the telling and retelling, and a new batch of undergraduates
still thronged to hear him. He was rather inclined now to
suggest that he had indeed murdered a colleague.

'People are apt to think,' he confided in Imogen, who had for once succumbed to blandishments and brought him his cup of coffee where he sat, 'that scholarship does not matter. Not really. They think nobody could kill on a point of scholarship. But some of us have spent our lives in the pursuit of learning. To us, nothing matters more.'

Imogen smiled. He was not soon going to let his laurel crown as a killer for truth fade from memory. Susan Inchman was studying law somewhere in the Midlands, and of Dave Inchman she had heard nothing further.

But the major change in Imogen's life was that Dennis Dobbs had left her. He had slipped from sleeping peacefully in his armchair into eternity while Imogen was in his house, making him a cup of tea and a rack of toast. Like most easy deaths it was hard on those left behind with no warning, and Imogen had indeed taken it hard. She had become depressed, a state for which she obdurately refused medication, and the flattened mood had dragged on. It was probably to cheer her up that Malcolm Gracie had asked her to accompany him.

He booked rooms for them in a pub in Loweswater – separate rooms – and when they had exhausted themselves on Rannerdale Knots, and Catbells, and Haystacks, they decided to award themselves an easier day, by driving round to Wasdale. They parked the car at Wasdale Foot and walked towards Wasdale Head, lured on, through scenes almost too austere to be beautiful, by Malcolm's recollection of oatmeal and onion soup eaten years ago in the pub at the dale head.

Past flint-coloured water, and near-vertical grey scree across the lake, they walked along the lakeshore road to their destination. No such soup was on the menu, but there was hearty food of other kinds.

They emerged an hour later to look around the dale head. The levels between the top of the lake and the abrupt steeps of the surrounding towering hills were laced with a network of stone walls, almost shoulder-high. In the corners of the tiny fields were domes of piled-up stones, like knots in the netting.

'Were those for anything?' Imogen wondered. 'What were they for?'

'A shepherd told me they were just dumps. Nobody would want to carry the stones from clearing the ground any distance; they were just piled at angles of the fields. There's a church here, somewhere,' he added.

Imogen looked around. At first she couldn't see any such thing; then she spotted a long, low slate roof nearly out of sight among a ring of evergreens. Squinting at it against the sun she saw the little belfry, a single bell hanging hardly a foot above the roof. 'There,' she said. They set off down the rough track towards it, past a finger post that said 'St Olaf's'. As they walked away from the pub the silence of the valley descended on them. The church seemed intimidated by its surroundings, crouching low beneath the mighty looming hills around it. Malcolm named them for her: 'Kirk Fell, Great Gable, still highlit with bands of snow, Scafell and Scafell Pike, and Great End . . .'

'Malcolm, are there people up there?' Imogen asked, amazed. 'Those spots of colour, far far up . . .'

Malcolm got out his binoculars, and scanned the view. 'Yes. Three or four climbers on Scafell Pike,' he said. 'Want to look?'

While she did so, he said, 'Mountains are beautiful, I know, but why not see them from below?'

'Clever, Malcolm. Just how I feel,' she said, handing back his binoculars.

'Not mine, I'm afraid. Belloc, I think.'

They lifted the latch at the churchyard gate, and entered a small grassy walled space. They looked in the tiny church with its pitch-pine roof beams, very dark and low, and a set of notices about births, marriages and deaths. Then they looked round the tombstones set in the lush grass. And those were remarkable. There were some parish burials there: surely the little stone for a baby must have been a death in this tiny parish. There was a memorial to the last schoolteacher in the dale, who had died in 1947, but most were memorials to climbers. A beloved son who died on Great Gable, who was the President of the Fell and Rock Club, but that had not saved him. There was a stone to five members of a Batura Muztagh Expedition, lost in the Himalayas in 1950 and touching lines to a party of five lost on 'Skawfell', and lying in view of their doom:

> One moment stood they as the angels stand
> High in the stainless immanence of air,
> The next they were not. To their fatherland
> Translated unaware.

How could this first line not remind Imogen of Martin Mottle's spectacular farewell to his friend?

So she was not surprised really to find by the southern gate out of the churchyard a stone of the greenish local slate which said:

> John Talentire, 1976–2004
> Who fell from a high place.
> An irretrievable loss to scholarship,
> and to his grieving family and friends.
> RIP

'May he indeed,' said Malcolm. They began the walk back to the pub, and their car. The pub itself, such a short step away, was dwarfed by the mass of the hill behind it. The climbers had moved up a bit, and were now so tiny that you wouldn't have seen them if you hadn't known they were there.

'I wonder what it is?' Imogen mused.

'You wonder what what is?' asked Malcolm.

'What draws them. Whatever it is that can't be seen from below. Is it danger itself, do you think?'

'Some super-human perspective,' he said. 'Some great simplicity.'